# AMBUSHED

The coming silver moon glazed the snow peaks and turned the grass under the horses' hoofs to moving quicksilver. Lacroix turned back in his saddle to say something, when he was violently taken from his horse. A dozen Utes leaped onto the trail, soundless as the night. Lacroix was set upon like a bear by enraged bees, and he fought back like a mountain lion.

Striking out with his massive fist, he felt a face collapse under it. An overeager brave drove a knife at Lacroix's chest, but it did not even penetrate the layers of fur the mountain man wore, and the brave paid for his mistake by taking a crushing fist to the ribs.

Greatly outnumbered by the Indians, Lacroix sidestepped a knife, hiprolled another brave—until he felt a horrible blow low in his back, where a Ute lance had buried its head. . . .

# UTE REVENGE

## BY PAUL LEDD

**ZEBRA BOOKS**
**KENSINGTON PUBLISHING CORP.**

ZEBRA BOOKS

are published by

KENSINGTON PUBLISHING CORP.
475 Park Avenue South
New York, N.Y. 10016

SECOND PRINTING: December 1986

Printed in the United States of America

# 1.

The big man with the impenetrable gaze stood on a narrow outcropping near the pinnacle of Homestake Peak in Colorado. He carried a musket, a short-handled hatchet, a long skinning knife, and a pack full of personal belongings.

Below, the mountain crumbled away into primordial chaos, ridges and outcroppings flaring up, merging and breaking off without apparent pattern or reason.

Georges Lacroix had scaled the peak in the bitter cold only to look at that which he had not seen before. This motive was not a new thing with him. It was the way he had lived the bulk of his forty years. He had seen places no man had seen, walked where no foot had fallen; this black-bearded giant.

The wind nipped at his shoulders, standing the hairs of his badgerskin tunic on end. This was a place, by the Lord. The whole string of blue mountains lined up like jagged teeth tearing at the belly of the low hanging sky. That was the Continental Divide, the way she looked then and had for millions of years, and would for millions more. Snake-sided long canyons where nought but a mountain goat could clamber, shale-slick sheer cliffs glazed with never melting ice, broken weather-shattered spires and curls of wind-carved shelf.

Lacroix squatted on his heels and filled a pipe. Those dark eyes, set deep in the Frenchman's massive skull took it all in with an understanding that only his sort of man has of true wilderness.

It was 1850. Georges Lacroix had come home again—again into an uncharted wilderness where no white had ever walked, and by the absence of sign, few Indians. Since leaving Quebec hurriedly under difficult circumstances twenty years earlier, the brooding mountain man had wandered the farther parts of the American wilderness on both sides of the Canadian border from the Yukon to the Dakota badlands. But Lacroix had seen little to match this.

Two dozen great pyramids of blue-gray mountain surged up mocking the small men who would never scale them. Below in the spruce lined valley, grayed by the late hour and the misting clouds, he could make out the tea cup of a frozen lake which was the source of the Eagle, and ultimately of the Colorado. There would be beaver there, otter, and brown trout surging through the white water. I will stay, he told himself. For a time.

He threw up a lean-to of pine boughs carefully interwoven and overlapped and there he spent his first winter, huddled over a small fire when he was not setting his trap lines. The winter was harsh, the pelts good.

Lacroix trekked to Julesburg in the spring, got drunk the first night and set fire to the town's only saloon, leaving before he could collect a cent for his furs. He built his two room cabin snugly, aloft on the sandstone bluffs along the Eagle where there was an unobstructed view of the surrounding valleys.

The Utes had been there.

Curiously, they had sprung several traps. Lacroix found blood and footprints. "They will come for me," he decided.

The Utes would come out of curiosity, and in hopes of finding booty. Lacroix had weapons, a hand mirror, and the pelts. He was also an intruder.

The following winter was exceedingly bitter. Georges Lacroix seldom ventured forth to check his traps. In fact, he seldom set them. His snares for food were close to the cabin. He spent hour after hour, month after month in the close, cold cabin in the dark, brooding.

Lacroix was a brooding man by nature. And he brooded the winter long. The constant wind thundered against the cabin, the snow drifting to sixteen feet or better. He emerged only for wood or for food. And when spring had finally, tentatively arrived, melting bright green patches through the snow bound meadows, Lacroix moved as a tangle-haired, hollow-eyed, long-bearded bear across the deep valleys.

He saw Utes the third day. Six warriors, all mounted, pointing toward the beaver dams where a number of his traps were staked. He watched them without moving for hours as they tore up the traps, slinging them into the Green Fork Creek. The following day they burned his cabin.

"I'll pay you for this," the Frenchman swore. "Lacroix will pay you."

He watched the smoke rising in lazy spirals into the pale sky, lifting toward the snow-peaked mountains. It would be cold that night, he knew. "You will not have Lacroix so easily."

He found the Ute camp two days later, at sundown

7

when the fire of the high sky bled onto the snowy mountains. There was fire in several tents. A remuda of horses to the south. From there, high on a forested bench, he could hear the sounds of chanting. A celebration was in the planning.

"I'll give you what to celebrate. Filthy things. You think Lacroix will run? Never."

He waited till full dark then inched down the hillside to the camp fringes. Inside the camp the Ute party celebrated wildly, singing around the flaring communal fire. Lacroix, puffing, sliding over the snow, pushed his musket before him, a bag of powder over his shoulder.

And then he saw the woman.

She struggled uphill through the deep snow in the ravine, a root sack over her shoulder, a lost, almost worried look on her sturdy features. Po-Ta-Liki. Timid Morning Light was her name. The village was a joyous place that evening, the hunt had been good, but her thoughts were not on the festival.

Morning Light had never been a participant, but only a silent, hesitant observer, her nervous gestures revealing an uncertainty of the heart. She was a stolid worker, an obedient daughter, a fine weaver. But there was little else to distinguish her from the other women. Yet within her was a sight which observed more than she ever told, which was to her a sacred thing. She knew the animals intimately as did all the tribe; but they seemed to recognize some kindred spirit in return. They approached Timid Morning Light as brazenly as one another.

*Sad blue night*, she thought. *So far-running this night which weaves through the mountains. Stars deliberate and graceful in their rounds. I think you must see me too.*

She sat on a low knoll, trembling slightly, watching the fire of the camp below where the people, like frenzied insects danced in response to its heat. The grass, black in the empty night swayed with the whims of the east wind, a night hawk darted in sudden, arcing dives, chasing insects. The river far away murmured over the rocky depths. The hand took her violently by the waist, and another, equally strong, bear-like, clamped over her mouth, bruising her pale lips against her teeth. She kicked out urgently, twisting with all of her strength. Her vehement objections were choked off in her throat.

"Bear," she pleaded, "release me. I am a simple person. Bad monstrous thing, go away!"

Lacroix held her tightly, in massive arms tempered by thirty-five years of wilderness living. Few men were a match for him. No woman. But she fought like a bobcat. For only a second.

"Has she fainted?"

The woman had slumped limply, offering no more resistance than a sack of potatoes. Lacroix arched his thick black eyebrows questioningly, but continued dragging her away from the Ute camp.

The night had gone black, but for the faint flickering of stars through the sheer clouds above the pine forest. Lacroix dragged her onward, breath steaming from his lips.

The girl was inert, sketching a long, jagged groove through the snow. "Bear ... let me loose," Timid Morning Light whispered through compressed lips. But the event had taken an unreal air. A savage, driving force had snatched her from the bosom of the tribe. The only reality was the slogging beast towing her along. The black pines above. The scrape and swish of

9

snow under her body as they moved. A moon, half orange, half black burst from behind the deep rows of high pines, glossing the world.

Lacroix was panting deeply, but his mind was abstracted from his physical movements. He was only dimly aware of the sweat pouring from his burly body, the effortful upclimbing, the cold.

"Woman, you are my repayment," he told her as they rested briefly on the hillside, in a crooked notch between two jutting boulder stacks.

Morning Light glanced fearfully at this bearded apparition. She had never before seen a man with hair on his face, a man of such bulk, clad in skins and hair.

Lacroix stopped to rest only once, around midnight. The snow had begun to fall lightly, but enough to cover his tracks. He slung the woman over his shoulder, feeling the shape of her curves through the buckskin she wore. He walked more quickly after that.

The beast seemed tireless to Timid Morning Light. It slogged on through the drifting snow, climbing forever up into the high reaches of a mountain she had never climbed. They passed through the timberline and onto the naked stony slopes of the high pass. Once the moon broke through the thin cloud, lighting the creature's ferocious, bearded face. Broad, powerful features it had, and deep demon eyes.

"It takes me to its nest in the pinnacles," she thought.

It was dawning spectacularly before they finally halted. The snow fields before them flushed a vague pink and then a deep rose. The tips of the pine trees flashed with silver, the ice on their boughs brilliant as if hung with a thousand mirrors. The shadows fled the deep, barren canyons and vanished before the great red ball of the sun.

"Now we stop," Georges Lacroix grunted. "Up there—a cave I have seen before. It will do for now."

He glanced at the girl, suppressing a thick smile. She was such a forlorn looking, unhappy mudhen of a woman.

"I will not hurt you girl. I'll give you all you would have had with them."

But when he stretched out a gnarled, black-haired hand to her, she drew back.

"No matter. I'll have you anyway. You'll see I am a good hunter."

The cave was dry, empty, tiny. Timid Morning Light glanced around fearfully, finally folding up into a tight ball on the bearskin Lacroix had spread on the floor. The mountain man stood in the cave opening studying the long, sweeping mountain flanks below.

"They'll not come." If the snow did not cover their tracks, the Utes might follow as far as the timberline. From there, across stretches of slate gray, bare stone, he could not be tracked by any man.

"Maybe they do not even know you are gone yet, little one," Lacroix mused, turning his eyes on the woman. "Maybe no one wanted you at all."

The creature moved around the cave, muttering in his strange language. She watched him fearfully as he stripped off his skins and stood naked before her for a moment, massive, hairy as a great black bear, before he lay down beside her, pulling another fur over them.

# 2.

The baby was born in the spring. Lacroix was not there, as he was usually not there. He roamed the mountains far and wide, trapping where the pelts were to be found, worrying little, if at all, about the small Indian girl he had left in the new cabin along Red Falls Creek beyond the Cottonwood Pass flats.

Alone, as the women in her tribe had always been at birthing time, the girl delivered her own child, standing in the doorway of the cabin, catching it as it emerged in her apron.

Sweating, shaky, uncertain, she wiped it clean, saw that it was a sturdy, red bawling boy, and wrapped it in the blanket she had woven from the soft wool of a young mountain sheep.

"Man child," she said, and she smiled. She lay him temporarily on the bed while she pulled on her moccasins. Hurriedly, for no reason she could define, she snatched up the infant and walked down the narrow river trail to the icy creek.

Once there she unwrapped him and bathed him in the frigid, quick running water. The baby caught its breath, went a purplish blue, then squalled with all of its might, its tiny fists clenching.

"So cold," she murmured anxiously. "But you are strong. Strong like your . . . mountain."

Tenderly she wrapped the still-crying baby back into its blanket and put it to her breast, suckling it as she walked the treacherous, stony path along the gray rock cliffs.

Once home she sat on the doorstep, waiting. The baby ate eagerly, its color returning to normal as it warmed. It was a beautiful baby. She decided she had never seen one so handsome.

He had dark eyes, long dark lashes. Stubby, powerful hands and a deep chest. She held it to her, nursing it, petting it until the sun filtered behind the long stands of cedar and pine, reddening, and sank into the ranks of far running mountains.

It was full dark with a rising, cold wind twisting up the canyons before she rose and went inside, barring the door.


It was October, the long valleys clotted with blue, fresh snow forming delicate, treacherous bridges and sweeping majestic cornices before Lacroix returned, towing a nearly black jenny mule laden with trade goods.

He stood, panting, on the far side of the deep vale, the wind cutting at his seamed face. The woman was there sitting on the step, wrapped tightly in a red and brown blanket, with something smaller in her arms.

The Frenchman tramped the last quarter of a mile as he had the first one hundred-fifty of his journey, evenly, without haste.

He unpacked the mule and put it in the stable, taking

a handful of trinkets from his heavy pack.

"Have you got to eat, woman?" he asked in his rasping French. She did not understand until he made shoveling motions near his mouth.

Timid Morning Light nodded and got up heavily. Hesitating, she held the boy out for him to see. Black-eyed, with a mop of fly-away, dark hair, the baby hid his face.

"Boy?" Lacroix asked.

She unwrapped the blanket from the baby. Lacroix looked, grunted and stamped the snow from his feet. He walked past her, rubbing his hands together, throwing down a few beads and a bolt of twill cloth he had picked up in Hewitt.

Morning Light warmed the stew pot, working hurriedly, with the baby on her hip. She put the plate of food, along with a loaf of corn bread, a quart of goat's milk and a handful of currants in front of Lacroix.

Still in his great bearhide coat, Lacroix ate every bit of it without looking up. Then he curled up by the fire, snoring softly as Timid Morning Light, nursing the boy, looked on.

The boy grew, and to him it all seemed so natural. Living alone in this high country cabin with the dark-eyed, loving woman.

He followed her through the woods almost as soon as he could walk, watching her way with the animals, understanding her solemn, quiet moods. He grew strong on trout snatched from the icy, quick running rivers, gooseberries, currants, raspberries stolen from the thorny thickets and the black bears. He did not know what lay beyond the mountains, hardly believed that beyond the gray evening mists, the long stretches of

14

cold, high mountain grandeur there were other people. There was, for him, only this quiet woman, the great bulk of the wild country, the hidden secrets, the ranging lion and bear.

At long intervals the man returned. A great grizzly that sent his mother's blood racing, causing her lips to tremble, her placid actions to become hectic, worried.

The boy, whose mother called him Mantaka, after the first Poche Ute chieftain, huddled in his pile of skins, watching the silent hulking ghost of a man who came from time to time, bringing trinkets which brightened his mother's eyes but a little.

Yet he never stayed longer than three winter months, and he always brought needed cloth, smoked meat, white flour and whatever else he had picked up on his forays into the outer world. It was only occasionally that those deep, dark eyes were turned on the boy. The firelight painted the face of the grotesque bearded man, sinking his glittering eyes into deeper shadow.

"Don't be afraid, boy," Lacroix would say. "I am your father."

But the boy invariably sunk deeper into his concealing pile of furs, with only the black eyes, the straight fly-away hair showing.

"What do you tell the boy? That I am a bogey-man?"

Timid Morning Light could only shrug. Her French was as incomplete as it had been five years earlier.

"He is frightened," she said in Ute. "He does not see you much. So long, Lacroix."

The woman shrugged helplessly. The mountain man grunted in return and fished for a bottle he had brought with him. He drew the cork and drank half of

15

the whisky before speaking again.

"Boy? I have for you." Clumsily he reached into the pack and drew forth a silvery top and string. "You know what this is?"

His thick, weather cracked hands wound the string around the top uncertainly. Fascinated, Mantaka watched as he drew the string taut and cast the top onto the table where it spun, flashing silver in the firelight.

"You like it?"

Mantaka, for all his interest, could not look the big man in the eyes. Those fearful black eyes.

"Well!"

The boy said nothing, drawing the furs tighter as the top faltered and toppled, dying in a crazy, tight circle.

"He is afraid to like," Timid Morning Light said, but Lacroix did not understand.

"It is for you, anyway," the Frenchman said. But he did not move to pick up the top. He drank again, deeply, of the whisky.

They slept heaped in furs that night. But the great bear had taken his mother to the other side of the cabin. Stealthily Mantaka crept out from under his covers into the icy air to recover the glittering silver toy. He slept with it clenched tightly in his tiny hand.

The man was gone with the first melt. They watched him from the doorway as he ambled down the long, snow-rich canyons. The woman did not tell him where the man went, and Mantaka did not ask.

Their life seemed suddenly lighter, despite the lingering bad weather which brought intermittent snows and roaring winds which tore at the cabin, booming up the deep gorges. Spring did not settle in until late May.

Then the long grassy valleys exploded with brief, brilliant color. They walked together among the heartleaf, arnica, purple lungwort, far-reaching beds of black-eyed susan and rosecrown ferreting out an existence in the bleak, awesome wilderness.

In June Mantaka was startled by a surly, argumentative badger and had to take refuge in an aspen tree. The hills were alive with beaver and yellow porcupine, deer and broad racked elk. In July the Utes came.

Timid Morning Light had a basket filled with blackberries and wild plum. Smiling indulgently, she watched as the boy played, darting after gray squirrels. Then he found a leaf of grass and, placing it between his thumbs made a shrill whistling noise. At that moment they crested a low rise. Below them she saw the horsemen.

"Get down, boy!"

She practically clubbed Mantaka to the ground, a violent gesture that startled him. Her manner was totally strange.

"Now we are quiet. Now we are still!" she whispered harshly in his ear. Then Mantaka saw them too. Six men with paint on their flesh, weapons in their hands. They looked toward the hillrise where they lay, one of them pointing toward it.

Through the tall grass Mantaka could see them plainly. Slender men, small compared to his father, they watered their horses at the gray granite basin under Skunk Falls. His mother's hand gripped him tightly, squeezing his wrist until the hand turned white. The summer smell of the grass was pleasant, but it itched. A red ant scurried across his thin forearm. They did not move.

17

Finally they did. The one Indian shook his head in argument. His companions talked him out of the long ride up the steep crest. They ran home that evening, and for weeks afterward they did not venture from the cabin in the high reaches.

"Poor boy," Timid Morning Light said as she stroked the sleeping boy's dark head. "How could you know? Why have you come into this world as it is—bloody, wicked place?

"The tribal memory is long. They have not forgotten Lacroix. And there are ways of repaying him. You would be the victim, harmless child, I, perhaps.

"Sleep." She kissed him tenderly, a damp spot appearing on his cheek as she touched him. Morning Light dried her eyes and stood for a long minute, watching the star-tree across the mountains. Brilliant silver fruit filled the black, deep boughs of the tree of the gods.

"He is a fine child. He deserves a life."

She drew the bolt firmly before turning in to sleep. Men—they killed always the innocent, things better than themselves but weaker, more fragile. But not this boy. From the moment of his conception it had been too late for her to return to her people. They would kill the baby, or scorn it as it grew.

But Mantaka was all she had to make her life fruitful. Outside of that, what was she? In his way perhaps Lacroix was the kind of father he needed. He came with provisions then went away, never loving the boy, but never harming him. Not a hair on his head.

As for the loving, she doubted Lacroix knew how. His loving was only for the wild places, a loving she understood.

The boy must learn both sorts of loving, it was his right to learn them. He must know he belonged in the world; that nature was a part of him, that human warmth was necessary. If only they would stay away . . . these others.

# 3.

When Lacroix came it was after a long absence. He rode a horse this time, leading another behind him. Mantaka was ten years of age and as wild and free as any forest creature.

The mountain man said nothing until the day before he was to leave. Then he told her, "The boy must hunt now. He will come with me."

Timid Morning Light got some things together: Pemmican made of jerky, fat meat and wild berries, a new white Hudson Bay blanket, and his first pair of boots. Lacroix had a skinning knife he gave the boy.

Together the man and his son rode away in the first hazy gray of morning. Mantaka turned in the unfamiliar saddle to watch his mother. She stayed, arms crossed, back rigid in the doorway until they had crested the low line of black hills and disappeared.

"What does she call you, Mantaka?" Lacroix asked without turning his head.

"Mantaka," the boy affirmed, half understanding the question.

"That's fine up here, but not out in the world. You must learn French, understand?"

"Speak."

"Speak French."

Lacroix studied the boy for a time, liking the way he carried himself in the saddle of the stubby dun mustang, the proud tilt of his head, the even gaze in his eyes.

"I'll call you Jean-Paul. Understand? Jean-Paul."

The boy who had been called Mantaka nodded his head uncertainly, pointing to his own chest. "Jean-Paul." If it pleased the man . . .

"Good," Lacroix roared with approval. "You're a clever boy, Jean-Paul."

Crowder was waiting in the tiny camp among the blue spruce low on the South Platte bluffs where the river broke back in a crescent-shaped oxbow before merging with the Little Crow Creek. A stubby, fair-skinned man with a twinkle in his pale blue eyes, Crowder watched as Lacroix wove his way through the trees, approaching.

"Thought you'd got lost," Crowder said with a quick smile, holding the bridle as Lacroix got down. With interest the stubby man's eyes studied the kid with Lacroix.

"Indian boy?" Crowder wanted to know.

"My boy," Lacroix grunted. Already the Frenchman was unloading his pack, slinging his roll down beside Crowder's. He checked the coffee pot and took a swig from the pot.

"How you doin', boy?" Crowder asked, thrusting out a hand.

"He don't speak French," Lacroix apologized as the boy drew back.

"English?"

"No English," Lacroix spat. "Damn savage tongue!

21

Some Ute. But we'll learn him. He's come hunting the first time."

"All right, fine." Crowder started to say something else. The boy just sat his horse, a faintly apprehensive look on his slender features as if he had never seen a man before.

"How's beaver?" Lacroix asked around a mouthful of sourdough.

"Not good this year, Georges. Too warm too early for much. Elk trampling on each other's heels though."

"I don't hunt for meat."

"I don't either, usually. Can't carry enough fresh enough to anywhere near enough," Crowder said, stoking up the stubby pipe he smoked. The boy still sat the dun pony, a fact that didn't seem to bother Lacroix at all. "But there's a market, Georges."

"Oh?" Lacroix glanced up expectantly from under massive eyebrows, wiping his arm across his mouth.

"Miners. They've found gold down near Milk Creek."

"The devil!" Lacroix shook his head wonderingly. "Now they'll come." He spat in disgust.

"They're here. There's a town sprung up. Maybe a hundred men. So busy digging holes in the ground they've no time to hunt."

"I've seen that kind. Rather starve than miss out."

"What do you think, Georges, are you for it? The pelts are thin until the weather cools."

Lacroix studied his partner's face quietly for a long time before finally nodding his massive head. "I hate like the devil to feed the vultures, though. They'll gut the mountains with half a chance." Suddenly his thoughts shifted. "Get down, boy! Eat your fill."

With little urging the boy called Jean-Paul squatted on his heels and began spooning the sourdough and bacon grease into his mouth as he watched the two men chattering away in their strange tongue.

He wanted nothing more th ⌐ to turn around and go up the long mountains, but his mother had told him he must come. So he came. He washed later in the day, in the creek when the men did, and that night he rolled up to sleep when they did. In the morning they rode. The frost was still on the grass, their horses leaving green circles behind them where they stepped.

Crowder knew where he wanted to go, and they followed him across the vast meadows between the long rows of surrounding hills thick with aspen flushed delicate yellows and gold in the dawn. The air was crisp, biting at his nose and ears. The horse steamed from the nostrils, but seemed to enjoy running, stretching its muscles after the stiffness of the cold night. They turned up a long, rocky canyon cresting a low green velvet saddle to find the elk before them.

Spread out across the grassy depression, heads down or lifted in vigilance, they made a remarkable sight, each bull tremendously racked with his harem and calves clustered around him, trusting his skill in combat. They sat their ponies downwind from the herd perhaps three hundred yards off, the twitching of the horses' tails the only movement they made.

Suddenly, but smoothly, Crowder swung down, unlimbering a long-barreled Remington fifty-caliber rifle. Lacroix did the same, slipping his new favorite—a Sharps—from the boot. Jean-Paul sat very still in the saddle, eyes fixed on the elk, the wind lifting a lock of dark hair from his scalp. He jerked in a reflex of astonishment when the two hunters suddenly touched off simultaneously, the rolling echo waning. The heads of the elk seemed to come up in unison, but they did not run at once, milling in confusion. Crowder had shoveled a second cartridge into the breech of his rifle before the massive bull elk, far across the valley, keeled over, legs thrashing at the grass, dead from the marksman's first bullet.

They fired continuously, a never ending salvo roaring in the canyon, and the air filled with acrid black powder smoke as the elk turned heel and bolted, leaving six of their number behind.

They fleshed out the carcasses, saving the hides for the Indian trade and their own clothing, leaving only the antlers, hooves and entrails steaming on the grass. The livers they ate.

They stopped to wash the blood from them at the Black Tongue Creek, letting the horses rest before repacking them, and leading them, descending, into the tiny funnel-shaped valley where the boomtown of Deep Water had sprouted up.

Lacroix remembered the tiny valley well. There had been cedar on the high ridge, a shallow stream called the Pullet. He had tussled with a three footed black bear once not far above where the gaping, ugly hole had been bored into the barren, ore-littered hillside. The stench of sulphur was in the air, a rising column of yellow smoke drifting away in the soft breeze off the high country. There was no grass in the bottomlands now, just a collection of ramshackle buildings thrown up with whatever was on hand, and farther up the hillside a swarm of canvas tents, some with wooden framing, clinging like parasites to the yielding mountain.

In the streets wagons rumbled past, drawn by picket-ribbed mules, driven by faceless men. A woman in yellow and a faded red smile waved from the porch of one of the more permanent buildings as they passed.

Men sat drunkenly in the street, and one obviously dead miner was left sprawling back in a narrow alleyway. "Let's be done and gone," Lacroix growled.

Crowder agreed. He wanted no part of the town either. He gaped in awe at the collection of people, equipment and buildings. The town, in its turn stared back. The days of Lacroix and his kind were nearly gone. These two bearded, fur clad mountain men were an oddity.

Lacroix stopped a passing citizen, grasping the man's shoulder firmly. "Where's business done in this god-neglected hole?"

The man, a well set up individual with yellow hair and an unhealthy pallor turned angrily but held back at the sight of the massive, bearded Lacroix.

"I don't speak no Frenchy," the miner said irritably.

"We've goods to sell," Crowder said in English. "Meat—who's likely to buy?"

"Parillo's mine boss of the Angel Sink," the miner said with a toss of his head. "You'll find him likely in the Fire Eye Saloon."

"*Merci*," Lacroix said, slowly letting go of the man's shoulder. With a scowl the miner turned and stalked away, thumbs hooked in his suspenders.

"Let's talk while the flies are off the meat," Crowder suggested. Lacroix nodded in agreement.

"Boy!" he called Jean-Paul to him. "You see what these towns are like. Here's a penny for you. You can have something at that place." He turned the boy's

25

head toward a general store after pressing the copper into his hand.

Jean-Paul nodded, understanding only that he was to go into the store.

"Sweet foods," Crowder added in the Ute tongue, but Lacroix scowled so fiercely at the sound of the Indian language that Crowder shut up.

The boy, who was sometimes called Mantaka, watched as his father and Crowder disappeared into the squat, faintly green building, then he turned back toward the store.

"What ya got?"

Mantaka blinked, studying the Irish boy in knickers and cap. He held out his palm, displaying the penny.

"You'll give it to me now, won't you?"

Mantaka shrugged and handed it over. The boy laughed viciously and turned to go into the general store himself. Mantaka followed him.

The storekeeper, whose rightful name was Sorley—a name he had abandoned in the states—watched as the O'Reilly kid shouldered through the door, followed at a tentative distance by another boy.

"Le' me 'ave the lemon drops," the O'Reilly kid demanded. Like his father, that brawling miner, this kid was.

"Where'd you get the penny?" Sorley wanted to know.

"Y'ask that of all yer customers, do ya?"

"The likes of you," Sorley snapped. The other kid, a rangy, dark-eyed boy of ten or eleven wrapped in an Indian trade blanket, stood quietly, watching the transaction with interest.

"All right," Sorley mumbled, scooping the sugary

yellow drops into a white bag which he twisted shut. He handed it over with a shake of his head.

"Thanks," the Irish kid said with a twist of his mouth.

Mantaka waited, understanding that a trade was being made. He grinned when the boy came back with candy. He must be a shrewd trader, this one, to have gotten so much for so little. He stuck out a hand for his share.

"Get lost, ya dumb savage," the town boy told him. He shoved Mantaka aside and went out, popping a lemon drop into his mouth.

Mantaka tugged at the boy's ragged, filthy shirt.

"Get lost, I tol' ya."

The boy laughed once, harshly, then stepped into the street, waving a hand to a friend, a boy several years older.

"What d'ya got, Tim?"

"Lemon drops."

"Gi'me some."

The new boy was broad in the shoulders, hat tipped back that allowed rust red hair to spill out across his lumpy forehead.

"Two! No more, Stinger," the O'Reilly kid said.

"Shaddup," the kid called Stinger said, grabbing a handful which he stuffed into his freckled cheeks. "What's he?" Stinger asked around the mouthful of sweets.

"Who? Him?" O'Reilly shrugged. "Some kinda Indian or what—I don't know."

They walked away, talking, teasing, punching each other. Mantaka followed, fascinated by his first sight of boys his own age. They walked down past the livery and toward the blacksmith shop where they were used to passing time, sitting in the loft.

"He's still there," Stinger said finally.

"What? Oh . . . him, that don't matter. We'll have us some fun."

The O'Reilly kid stuffed the bag of candy into his hip pocket and rolled up his sleeves.

"Hey, you!" he shouted, stepping boldly toward Mantaka. "Get on out now. I'll show your nose a new way to go."

"Get on!"

Mantaka smiled and stuck out his hand, expecting a lemon drop from his new friends. Instead the boys stepped as one toward him, each taking an arm. Still Mantaka smiled, nodding his head.

Stinger suddenly unleashed a right-handed fist, catching Mantaka in the wind. "Now get out of here," the boy hissed.

Hurt, the half breed pulled back, holding his stomach.

"You unnerstand!" O'Reilly shrieked. "Get out of here."

"No speak," Mantaka said, smiling weakly.

"No speak. No speak," they taunted. Emboldened, O'Reilly stepped in, face screwed into a vicious, puckish grin. It was a mistake.

Mantaka, wielding his fist like a club chopped down on the top of O'Reilly's skull. The kid dropped like a poleaxed steer, his eyes going blank.

Mantaka shrugged and stepped over the dazed boy, reaching for the lemon drops in his pocket. With a hysterical roar, Stinger flew into him, enraged by the sudden turn.

"Damn savage," the boy growled. His shoulder hit Mantaka at the knees, sending him tumbling to the ground where they rolled in a ball of yellow dust, fists and feet flying.

Mantaka came to his feet, wary of the blows. O'Reilly still sat, wide-legged on the ground, holding his head. But Stinger was a hardier sort. Winging amateurish punches from the ground he came in like a windmill, taking aim with each shot at the younger boy's head.

Mantaka stepped aside from a left, ducked under a wild right and slapped down a powerful uppercut.

"Friends!" Mantaka shouted, fending off the blows with his hands. "*Ami!*"

But Stinger came ahead, lifting a foot to protect himself. Mantaka shrugged, grabbed the boot with utter instinct and twisted it, throwing Stinger face down on the earth.

"Sweets." Mantaka picked up the bag of candy once again, and once again Stinger waded in, tears dripping from his eyes, dirt streaking his face.

"I'll kill you!" he shrieked in a voice which broke. His stubby fists bore in, but seemed never to find their target. Finally, tired of the game, wishing to eat his sweets in peace, Mantaka waited and took Stinger's incoming arm at the wrist, twisted it violently back, at the same time jerked the boy's feet from under him with a heel.

Stinger hit the ground with a whallop that ripped the breath from him. His head spun with red and green lights. Slowly he came to a crouched position. The savage was standing there, sucking on a lemon drop. Stinger started to growl menacingly, to come to his feet, but the fist darted out instantaneously, catching the point of his chin, and Stinger collapsed into an insensible heap.

"Town boys," Mantaka said softly. Lazily, enjoying the warmth of the day, he walked the main street in the late hours, looking for Lacroix, sucking idly on the sweet candy.

# 4.

Michael O'Reilly was roaring mad, roaring drunk. His boy had been beaten up by a gang of Indian kids. He stood at the weathered bar of the Single Jack Saloon complaining bitterly.

"Took his candy away from him," O'Reilly complained. A tear actually rolled down his red cheek, but he was not taken seriously. O'Reilly kicked his kid in the pants now and then and fed him if there was anything left from his drinking bouts, but every man on the shift knew O'Reilly had no real tenderness in him for the boy.

Snot-nosed, snivelling, the kid stood beside his father, nodding his head solemnly, showing the egg-sized knot on his head to anyone who evinced a casual interest. But there were few among the hard-bitten miners who paid any attention, fewer who believed anything the O'Reilly brat said.

"I ain't seen an Indian kid in three months, let alone a gang of 'em," the man in bib overalls, Paulsen, said. He was a lean man, a retarded smile playing on his lips as he hoisted a shot glass.

"They was a gang, Mister Paulsen," the kid insisted.

"They gets around me and they kicks me. One of 'em had a warclub like. That's how I got this on my head."

"Bull snort!" Paulsen snapped.

"Shut your mouth, Paulsen," O'Reilly said. He was literally trembling. A huge, flaccid man with the lines of hard work and liquor on his face, he was unused to being mocked.

"If there is a bunch of Indian kids hanging around," Sam Reems said thoughtfully, "we should know about it. They get to looking around, slipping off with stock and whatever's handy. Happened in Farragutt when we first opened the Princess Lynn Mine there."

"You fellows ain't got nothing to do for excitement?" Paulsen said with a thin, broken laugh.

"Maybe," O'Reilly said cruelly. "And maybe it'll have to do with you."

Paulsen snapped down his glass and slid a nickel across the counter before pulling on his hat. "Not me, O'Reilly. I got better things to do than going around making an ass of myself."

The implication was there, but O'Reilly, in his current state was slow to grasp it. He stared blankly at Paulsen. It was then that the Indian boy came in the doorway.

Mantaka had wandered around the town until dark, fascinated by the smallest wonders—a plate glass window like frozen water which never melted, a place where men went and sat in a chair to have their beards removed. This shop smelled like lavender and wild rose.

The strange boy from the high country had frittered the day away, absorbed in the pace, the size of this vast town of one hundred souls. After dark he realized he had failed to meet Lacroix in the appointed place.

32

Rushing to the building, the Fire Eye Saloon, he had burst through the doors to find a collection of dirty, hard-looking white men lifting glasses or playing cards. They glanced curiously at him, but when he asked for Lacroix no one could answer him in the Ute language.

He had tried three other places of business first—including one where several half-dressed women lounged on cots, smiling up at him—before opening the splintered door to the Single Jack.

"That's him! One of 'em!" the O'Reilly kid screamed, nearly apoplectic with the sudden appearance of Mantaka.

O'Reilly was on his feet in a second, and someone snapped the door closed behind Mantaka. The bartender watched disinterestedly, barely stifling a yawn.

"Kill him, Pop!"

O'Reilly had Mantaka by the neck, hoisting him from the floor, his face a mask of cruelty. Paulsen stepped up quickly, taking O'Reilly's shoulder.

"Best put the boy down, O'Reilly. You know nothing of this boy."

"Get the hell out of here, Paulsen!"

"I'm advising you ..."

"I'm advising you to swallow your tongue!"

"Paulsen's right," Sam Reems put in. "You don't know whose kid he is."

Mantaka struggled wildly, but O'Reilly's grip was vise like. "He ain't nobody's kid," O'Reilly argues. "A thievin' Ute."

"I seen the kid with a Frenchy this morning," someone said quietly. "Trapper or something."

"Then I'll take care of a Frenchy too," O'Reilly

boasted. "Where's the rest of the Injun kids?" he demanded, turning his full attention to Mantaka.

Mantaka could only shake his head with fright. O'Reilly's hand snapped his head around as he slapped him full across the face.

"Now you speak? Now you speak, boy!"

Again the meaty hand of the miner fell on Mantaka's face. What was happening? Why did these men allow it?

"You tell me or I'll bat your brains out, boy."

There was a cool draft as the door opened behind them, and the soft fall of several footsteps to warn O'Reilly, but his attention was focused only on the helpless boy. When he did look up, it was too late.

He heard a low, throbbing growl, and felt the rush of a massive, hairy body against his. Then he seemed to be caught in a rockslide, the battering knocking his sense from him as he thudded to the floor, blood streaming from a broken nose.

"Get you up!" the bear said. There was something irresistible in the command, and despite himself O'Reilly came to his feet, swaying before the huge Moses-bearded mountain man.

Lacroix's fist fell like a battering ram, splitting O'Reilly's lips, spraying the floor with blood.

"Come up again," Lacroix invited him in his fragmented English.

The bartender had come up with a gun and he held it tentatively across the bar. Lacroix's glance made him uncertain that a simple load of buckshot would stop such a man.

"Come up again."

"No . . ." O'Reilly panted, and in response Lacroix's

boot struck out and leveled O'Reilly, his head thumping against the floor, lolling there.

"That's enough..." Paulsen managed to spit out.

"This is my boy!" Lacroix roared. "A good boy."

"He said a gang of Indian kids attacked his boy."

"No gang. I have one boy. This boy!" Lacroix said. He threw a massive arm around Mantaka's shoulder and with a single, vengeful glance around the room, stormed out.

O'Reilly came slowly to his knees, head reeling, blood dripping from his nostrils and ears. "I'll kill him," the miner grumbled, but there was little impact in his words.

"Best let well enough alone," Sam Reems advised him, "and count yourself lucky. That there was Georges Lacroix." At that O'Reilly's face fell. He had heard the stories.

"Said there wasn't no gang of kids, O'Reilly," someone advised him, "just his kid."

O'Reilly's head cleared slowly. Clutching it gingerly, he climbed up to the bar. Then another thought occurred to him.

"Boy...!" he bellowed.

But whatever else the younger O'Reilly was, he was not slow. He had been inching toward the door already, and at his father's roar he made a dash for it, scrambling under one table and over another, spilling beer and chips, with O'Reilly after him, holding his pounding head as he trotted out all the cuss words he had learned in twenty-three years of deep rock mining.

He got the kid by the coat, but the kid shed it, streaking out the door as the saloon erupted into hard, tear-producing laughter. The laughter echoed up the dark, nearly empty streets of Deep Water, but the sound of it brought not a whisper of a smile to the faces of the three who rode slowly out toward the long, black hills.

Lacroix rode close beside the boy. It surprised Crowder to notice it. It was the first affection the Frenchman had shown the boy on the trip. Perhaps, the stubby man decided, it was the first affection he had ever shown the boy. Lacroix seemed as surprised by it as he did.

The coming silver moon glazed the snow peaks and turned the grass under the horses' hoofs to moving quicksilver. Crowder had fallen back some as they came up the cedar cropped knoll, following the high rim trail toward Green Fork Creek which showed only as a restless dark line through the willows far below.

Lacroix turned back in his saddle to say something and they took him from his horse, violently. Utes—a dozen perhaps—leaped onto the trail, soundless as the night. Crowder saw a knife flash, and another. Lacroix roared like a wounded bear, slapping the flank of the stubby dun pony the kid rode. Then he fell.

"Get out of here!" Lacroix bellowed.

The pony lurched forward, stumbled, and darted into the thick forest. A Ute clung to the mane of Mantaka's horse. Without thinking about it Mantaka drove his skinning knife through the brave's forearm and with a grunt the man fell away, angered surprise in his moon bright eyes.

Lacroix had been set upon by them like a bear by enraged bees, and he fought back like a mountain lion. He struck out with a massive fist, feeling a face collapse under it. An overeager young brave drove a knife at Lacroix's chest, but it did not even penetrate the layers

36

of furs the mountain man wore, and he paid for his mistake taking an answering fist to the ribs.

Lacroix sidestepped a knife, hiprolled another brave and felt a horrible blow low in his back where a Ute lance had buried its head.

"Lacroix!"

Crowder had whipped his horse forward, unlimbering the Remington. His first shot was hasty and missed the mark, lighting the painted face of a broken-toothed brave. Hurriedly he opened the breech and thrust home a second cartridge, catching an Indian in the chest as the man grabbed for his horse's reins. Lacroix spun around, his face utterly savage as if incensed at the audacity of the attacking Utes.

"Lacroix!" Crowder shouted again.

Lacroix spun around, grabbed for the back of Crowder's horse and was taken from behind by a steely forearm around the throat. Lacroix ripped the arm from him, throwing the man over his shoulder.

Crowder, trying desperately to shovel home another cartridge in the breech loader, was hit with a musket ball in the leg, the flash of the antique weapon lighting the marksman's face so that Crowder was able to see it wash out with pain as his answering bullet found its mark.

Lacroix stood in the open, swinging with both fists, a giant angered to madness. He caught a Ute on the point of the chin and the brave fell as if it had been a sledge hammer. Another lunged at the Frenchman with a knife, drawing blood from a deep gash across his hand, but Lacroix calmly took it and responded with a violent kick to the Ute's groin.

"Lacroix, get aboard!" Crowder shouted, but it was

impossible. The Indians swarmed over him now. An angry cut had opened across his forehead, another below the eye.

Crowder circled the frightened pony, trying for a clear shot, but there was none as the Indians pressed close, dragging him finally from his horse.

From the perimeter of the woods Mantaka watched, his heart urging him to fight, his fear holding him back. He saw his father go down under the massed weight of ten armed warriors. Crowder had wrestled free, lunging again for his horse, the Remington again exploding with deadly fire. Crowder reached his horse, dragged his injured leg up and swung the pony's head around. He took one final look at Lacroix and rode for the shelter of the night-darkened cedars. A knife blade flashed in the moonlight as the Utes worked on Lacroix.

"Ride, boy!" Crowder shouted, coming up on Mantaka suddenly.

Mantaka hesitated a moment, but there was no hope for the big Frenchman, so he turned his horse, his head filled with dizzy horror. Together he and Crowder rode into the rock strewn dark hills, the sounds of Ute war screams echoing in their ears.

"They're afoot," Crowder gasped. "We'll be far away at first light."

Silently they wove through the rocks and scattered cedar and pine. Crowder's mouth had fallen slack, his thin hair damp and tangled. He held his badly bleeding leg as he slumped in the saddle.

"Where's the house, boy? The cabin."

Mantaka indicated the high, barren peak with a nod of his head. Crowder grunted.

"It figures," he said appreciatively, surveying the

high reaches. "The grizzly ranges high."

They had gone not a mile when Crowder suddenly slid from the saddle, hitting the earth with a bone-jarring crunch.

Mantaka found a scarf in the woodsman's kit and tied a tourniquet above the musket wound. It was a time before Crowder came around, the loss of blood telling heavily.

"Well then..." he panted. "Upward. Ever upward." Crowder was breathing heavily in the cold altitude. The wind growled in the canyon depths, swaying the largest of the pines, cutting through even their heavy clothing. Mantaka took Crowder's reins and led the horse behind his own. The cabin was there. Timid Morning Light would be there waiting. She would know what to do.

Dawn was coloring the far running clouds before they came in sight of the tiny cabin. Crowder had come around again. With clenched teeth he gripped the pommel of his saddle, his face waxen, the skin taut across his cheekbones. The blood seeped from his leg, staining the patches of snow.

Mantaka swung down in front of the cabin. He made for the house.

"Boy!" Crowder growled in a strangely hollow voice. "Get me down!"

Mantaka nodded and braced himself as the man half stepped, half fell from the horse, staining Mantaka with his blood.

"No," Crowder said as the boy turned to go, "I'll see!"

There was an edge to the mountain man's voice that Mantaka did not understand at first. Then he noticed the faint, unusual odor. The goats Lacroix had brought from Falls Church were not in their pen. Neither was the mule in its corral. Mantaka felt his muscles tighten in despair, his stomach turn over. Crowder pushed by him and hobbled unsteadily to the front door, pushing it open with the muzzle of his rifle.

"God!" the mountain man groaned.

Mantaka was at his shoulder. Crowder turned and screamed at the boy. "Get out of here! Get the hell out of here!"

But it was too late. Mantaka had seen through the crack of the open door. The dark, limp form which had been a dark-eyed, kind woman. Which had been mother, home and all that was warm in the cold world.

# 5.

Timid Morning Light was buried near the Green Creek where the sunlight filtered through deep fern and a tangle of wild blackberries. Crowder's grave was near to the cabin, a great bleak gray stone for his marker.

Mantaka put the torch to the cabin early in the morning and with all the supplies he could carry on his back, Crowder's Remington in his hand, he strode down the long highlands toward the shelter of the forest below. If the Utes had come once, he reasoned, they might come again. Well, let them. Let them have the charred timbers, the barren mountain, the eternal ice. They would not have his blood.

The horses he had set free, reasoning that the problems of concealing them and constantly foraging for them at this harsh time of year outweighed the advantages. This way he had only himself to worry about. He would find Lacroix's remains first of all, then with winter looming, he would find a fortress for the long, dark months. He kept to the ridges, just below the skyline, among the timber. He saw no sign of Indian the first day. Lacroix was where they had left him, hardly recognizable.

"What were they thinking?" he asked himself. They had cut Lacroix's hands off, as if taking the claws from a grizzly.

The soil was hard, and he had nothing to dig with but a pointed stick, which made for slow going. Finally, under a lightning-struck, broken-limbed pine he had scooped out a grave for his father. On the white, barkless trunk he scratched, *Lacroix*, 1864.

He had no certain destination in mind, but he wanted to be as far from the Ute territory as possible. The mountains, all appearing the same despite their distinct angles and dispositions, offered little to choose from. Finally, choosing the eastern slope of Pyramid Peak as a relatively safe and wind sheltered refuge, he began the long walk.

He walked without thinking consciously of his situation, but there was no escaping his position. Surrounded by hostiles, he was a scant eleven years old. He spoke only Ute, the language of his enemies, with a bare smattering of French. Of towns and townspeople he had early learned a bitter lesson; besides, he was bred to the wild country and knew only these ranging broad peaks. He did not allow himself to think any further.

Near the creek called Coscobo he set his snares and built his house on a high, bare ledge. His "house" was a massive Jeffrey pine with dead boughs woven through the lower branches for a floor which was covered with green boughs. Then, carefully, he built the walls, weaving other branches, overlapping them as he went down, drawing them tight against the wind.

He had chosen well and finished just in time, for the snow season was already upon him. Mantaka awoke in his tight, tiny nest one morning to find the snow two feet deep at the base of the tree.

"I must build higher," he told himself. Diligently he set to work on a second story. From there he could walk out onto an upper ledge of stone which butted against the tree. Along an eyebrow of a trail he was able to ascend farther yet, to the windswept crest.

Surveying the snow-blanketed lowlands he doubted if the Utes were about. He doubted also that he could be found, but he moved warily from snare to snare, the Remington always near at hand. The ammunition had to be kept dry. He had but a dozen rounds and no way of obtaining more. The days were short. There was no time to think, but only for the work of checking the now usually empty snares. It was the nights which caused Mantaka to feel even more empty.

Outside the winds howled, and the snows freshened the winterscape. Mantaka sat huddled inside his tree house, wrapped in buffalo skins, the smoke from a tiny cooking fire seeping through the upper boughs.

"What is it that's brought me here?"

There was no answer to his voice. There never was an answer, but only the groaning of the wind, the sounds the wilderness made: snow sliding from a ledge, the howl of the far gray timber wolf, an occasional owl in the high forest. "What is it that's brought me here?"

He slept as he did each night, a tiny huddled figure, clinging to a life he could not understand, which barely admitted his existence. But he survived the winter. That first awful winter when his belly shrunk and cried for food. Once he managed to club a porcupine, devouring almost all of it raw, saving the quills for needles and hooks. He learned the art of trapping beaver using a simple log fall.

Crossing the Coscobo late in the winter he fell through the thin ice and was saved only by an instant reflex which brought his arm up, driving his skinning knife deeply into the solid ice for a hand hold. But he survived.

In May, with the grass high and green, the harebell and black-eyed susans rife in the meadows, he found the men working along the Coscobo.

"And what in hell are you?" the gravel voiced man with the yellow beard asked.

"What's that?" Weiner asked.

"Indian kid."

Weiner, a wiry one-eyed man scratched at his chin and examined the boy. He had been standing there for hours, just watching as they panned. Matted hair, deep eyed, the boy said nothing in response. Mantaka did not understand their English, nor did he understand what they were fishing for. There were no trout this low on the Coscobo. The big yellow bearded man tossed a rock at him.

"Leave off," Weiner said to Cooms. "The kid ain't bothering ought."

"I don't like nobody around the claim," Cooms replied brusquely. He straightened up, pressing a meaty hand to his aching back. "Never know who the kid'll talk to. Who sent him."

"Boy," Weiner called, ignoring his partner, "come have to eat!" He showed the pot to Mantaka who hesitantly took a half step forward.

"Come to eat," Weiner said with a smile that broke Mantaka's resistance. He came down off the knoll, the rifle in hand. He was wary, but hungry for human com-

44

panionship. He had not seen a living human being in six months.

"Look at 'im get to it," Weiner said with a delighted chuckle. Cooms sucked dourly on a corncob and wagged his head.

"I don't like it," he muttered. After a cup of coffee he went back to his panning along the stream.

Mantaka watched it all with interest as Weiner watched him, curious about this straggly boy with the pathetic home-made clothes.

"No," Mantaka said quietly after a time.

"What?"

"No," Mantaka repeated. In the dirt he sketched a fish, rubbing it out with his foot. "No." Then he pointed upstream where the Coscobo took a long slow turn through the high cliffs.

Weiner burst out laughing. "No, boy. Not fish. We're not fishing." He had to wipe the tears from his eyes.

"What's so funny?"

"No wonder he's watching us. Thinks we're trying to catch fish in our pans, I guess. Must seem almighty amusing."

Cooms turned away with a grunt, walking farther into the shallow stream.

"This is what we want," Weiner said. He opened a leather pouch, spilling out a thimbleful of gold dust. "Gold!" he winked.

"Gold," Mantaka repeated with a shrug.

"You talk too much," Cooms shouted angrily.

After eating Mantaka wandered off upstream, his thoughts for the first time in months not on how he would come by his next meal, but how to repay the

45

kindness which had given him his last meal.

Weiner, sleeves of his sweat stained shirt rolled up, worked in the icy, quick-running water beside his partner, eye fixed on the pan which he rocked ever so gently. Well, there was nothing to it, Mantaka decided. He knew where there was plentiful gold. Near the crumbled quartz chutes of the Little Gorge River the water spewed out of the high cliffs, circling a bowl shaped depression of nearly white granite before tumbling out again into the upper reaches of the Coscobo. Deposited in that depression was pounds of the glittering yellow stuff Weiner and the yellow bearded man fished for.

In that place, called Rose Canyon for the profusion of deep purple wild roses clinging to the sparse soil, Mantaka, the French-Indian boy collected this ... gold. Wading in knee deep into the cold waters of the basin he collected what he could in his hands, stuffing it into his rucksack.

It is not much, he reflected sadly, only a pound or so. There was more, much more, but his sack was small, the water chilly, and the hour late. Perhaps it would be enough to repay Weiner for his stew.

Weiner was hunched over the fire, weariness evident in his face as he cupped his coffee. Mantaka walked in easily, not realizing that Cooms was missing until the dirty, bulky man emerged from the shadows of the underbrush, the cocking of his huge Navy Colt sounding loud in the night.

"Stand where you are, boy!" he growled.

Mantaka, not understanding, smiled and took another two steps before Cooms fairly leaped forward and swung his heavy pistol against the side of Mantaka's neck, dropping him to his knees.

"I said stand fast," he panted.

Weiner was beside him in a second, restraining the gun hand. "The boy don't speak English," he sputtered.

"What's he doing here?" Cooms demanded, his eyes furious.

"How would I know?"

"Just a bowl of stew—and you thought he'd wander off. The little beggar." He glared at Mantaka who sat rigidly, afraid to twitch.

"There was no cause to hit him."

Weiner crouched beside Mantaka, turning up his long straight hair to examine the ugly bruise. "No need for it, Cooms."

"Well, what's he lurking about for?" Cooms snarled, but even before he had finished his question, his eye caught the glittering dust that had spilled from Mantaka's sack.

"Holy . . ." The firelight illuminated the odd, gawking smile on the big man's face. Gingerly he stretched out a hand and pinched up some of the dust, spreading it across his palm. Mantaka rested on his hands and knees, half afraid to rise. What he had done, he could not guess. He had meant to please.

"There's a pound of it here easy," Cooms said in a subdued voice. He sucked thoughtfully at his yellow mustache before his eyes flashed toward Mantaka.

"Where, boy!"

"Don't scare him," Weiner said. Carefully he helped Mantaka to his feet.

Mantaka's first instinct was to bolt for the woods, but something held him fast. He liked Weiner, and perhaps Cooms was not so bad as he seemed. He watched the

47

big man finger the gold dust. He is a fool for this gold, Mantaka thought.

"This is more than we've panned all month," Cooms admitted. "Give the boy some stew, Bob."

Weiner barely suppressed a grimace of disgust, but he ladled out another bowlful of the nearly warm stew. Cooms had hoisted the boy to his feet and was dusting him off. Mantaka, for all his bewilderment, looked pleased about the attention.

Cooms sat on the broken log near the fire, hands dangling. He watched the boy shovel the food down. When Mantaka was through he slapped his legs expectantly.

"Well, now. Where did you come by this, boy?" He had moved behind Mantaka, putting his hand on the boy's neck.

It was a rough, work-hardened hand, and Mantaka was not sure he liked it there. Cooms rubbed his neck in what was meant as a gesture of affection, comradeliness, but emerged as a clumsy, rough squeeze. Mantaka lifted his eyes to Weiner. The little man had not moved, keeping his eyes turned down. There was no understanding people, Mantaka reflected. Now it was Cooms who came to him, Weiner who withdrew. It was the gold.

"Where did you get this?" Cooms repeated.

He showed Mantaka a pinch of gold, shrugged and pointed upstream. "Where? You take me?" he asked, speaking this time in broken Ute. Mantaka nodded.

"You see!" Cooms shouted, throwing back his head. "We'll be rich, Bob." He lowered his voice to a rasping whisper. "Rich, man."

Cooms did not sleep that night, rolling in his blankets

with excitement. He was up with the first chill gray light of morning, already dressed, the fire going under the smoke blackened coffee pot. Weiner pulled on his boots sullenly, turning down the coffee. They tramped up the Coscobo until they crossed the Little Gorge. From there it was a steep, gruelling climb through the brush and broken rock to Rose Canyon. Cooms was sweating through his shirt by then, cursing the rocks, the climb and all of nature. "Damn it, boy," he muttered, "you better be right."

Weiner moved almost silently, deeply worried. He could not put his finger directly on the cause of his concern, but he had bad feelings about this. Very bad feelings. At noon they reached the depression. Weiner sagged onto the sandy shore beneath a stand of scrub oak, his face waxen. Cooms, on the other hand, threw down his pack and waded immediately into the icy water. Almost instantly he straightened up, his cupped hand streaming water, a glittering thimbleful of dust in his palm.

"God!" He let out a long, joyous howl. "We're rich, Bob! It's here! A ton of it."

As he spoke he wandered in circles in the knee-high water, snatching at the bottom here and there, working toward the plummeting falls which drowned out his voice as he neared them.

He stood nearly under the falls, the mist swirling around him, the foam churning at his feet, arms outstretched in ecstasy. Weiner slumped miserably on the bank, Mantaka standing beside him, confused by the stark contrast between the gold miners.

Cooms waded ashore breathlessly, throwing himself down on the earth with a sigh, rolling over to face the sun. "We've hit it, Bob!"

"It'll be the end of us," Weiner said.

"It's the *beginning!* The beginning, old timer." Cooms scowled briefly, deeply. "You'll see. The boy's made us rich. What did you want? To break your back for a few dollars in this forsaken country?"

"Maybe so," Weiner nodded. "Maybe so. They'll come," he said suddenly, turning to the big man. "Others will come. They'll find out."

"Never," Cooms hissed, wagging his head, but he knew what Weiner said was true. The first trip to the bank to purchase supplies with the new gold, to register the claim ... "We'll stand our ground," he vowed, "or ..."

"Or die trying?" Weiner suggested painfully.

"Or die trying."

# 6.

It was already late in the year when Cooms and Weiner trekked out of the high mountains, bringing a reluctant Mantaka with them. They walked side by side, Cooms leading their only horse which was heavily laden with gold from the Rose Canyon claim. There had already been one hard snow in the high passes, and the miners knew it was now or never if they were to register their claim in Deep Water, the nearest community with a territorial recorder and assay office. Cooms figured they didn't need the assayer. They knew damned well what they had, and it was high grade.

What they did need were supplies to hold out against the Rocky Mountain winter. Men had been known to eat their boots, their dogs and each other during a hard winter. Weiner didn't appear to have much meat on him.

"I sure don't like this." Weiner was apprehensive. Below, in the long valley sat Deep Water. From what they had heard the ore was nearly played out in and around Milk Creek. Showing new color to the men down below would be like waving a red flag at a bull.

"I don't like it any better than you," Cooms spat.

They sat on that high ridge, the cold wind rolling over them, and Cooms shook his head. "But we can't spend that gold in them hills. the claim ain't ours yet . . ."

"Yeah," Weiner agreed harshly, "but nobody's shootin' at us over it yet either."

"You always look to the dismal," Cooms said, digging his worn out chaw from his cheek, spitting out the leavings. "You sure got a way of lookin' to the dismals."

Cooms decided Weiner was an odd case. His partner had uncomplainingly clambered over mountains and deserts, digging hard rock from sun-up to sun-down, suffering cold and privation. Yet now that they had struck it, Weiner was as unhappy as a man could be. Cooms himself had no such doubts plaguing him. Growing up in a war-blackened Georgia, watching his father work himself to death on a hard rock Missouri farm, Cooms knew exactly what he wanted. It was gold that could buy it.

Not a night since he had come west had he failed to dream of the women, the fine house, the horses that a rich strike could purchase. Now they had struck it—the rest was only a matter of time.

"Let's get on down," Cooms said impatiently. Nevertheless he took the time to thrust his Colt Navy revolver into his belt and button his coat over it. He nodded to Weiner and then to Mantaka.

"Come on, kid."

"No." Mantaka squatted on the grass, rifle across his knees. He had memories of the town and no urge to revive them.

"Get up and get moving," Cooms said sharply.

"Leave him be," Weiner said. He half understood

Mantaka's reluctance. Towns had always been anathema to Weiner as well.

"He could hotfoot it back to the strike," Cooms argued.

"And what? Hell, if he'd wanted gold he damn sure could have had it before us."

"He didn't know what it was for," Cooms said in exasperation. He glared at Mantaka and Weiner a moment longer, failing to comprehend either of them. "Hell," he grunted finally, "let's get on down."

Cooms led off, taking the horse. Weiner waited a moment. "Want me to get you something, kid?" he asked Mantaka. Mantaka did not understand at first. "Want some sweets or something?"

Sweets? Mantaka smiled wryly. Now he understood the question and he dipped a hand into his buckskin pouch, showing Weiner what he wanted. Weiner picked up the brass cartridge, turned it over thoughtfully and handed it back.

"Fifty caliber. Remington."

Mantaka smiled faintly. The wind drifted his long, silky hair across his face as he watched Weiner stride off after Cooms who was looking back in disgust.

Sweets ... Mantaka looked again toward the town. A dirty yellowish blotch against the green mountains. Winter was coming in once more, and he had but four bullets left. Now it was time to do his hunting, to find his winter home. He had no intention of spending a winter with these prospectors.

He had been hungry for company, for the sight of a man's face. Now he had seen enough for a time. Cooms and Weiner disappeared around a tight bend in the trail, Mantaka's eyes following them. After he could no longer see them he climbed up onto a nearly square yellow boulder where brush screened him from view. Now too he was out of the wind, and Mantaka let his eyes droop shut and he napped, the Remington still across his lap, his hand near the trigger.

Weiner trailed Cooms into Deep Water, not liking the scent of the town any more than Georges Lacroix had a year earlier. Half the buildings which were occupied when Lacroix had been there were already closed down, being torn apart for firewood as the ore played out, the town died.

"Over there," Cooms nodded and Weiner's eyes lifted to the faded, hand painted sign which identified the assayer's office. Tying up at the rail Cooms unloaded the canvas sacks from the horse's haunches and they tramped in, finding a sleepy-eyed man with his boots propped up on a table out front.

"He'p you?"

"Need an assay," Cooms grunted. He took off his hat and wiped back his sweat soaked, stringy hair. The assay he needed only because it was required for the claim papers and would be necessary if the time came when they needed outside capital to develop their claim. Cooms knew what he had, and so did the assayer—instantly—as Cooms dipped into a small sack and thumbed a nugget from his palmful of samples onto the counter.

The assayer's eyes lighted and he picked up the nugget. "I'll need some typical rock," he said, eyeing the ore.

"That's about typical," Cooms replied coolly. The assayer blinked and turned the nugget over.

"I'll have it in a couple of hours," he told them.

"Those more samples?" he glanced at the heavy sacks a nervous Weiner held.

"That's dust," Cooms said. "And I don't need no assay on that. It's purely fine."

Weiner nearly winced. Cooms was normally cautious, but he was enjoying the envy in the assayer's expression.

"The express office will weigh it out and trade for coin," the assayer told them. "it's in the same building as the recorder."

"Thanks," Cooms said. He plopped his hat back on and told the man, "Have that assay as soon as possible, will ya? You keep that sample in payment. I figure that's a fair exchange, don't you?"

"Fair enough," the man answered.

He walked with Cooms and Weiner to the door, watching them move up the boardwalk toward the peeling, weathered recorder's office. Sam Courtney sat on the boardwalk not twenty feet away, whittling a piece of soft pine. The assayer called to him. "Sam. Watch the office, will you?"

"Sure." Courtney shrugged then watched as the assayer slipped into his threadbare coat and took off uptown after the two prospectors.

Sam Courtney had been born lazy, but he wasn't stupid. His eyes narrowed a moment, watching the hurrying assayer, the prospectors staggering as they walked with those heavy canvas sacks. Putting two and two together, Courtney walked to the assay office, put up a "closed" sign and shut the door, walking quickly toward the recorder's office himself, leaving his whittling behind. The assayer, whose name was Charlie Peck, was an Ohioan who had never wanted to be an assayer.

He had come west to get rich, like most of the residents of Deep Water. But like most of them he had always been a hair late, in the wrong place, too slow.

This time he meant to be first. Peck waited outside the recorder's office until Cooms and Weiner had finished recording their title and had exchanged their dust for gold coin. Then as the prospectors, laughing, arms around each other's shoulders, crossed the street to the Single Jack Saloon, Peck hurriedly slipped into the office himself. Ross Hazard was stretching his arms overhead. The recorder was a big, slack-jawed man with only a dusting of hair. He finished his stretch while Peck waited impatiently.

"What can I do for you, Charlie?" Hazard asked with a yawn.

"I was looking for two men. I just ran an assay for them. Cooms and Weiner?"

"They just left." Hazard leaned forward, planting his huge forearms on his desk, suspicion creeping into his expression. "How'd it assay out?"

"Only fair, Ross," Peck said with a shrug of indifference. "Where did they file?"

There was a forced casualness in Peck's voice, but Hazard was reading something else in Peck's tight smile, the way the assayer's eyes refused to meet his.

"Rose Canyon," Hazard answered finally. He had picked up a pencil and was toying with it.

"That's up along the Coscobo, isn't it?"

"Near." Ross Hazard was silent, waiting for Peck to come to his point. "But you say it doesn't show much promise?"

"Average. Not enough for a man to sell the farm for," he laughed. "But you know," Peck scratched his

56

head as if he had just now thought of something, "my cousin, Henry, back East, has been wanting to go prospecting. Just for the heck of it, to get away from his wife, I think ..."

Peck laughed again, unconvincingly, and Hazard responded with a fraternal smile.

"He's been asking me to find something for him—through the office—with just enough color to make wages." Peck waved a casual hand.

"You going to file?" Ross asked, cutting through it.

"Sure, why not," Peck laughed. "In my name. I'll sign it over when he gets out here."

"Ain't legal unless you've been up there and marked out your patch," Ross reminded him.

"I know. But Ross, we're old pals." Hazard nodded and Peck said off-handedly, "Maybe the downstream adjoining parcel from the Cooms-Weiner claim."

"How about upstream?" Ross Hazard replied. He leaned far forward, hands clenched together. "Me, I'm taking downstream."

Peck's face whitened and his lips compressed. Ross was glaring at him, jaw set. "How about it, Charlie. What kind of color have they got?"

"It'll run ninety-nine and a third," Charlie Peck muttered. "The best I've ever seen."

Hazard smiled thinly, taking out an application form from his desk drawer. He handed it to Peck and gave him a pen, taking another for himself.

"Upstream?" Hazard asked. Peck stifled a curse and nodded his agreement.

The door clicked shut and Hazard glanced up to see that loafer, Sam Courtney lounging against it, his torn hat tilted back on his head. Courtney was grinning.

"What the hell do you want?"

"In," Courtney replied. He walked over to the desk, putting his palms on it. Ross Hazard could smell the whisky and sweat on the man.

"You're in."

"Not in the door, damn it," Courtney exploded. Then he smiled again. "In on the strike. I figure you two have already taken the two best claims, but I'll settle for an uphill."

"You got the twenty-five bucks for a recording fee?"

"No." Courtney rubbed his whiskered jaw. "But I kinder figured you boys might lend it to me."

"I'll be damned!" Hazard erupted, his fists tightening, the tendons in his bull neck standing taut.

"You can share with me or share with half the town," Sam Courtney said mildly. Then he planted his rump on Ross Hazard's desk and reached across for an application form.

Michael O'Reilly was nearly dead drunk, but even in that condition, he could realize that someone was buying another round of drinks. He lifted his head from the whisky stained table and through bleary, red eyes saw the bartender setting them up, saw the buckskin clad prospector paying with new minted gold.

The one that was doing the buying was a big man with a yellow beard and a snoot full of raw whisky. His face was flushed with alcohol. His partner was a narrow-built man with one eye gone. He seemed uncomfortable, more than anything else.

O'Reilly struggled to his feet, nearly tipping the table over, and he zig-zagged to the bar, not wanting to miss out. "I'll have one, Tyler!"

The barkeep turned to Cooms. "You buying him one too?"

"Sure!" Cooms slapped O'Reilly on the shoulder. "Looks like a man could use a drink."

Weiner turned away in disgust. They should be making their purchases, packing up and getting out of this town. Cooms never could drag himself away from a bottle until it was empty. Today was no exception. Yet it should have been. It was a time for caution, and Weiner knew it. Yet Cooms could not shut it off. Not that he had actually revealed anything about the claim, but he was making broad hints, doing the kind of boasting he had always enjoyed, the kind most prospectors did.

Most times when a man bragged it up, folks knew he was putting on some shine. It was when the bragging was accompanied by a flow of gold money that folks listened seriously—and Cooms kept on buying. Now the big Irishman was draped over Cooms' shoulder, encouraging him to try champagne.

"We got to be goin'," Weiner said. Cooms brushed him aside. "Cooms! It's time," Weiner said in exasperation.

"Wha's difference? T'day, t'morrow."

"It's time now!" Weiner persisted. The Irishman turned menacingly toward Weiner. O'Reilly wanted no one taking his meal ticket out of that bar.

"You don't like it here," O'Reilly said, thumping Weiner on the chest. "*You* leave!"

Cooms only seemed to think that O'Reilly was funny; swallowing his bile, Weiner turned and did just that—shoving through the crowd of free loaders. He stood on the boardwalk, taking in a deep breath of fresh air, hearing a glass break against the floor behind him. *The assay.*

Weiner strode across the street and up past the new brick Wells Fargo office to the assayer's. He frowned at the sign in the window. "Closed." Trying the door, Weiner found it locked; maybe the man had gone to dinner.

The miner hesitated, then went about his errands. He picked up a tough-looking seven-year-old mule and a pack. Leading the animal back downtown, he tied it at the rail before the mercantile and ducking under the rail went in, slapping dust from his jeans.

For a man who had spent the last six months in the mountains, the general store was a bountiful paradise. Weiner bought himself some new boots, two shirts and a pair of jeans. Guessing at Cooms' size he bought a pair for his partner as well.

He bought fifty pounds of flour, ten of sugar, two sides of bacon and two cases of beans. It was going to be a hard winter, and Weiner had no intention of being starved out. He asked for and got a case of canned peaches and a case of tomatoes. His sweet tooth got the better of him and he bought a handful of licorice whips along with a pound of chewing tobacco for Cooms who could not live without the stuff.

"You carry cartridges for a Remington, caliber fifty?" Weiner asked the storekeeper.

"I think. Maybe." The clerk climbed a ladder, looking in a dusty recess for the shells. "That's an odd caliber, not many men tote a Remington. Damned fine gun, though. That's what them American sharpshooters carried when they won the world trophy over in Europe a few years back. Here," the storekeeper slapped a green box on the counter. "There used to be a mountain man name of Crowder who carried a Remington—proud as a peacock of it he was too. Said he took down an elk at seven hundred yards with it. . . . Of course what's brag and what's fact? Anyway, I used to keep a box around for Crowder. He ain't been around in a year or so, I guess. Looks like the Utes got his scalp."

Weiner stifled a yawn, nodded with feigned interest and stowed the cartridges in his pack. "What do I owe you?"

The man scribbled on the counter briefly with a stub of a pencil and announced, "Thirty-two fifty."

Weiner counted it out slowly, moving his lips as he did so.

"How many of you boys goin' up into the mountains?" the storekeeper asked, dropping the gold and silver pieces into the register.

"How many?" Weiner was puzzled. "Why do you ask?"

"Hell, I'm runnin' low on everything. This is the best day I've had in three years. Folks been buying up every pick and pan, sack of flour and salt I got. Hell, boy," the clerk winked, "I been around gold country long enough to smell a strike. And," he added, "long enough to know better than to go chasin' 'em."

Weiner hardly heard the rest of the storekeeper's conversation. The man helped Weiner pack that mule and then went back to work, leaving Weiner to lean his head miserably against the mule's back, cursing the day.

"We got trouble," Weiner muttered. The mule twitched its long ears and rolled its eyes at Weiner who started morosely off up the street. Now he knew why the assay office was closed. And Cooms was over at that saloon still shooting his mouth off to make matters worse.

They had trouble. A peck of it.

# 7.

The shadows had grown long in the mountain valleys. A long-winging flock of Canada geese cut a wandering "V" across the darkening skies. Mantaka rose, stretched his cold muscles and climbed down from the rock. The sound of hooves had awakened Mantaka, and he waited now, expecting Cooms and Weiner to appear around the tight bend in the trail. After a minute they did. Weiner was leading a pack mule, and Cooms riding the roan—or trying to.

He sagged drunkenly in the saddle. His hat had been lost; his shirt was stained. Mantaka stepped forward to meet the prospectors, and it was then that his ears told him someone else was on the trail behind the two.

Weiner looked extremely weary. Dust rose from his plodding boots in tiny puffs as he walked forward. Cooms, lurching in the saddle, sang a tuneless, muttered song. And behind them came fifty others.

Mantaka's jaw sagged in an incredulous gape. Weiner did not even look back; he knew they were there and Cooms and Weiner were leading them into the wilderness like two grizzled, buckskin garbed prophets. Most rode horses, some led pack animals. All were bristling with picks and shovels. Three men were walking, singing a sea chanty as they strode the long hills in the fading light. One of these, a square-shouldered Dutchman pushed a wheelbarrow loaded with mining tools before him.

Weiner plodded past and Mantaka fell in beside him, his head swivelling back constantly to the swarm of men, not understanding.

"It's the gold," Weiner said breathlessly, "it's the gold they want, Mantaka."

Mantaka accepted the explanation but it made no real sense to him. All of these men leaving their warm village, traipsing into the high country with winter looming. Half of them had no food supplies, no furs, no rifles for hunting. Mantaka supposed they must all be good mountain men. Who else would so foolishly go into the high reaches this time of the year?

Weiner could only wag his head and repeat over and over, "Damned fools, damned gold."

He handed Mantaka the box of cartridges which he had kept inside his coat, and the boy took them gratefully. Now he would have meat for the winter. He had already made a decision. He would leave Rose Canyon immediately. There were too many men, and their eyes glittered like gold. One of them he even recognized. An unsteady, hugely built man with a shock of red hair. O'Reilly.

Once they reached Rose Canyon the men fanned out upstream and down, with only Peck and Hazard, trying to protect their own claims, respecting any order. Cooms was out cold and Weiner, although he objected, hadn't the heart to stand up to them. They splashed into the river, panning before they had unpacked their horses or rolled out their beds. Weiner took a last lingering look at them and, shaking his head, set up their tent, dragging Cooms inside to sleep it off.

Mantaka watched for a time, felt the bitter cold of night begin to settle, and wondered what these men would do when the snows fell. But already one man had found color and he stood shouting exultantly in the middle of the fast running stream, his clothes soaking wet, his teeth chattering.

Peck and Hazard had taken the time to stake out their recorded claims—whatever these fools managed to pan out they could keep. The assayer and the recorder meant to go about things in a businesslike manner. It was not a few ounces of placer gold they were after. Peck knew it was down there. He read the formation of the land, the volcanic float rock he spotted here and there, the wedge of quartz which streaked the bluffs on either side of the Coscobo, and he knew he had something big. Keeping it would be the problem.

"I figure we're in this together," he told Hazard. "And it's best we help each other. I'll sit guard while you work, if you'll do the same."

"All right." Hazard was a powerfully built man, and he had seen his share of Indian fighting and barroom brawling, but what he saw now frightened him. They were madmen storming up and down the creek. Sam Courtney had been one of the first to find more than dust and he was showing everyone who would look his thumb-sized nugget.

Michael O'Reilly, now seeming nearly sober, waded in the icy Coscobo, using only his hands. If O'Reilly came by any gold Peck had no doubt it would be some- one else's. Night and an icy wind only slowed them down. Lanterns were lighted and sat upon the bank or carried into the stream. The miners moved about like so many peripatetic fireflies, the yellow reflections of the lanterns glazing the black Coscobo.

Cooms, holding his head, staggered from the tent and his eyes opened in amazement. Angrily he grabbed for his rifle, but his head hurt too much, and his stomach was turning over. Gingerly he moved forward and sagged beside Weiner on the skinned log, taking a cup coffee which the little man offered.

"I'll run 'em all off tomorrow," Cooms promised. Weiner lifted an eyebrow and said nothing. Finally he observed.

"Fifty gold crazy men. You couldn't run 'em off with cannon. Wait—winter'll do it for us. Let 'em have the dust. We know what we've got."

Normally Cooms would have flared up again. Patience or any suggestion of it was foreign to his way of thinking. "Maybe you're right," he muttered. He finished his coffee and then went off into the timber to be sick.

Weiner sat in the flickering shadows, his coffee sending clouds of steam against the cold of night. It was a time before he noticed the boy.

"Goin' off are you? Can't say I blame you, Mantaka."

Together they watched the incessant activity along the streambed. Mantaka had his rifle with him, sheathed in a buckskin cover. The wind off the high peaks lifted the hair on his head and numbed his ears.

"All crazy," Mantaka said in English.

Weiner said nothing in reply. There was no gainsaying it. He turned back to staring into the low-burning, wind ruffled fire and when he looked up again, Mantaka was gone, moving silently through the shadows of the camp and into the timber beyond.

Mantaka moved higher, travelling the broken, slate-littered ridges of Homestake's eastern slope. It felt good to be moving once again, to be striding among the timber, listening to the night sounds, the wind working in the pines, the rush of water from an unseen waterfall, the questioning hoot of a horned owl. He liked his solitude, he decided, enforced as it was. Those men below—they swarmed like red ants across a sun-warmed anthill. The gold must give off a poisonous gas which makes men lose their senses, he decided.

It would be a hard winter, and they had no food, yet they would have their gold. Maybe it could keep them warm. What only Weiner, Cooms and a few of the others seemed to realize was that the snow would block the pass, the return to Deep Water with tons of snow in drifts up to forty feet high. Yet Mantaka put these thoughts temporarily out of his mind. They were older than he, old enough to know better.

His mind sifted through his own problems, which were immediate, basic. He must first find a stronghold. He dared not use the tree house of last winter. The Utes had had a year to discover it, and probably they had.

He knew of a cave—once before Lacroix had built the eagle's nest cabin and they had stayed there. So Morning Light had told her son. Then he must obtain meat, smoke it and carry his provisions to the cave. Wood must be gathered.

Mantaka broke out of the timber and came to a place he knew well. A ledge of bare granite thrust out of the side of Homestake like a tongue, and Mantaka clambered up. It was still warm, retaining the heat of the sun long after the empty land had turned chill. From there Mantaka could watch the distant, starlit Arkansas River meander eastward, and from there he could see far to the north where the broken spine of the Rockies stretched toward Canada.

The boy sat there and listened to the silence of night. A magnificent, empty wilderness swept in all directions. From where he now sat he could see no lantern, no firelight; he heard no human voices. It was here he belonged, for all of the loneliness, for all of the hardship. It was a shocking realization. All of last winter he had thought only of finding other men, of hearing their laughter, sharing their food.

He had found them, yet they hardly laughed. They shared only grudgingly and were liable to strike out at any moment. Utes, whites, all more savage than raw nature. Yet there was a gnawing emptiness inside Mantaka, and he leaned his head forward, letting it rest on his knees. He thought briefly of his mother, hardly recalling her face now, but more strongly her laugh, a pleasant warmth, a soft touch. . . . The wind chilled Mantaka's tears and he stood, wiping them away. There was meat to be hunted.

When the snows came they came in early and hard. Day after day great masses of black thunderheads gathered among the peaks, blotting out the sun, smothering the green and gray of the earth with layer upon layer of snow.

The Coscobo was fringed with needles of ice, though the quick-running stream still flowed. The pass to Deep

Water was closed. The first snow had sent half of the prospectors scurrying back to safety, seeing that it was useless to pan in the creek, lacking tools, supplies and claims.

To a man they vowed to return in the spring with their own gear, and to that end they had staked out claims up and down the hills, using mounds of rocks for their corners. Yet some of the men stayed on. Cooms and Weiner, of course, and Peck and Hazard, who had come equipped and had the only other legal claim excepting that of Sam Courtney, who like O'Reilly couldn't stand the thought of a winter without whisky. The two had gone off together after gathering enough gold dust for a three month drinking spree.

Weiner and Cooms worked through even the worst of the weather, piling the snow over their shaft high with snow, glazing it with their shovels. Cooms was anxious to get rich; Weiner was anxious to get out before spring.

The fire in the pit flickered across the wall of the small shaft and Cooms breathed a curse. "Look at that," he said with a respect he reserved for horses, harlots and gold.

"It'll likely play out," Weiner said.

Neither of them believed it, as much as Weiner hoped it would be so. The light glittered on a wide vein of pure gold which wound sinuously through the milky quartz of the vein.

"Jewelry gold," Cooms said. "You could take that and beat it out into jewelry as is." With his pick he pried against the vein, the rotten quartz falling away as a sliver of gold came free. Cooms held it in his hand, biting it, turning it over in the light as if he could not accept the reality of it.

"Ten years I've been looking for something like this—half of this. Smile, damn you!" Cooms shouted, slapping Weiner on the shoulder.

Weiner attempted it, but it was a sickly expression. It seemed to Weiner that the sinuous streak of gold was writing his death warrant in the stone.

A month's work only proved the vein to be richer. The vein did not peter out, but widened as it angled down. Weiner was still worried and now Cooms had caught it. There was twenty thousand dollars in gold sitting in their tent, covered with a section of canvas thrown over a pit in the tent floor.

"I can't sleep anymore," Cooms had to admit. His eyes swept the snow draped hills, the cold, aloof mountains beyond. "I'm afraid they'll knock our heads in, take the gold."

There was still men hanging on around the Coscobo who had no claims of their own. What they were waiting for, only they could say, but Cooms had his ideas.

"We should band together," Weiner suggested. His own face was doubtful, and Cooms was not receptive to it at all, but it seemed the only way. "With Peck and Hazard we've got the only working claims. We've got all the wealth. The rest are buzzards."

"Peck and that damned recorder are buzzards too," Cooms said hotly. "Followed us up here, brought the others. . . ." Cooms fell silent, realizing that his own big mouth had done more damage than Peck and Hazard.

"I don't see any other way," Weiner said. "It's the best way—it's been done in most mine camps. A sort of mutual protective agency."

"I don't like it," Cooms grumbled, but he was wavering. He needed his sleep. Together the two men tramped through the knee-deep snow to Peck's site. They had gotten within fifty yards when they heard the hard, metallic click of a hammer being drawn back. Both men halted, waiting as Hazard crept from the woods, his coat and beard dusted with snow. His eyes were red-rimmed, his face haggard.

"What is it?" he demanded.

"You don't need that," Cooms said, gesturing toward the rifle the man carried. Wearily Hazard lowered it.

"I guess not. But we've had trouble already."

Cooms and Weiner exchanged glances; as they walked to the claim where Peck, bundled in furs was digging, they explained what they had in mind.

"I'm for it," Hazard said quickly. He looked at Cooms and commented, "I haven't been sleeping any better than you. Peck and I have been alternating, but by the time I dig in my shaft, then sit watch over his, I'm worn down. I'm for it."

Peck also agreed quickly, and he had one other suggestion. "The Dutchman, Van der Walt, he's an honest man. The only reason he's around is to guard his own claim, but he can't work it until spring. He's upslope under a shelf of snow."

"All right," Cooms said impatiently, "what about him?"

"I want to hire him," Charlie Peck said, his glance going from Cooms to Ross Hazard who himself was caught unaware by the suggestion. "As a sheriff, guard, what you will. He can patrol back and forth between our claims."

"Will he do it?" Hazard asked.

71

"How much will he want?" Cooms interrupted.

Weiner was more interested in Van der Walt's reputation for honesty. Charlie Peck held up a hand for quiet. "Van der Walt was a deputy marshal in Abilene under Hickok. He knows the ropes; and when he came into Deep Water looking for work he was carrying a letter of recommendation from Wild Bill himself.

"As for pay," Peck went on, "I think he'd work for supplies. His food's damned near out. But to be fair and to maybe buy a little loyalty, I think we should kick in some cash as well. Say a hundred a month."

"A hundred. . . ! That's twenty-five apiece!" Hazard was stunned.

"You're still thinking like an underpaid civil servant, Ross. We can afford it now. I don't know if Van der Walt will accept," Peck went on, answering the first question last, "but in his position, I would. Anyway, we can talk to him."

"Ross said you all have had some trouble," Cooms said.

Peck sighed heavily and nodded. "It's true. Clarence Westhead." Peck's voice lowered. "A man Ross and I know but you wouldn't. He slipped into our camp one night and dipped into our gold."

"He got away?" Weiner asked.

Charlie Peck simply swivelled his head slightly and nodded toward a mound of snow back under the pines.

In that way the Rose Canyon Mine Owners Association was formed. Van der Walt was officially hired, and he was grateful for the work. With his supplies nearly gone the Dutchman would have had no choice but to try trekking out of the high passes which were clogged with snow. Two of the hangers-on tried it, Stout and

Brian. They were found in the spring, not three miles from the canyon. Clearing away the snow as it fell, constructing sloped roofs over the shafts, Weiner and Cooms were able to work through most of the winter, building fires in the shafts to thaw the frozen earth. As Weiner had foreseen, the vein continued to widen, still showing pure. There was a cave-in one Sunday and a second a week later, with Cooms buried up to his neck in rubble. Panting, he was pulled out by Weiner and Van der Walt.

"Well, that's about if for this year," Weiner commented. "We can't go any farther without shoring, and we don't have the tools for it."

Yet the two men were far from dissatisfied. Their hidden gold cache had blossomed to nearly fifty thousand dollars. Peck and Ross Hazard worked a while longer and then gave it up as a thundering blizzard buried their shaft in an avalanche of snow. There was nothing left to do but wait out the long, dark months, sitting watch over their gold with loaded rifles. It was decided that Charlie Peck and Weiner along with Van der Walt would make the trip into Deep Water at the first thaw, bank the gold and return with axes, saws, fresh supplies and a man or two if any trustworthy workers could be found.

It was the morose Weiner who said it, but they all shared his thoughts. "We've seen nothing yet. When that gold hits Deep Water we'll have men from all over Colorado storming these mountains. We'd better be ready for spring, gents. If we're not they'll gobble us up."

Outside it had begun to snow again. A heavy wash of white with a gale of wind behind it swept through Rose

Canyon, smothering tents, claims and the Coscobo River. The skies went dark and the tent ropes snapped in the wind. Cooms reached into his coat and took out the greasy deck of playing cards he had and started dealing to the men hunched around the packing crate.

Higher up, along the gaunt, snow washed flanks of the Homestake Peak, Mantaka ate his second meal of the day. A little elk jerky shaved into a pot with the Indian potatoes he had gathered. As the pot boiled, Mantaka, wrapped in his elkskin robe, stood near the entrance to his low cave, watching the snows twist and plummet through the empty skies. Below all was white, above it was a rolling black with an occasional patch of clear sky showing brilliantly through the low clouds. The wind shrieked in the timber above the cave mouth and pressed against Mantaka, sweeping his fine dark hair back. He reached out and broke a pair of icicles free from the cavern lip, wanting them for water. Then he turned and crossed the dark cave until he came to his wind-whipped fire. Dropping the icicles into the pot he stared for a long while into the flames, enjoying the golden arabesques the fire wove.

Rising, he stretched and walked to the far wall where the firelight played dully. Picking up the red stone he used for that purpose, Mantaka sketched a stick-figure elk on the wall, and then a rank of pine trees. Stepping back he frowned as he examined his artwork. Throwing down the red rock he crossed again to his pot, removing it from the fire. When it had cooled he dipped into the stew, cupping it with his hand as he slurped it down. Outside the storm thundered up the long canyons. The snow fell as it would for months.

Mantaka finished eating, shoved the pot aside and

wiped his hands on a bearskin. Then, arranging his furs, he made a bed near enough to the fire so that he only had to reach out to feed fresh fuel into it. Then he heaped his furs over his slender body and slowly fell off to sleep dreaming dreams of warfare, of a land of ice where grizzlies lived in towns, where raiding Utes murdered and scalped the bears in their sleep while a long-gowned woman shrieked from the mountain tops. Outside the snows fell.

# 8.

When they did come it was with a storm, in a volume which shocked even the pessimistic Weiner. In March of the following year, at first thaw, there were sixteen men working along the Coscobo in Rose Canyon. By June there were five thousand men tearing at the earth with pick and shovel, long tom and pans, dynamite and drills. Surprisingly, most of them were making wages, even as far west as Ute Chief Rock, and back along the breaks two new mines opened a day.

The Weiner-Cooms mine, which had been named Range West, and the Peck-Hazard entry, Colleen Number One and Number Two, still produced the bulk of the ore. The Range West had sixteen men working in shifts, the Colleen Mines even more.

By August the first peddler had arrived in a painted wagon and unloaded a variety of goods, including two barrels of whisky. That nearly shut down the mines for two days. Toward September the town of Rose Canyon saw its first building begin to rise and its first lady of the evening arrive. That did shut down the mines. Weiner and Cooms had tapped a seemingly endless vein of gold, and that first year they took an additional fifty thousand from the narrow shaft. The second year saw that doubled, the third tripled. Peck had begun building a house back along the breaks—and why not? The town already boasted a Wells Fargo office, a bank, sixteen saloons and three real ladies, one of them the wife of Van der Walt, who had finally proved up on his claim, finding rich ore after three years of painstaking work.

He announced it by turning in his badge. "I won't have time for this sheriffin' no more," he had told Hazard.

"No?" Hazard looked up at the man from behind the desk of his office in Colleen Number Two. Van der Walt was streaked with dirt, his face beaming. "Struck it, Van?"

"I've struck it, Ross," the Dutchman grinned in return. "We're every one of us going to wind up millionaires. Filthy millionaires!"


Mantaka was pressed against the hard rock. Just above him he could see their moccasins behind the screen of willow brush. His heart pounded, but he stilled his breath, holding his knife tightly in his big hand. They were Utes and they spoke his mother's tongue, and he understood them.

"Where did he go?" the big one asked. He muttered a Ute oath, breathing raggedly from the long run up the mountain. "I had my rifle on him and then he was gone."

"The bastard Ute, the savage," another man answered.

"Why doesn't he go down among the whites?"

"They would not have him."

77

"I will have him, have his scalp. That pony was my best hunting horse."

"He is stealthy," a brave admitted grudgingly, "to take a pony from our camp...."

"He is dangerous!" the big one interrupted. "Next time it may be your throat cut. This bastard son of the grizzly is as bold as his father. I vow he will end the same way."

Slowly their voices faded away as they crossed the dry creek and moved into the timber. Mantaka waited an hour before he moved, and by then his legs and arms were stiff, his body drenched with cold sweat. He had a notion to raise up suddenly, to holler after the Utes tauntingly and then race for the cave. But there was no point to such bravado, and so he skidded down the dry, water polished chute to where he had left the stolen Indian pony.

"Hello, my new friend," Mantaka said, moving around the paint pony, examining it as he did so. The pony snorted, unused to the strange scent of this man, his clumsy touch.

"We will become good friends. You will see," Mantaka laughed. Leading the horse he recrossed the dry ravine and strode up the cedar-studded mountainside beyond. A tall youth with coal black eyes, he already carried the muscle of a man at fifteen. There was no inch of the mountains he did not know, no trick of survival unlearned. He could outrun a Ute, as he had learned in a moment of panic, outshoot any man he had yet seen.

They said that Lacroix was a big man, and that was the way Mantaka remembered him—a grizzly bear. Mantaka was thin, but his shoulders were broad, his chest deep and he showed every indication of growing to great dimensions. His hands were strong as vises, broad and hard as leather. When he took off his furs he saw the slabs of hard muscle across his chest and shoulders. Muscle put there by necessity, by the wild life where weakness meant death.

The Utes had never forgotten about him. It was a matter of tribal honor. The Frenchman had stolen a Poche woman, dishonored the tribe. Now Lacroix was dead, but the remnant of his sin—this half breed youth—remained to besmirch their honor. As Mantaka had grown older, however, he found he enjoyed their searching. He had the skills now to evade them, to foil them with rockslides and false tracks. One day they might kill him. He recognized that without fear. But he would not make it easy for them. Twice he had taken ponies, once taken the weapons of a sleeping brave. Perhaps that only made them fear and hate him more; the knowledge that he was their match at stealth, that he could count coup as well as any Ute.

Mantaka startled a badger which bared its teeth menacingly briefly before waddling away, and then crossed a long meadow, riding the paint pony for the first time. Off in the distance he saw a herd of elk, but he was not hunting on this day. He splashed across a narrow mountain rill which wound across the high meadow and began to climb the pine clad hills beyond. He crested the first small peak and then stopped abruptly. Dismounting Mantaka crouched against the earth, his rifle across his knee.

Six men filed through the timber. He caught flashes of color among the pines and he fell back, holding a hand over the nostrils of the pony to prevent it from blowing. Silently he moved back into the forest.

"They have found this cave as well," Mantaka told the pony. "And with it my meat and skins."

The horse pricked its ears curiously and Mantaka stroked its neck. "No matter—it has happened before. Now we simply find a new stronghold . . . and then another."

Mantaka smiled grimly, swung onto the pony's back and looked around him at the high peaks. "But where?"

It had been a long time since he had wintered along Rose Canyon. Four years by his count—or was it five? The winters passed in weary progression, with scarcely days of spring to separate them in this high savage land.

"We will see Rose Canyon, little pony. There is a lovely waterfall there. Clear water to drink. Once, so long ago I lived in a tree house there."

Mantaka turned the horse's head around, away from the Utes. Perhaps the two white men were still in the canyon of Roses. Mantaka brightened. He would not mind seeing Weiner again, and perhaps Cooms had grown more friendly. The more he thought about it the more Mantaka decided he would enjoy seeing the men again, and so he rode that way, singing to the horse, the day, and the high mountains, with a song he improvised as he rode.

It was a day and a half to Rose Canyon, and the morning of the second day it began to rain hard. Mantaka guided the horse, which had become used to his hand through the long, water-heavy ranks of blue spruce. The skies had cleared by mid-morning and a twin rainbow arched across the sky. The returning sun had called the birds out of their shelters and they sat singing in the trees. A curious jay followed Mantaka for nearly half a mile, scolding and fluttering around. It was all familiar, joyful, wonderful to Mantaka; what he found at Rose Canyon was incredible.

Sitting the pony on a low, wind swept ridge he looked down into the canyon, scarcely believing his eyes. A town had grown there. The trees, pulled down for lumber were cut back some five hundred yards from the river. A black smokestack upstream belched yellow sulfuric fumes, men crowded the streets where new buildings of green lumber faced each other across a red, mud thick road. Down along the Little Gorge hundreds of tents formed a secondary town of their own.

A brick building was being erected, several white frame houses, and here and there the land was being tilled for corn or graze for the livestock. The river itself was awash with mud. The ground was trodden bare back two hundred feet along every inch of the river.

A stagecoach rolled in from the East and Mantaka watched as six men, one in a black suit, climbed down from the stage and rushed off toward the camps. A shot from the town echoed up the long hillside to where Mantaka sat on the stolen paint pony, and then another.

He had never seen so many people, nor imagined there could be so many in one place, despite what he had heard from Lacroix. Twice the size of Deep Water already, the new town was still growing. Lots had been staked out farther west and back from the town along a second road. A town with all of its anger and senseless activity—it had come to his mountains. Mantaka's head turned, the wind was full in his face as he glanced up toward the falls where he had first led Weiner and

Cooms to find their gold. The pool at the base of the waterfall was a dirty, litter-filled basin. The roses had long since been trampled underfoot. Mantaka swung his pony around, and with the wind at his back climbed higher into the mountains where the air was still fresh, where the smoke did not reach.

The man in the black broadcloth suit had stepped from the stagecoach into the ankle-deep red mud of Colorado Boulevard as Peck had christened Rose Canyon's main street. He stood holding his bag, watching as the shirtsleeved miners rushed off toward the goldfields as if they expected to gather the gold like Easter eggs, tuck them into their kit bags, and be home by nightfall, wealthy men. One of them, a man named Biminy, had come all the way from Maryland, as he had confided to his companions on the coach.

Adrian Staughton had no such illusions. He had spent most of the last ten years at various strikes throughout the west—Virginia City, Leadville, Reno—and to Staughton the gold fields were an investment, not an adventure. He was not looking to get rick quick; he was simply looking to get rich. A tall, narrow man who rarely smiled, Staughton was elegant in a rather stiff way with cool blue eyes and a touch of silver at the temples. The men he was to meet had never been called elegant, even by their mothers.

Staughton checked in at the half finished hotel, and walked up the stairs to his room. Leaving his bag there he walked back down the hallway and tapped lightly on the door to Number 25.

"Come in, Staughton."

Staughton did so, grimacing as he surveyed the faces

of the men in the room. He was used to dealing with such men, but somehow, Staughton thought, one never gets totally used to them.

"Who's the kid?" he asked Michael O'Reilly.

"That's my boy," O'Reilly answered. Tim O'Reilly was nearly seventeen, and it was clear that the youth fancied himself. He was tilted back against the wall in a wooden chair, thumbs hooked into his belt. The old Colt Navy he wore was prominently displayed.

"Get him out of here," Staughton hissed, waving a hand.

"Get!" the elder O'Reilly snarled, and the kid, sparing a glance of contempt for Staughton, sauntered from the room.

With O'Reilly was a positively dirty-looking unshaven man named Sam Courtney. He had filed the third claim along Rose Canyon, proven too lazy to work it, and had finally lost the claim when he needed to cover a fifteen dollar poker bet. That mine was producing ten thousand dollars worth of ore a month now.

The third man was Judd Fitch, the Pueblo lawyer. He and Staughton shook hands, although Staughton made no attempt to offer his hand to O'Reilly or Courtney.

"How does it lay, Judd?" Staughton asked, sitting to the unpainted plank table. "Any chinks in the claims?"

"Nothing has turned up yet. Of course this Ross Hazard who's a partner in the Colleen Mines was a county recorder, so I expect they're covered. Hazard also registered the Cooms-Weiner claim."

"How's their capital?" Staughton wanted to know.

"There may be something there. I think there's a chance that both Range West and Colleen Number One have gone as far as they can without steam drills and ore crushers. At least that's the impression I get from talking to the miners."

"That's something." Staughton made a mental note. The two big mines had taken the skim, made a good profit. Like many operators, however, these men might be reluctant to pour their resources back into the mines. It would take plenty of money, stock sales—an area in which Staughton was most experienced. Some of the stock he had sold in his mining properties was even good.

"Who owns the ore crushers?" Staughton went on.

"We do now," Judd said without a smile. He shoved the ownership documents across the table toward Staughton who only glanced at them.

Unless the Rose Canyon miners wanted to set up their own freight line they would now have to use Staughton's ore crushers. And since Deep Water had closed down, the nearest mill was in Pueblo.

"Double the per-ton on that effective now," Staughton said, idly flicking at a fly. His eyes now went to the puffed, red face of O'Reilly and to that of Courtney, whose mouth was open in a cavernous yawn.

"Has Judd sketched everything out for you men?"

"Yeah." O'Reilly scratched his armpit. "When do we start?"

"It'll be a while yet. First we want to try this on the square. A little nudge here, a prod there. . . ."

Courtney interrupted. "What the hell are we supposed to do in the meantime?"

"Stay sober," Staughton shot back. Those blue eyes were cool, harder than Courtney could believe. Their gazes locked for a moment, then Sam Courtney broke it off. "You're on salary as of now," Staughton said, reassuming his businesslike manner. "It's a good salary—if you don't want it there's others that do."

Judd reached again into his bag and he withdrew a black velvet sack. From that he took two neat stacks of shiny gold eagles which he placed on the table before O'Reilly and Sam Courtney.

"Stay loose, men," Adrian Staughton said, "But stay sober. If you can't do that, stay out of Rose Canyon. Drinking men talk."

After the two strongarm boys had left Staughton shook his head as if from weariness and took out two cigars, offering one to the bulky Judd.

"Sometimes it's damned near enough to make a man want to go straight," he said dryly.

Judd smiled through the blue, curling smoke of his own newly lit cigar, but he found the remark humorless. A bulky man in his early fifties with tiny eyes and a narrow, hooked nose, Judd Fitch had been markedly unsuccessful as a trial lawyer and after one scandal-ridden term as a state supreme court judge in Indiana he had come west to specialize in goldfield actions. In that, too, he had been less than shiningly successful. Twice he had been shot at by his own clients in California, once dragged nearly a mile by a disgruntled miner. Then he had found his star, and he had hitched his wagon to Adrian Staughton.

Staughton had made him a wealthy man. The man was uncanny in his ability to find the rich claims, buy them out and turn them over before the bottom fell out. Judd Fitch owed everything he was to Adrian Staughton, and they had done some dirty work together. Still Fitch had managed as always, sometimes in the face of compelling evidence, to convince himself that he was an honest lawyer working for a shrewd businessman. It pained Fitch to hear Staughton so blithely admit they had fallen so far from the bar of justice.

"This will be a big one," Adrian Staughton said. His cigar jutted from the corner of his finely contoured lips. He sat, fingertips pressed together, eyeing Judd Fitch through a screen of tobacco smoke. He spoke as if reassuring a child. "This will be the biggest yet, Judd—have no doubt. And the easiest. We already have them by the throat; it's only that they have yet to feel the pressure being applied."

Then Staughton laughed. It was a dry, mirthless chuckle which caused Judd Fitch's skin to crawl. Fitch swallowed hard, choked on his cigar and offered a pale imitation of a smile in return.

*Someday*, he thought with sudden, stark awareness, *Staughton will get me hung*.

# 9.

Charlie Peck was concerned, Hazard was brooding. Cooms was livid, and oddly, it was Bob Weiner who seemed in control of himself.

"I take it you got an offer," Peck said as Weiner and Cooms crossed the office of Colleen Number Two and sat down, Cooms fidgeting, running a finger around the inside of his stiff collar. Cooms had never gotten used to tight boots and stiff shirts despite the fact he was now a millionaire.

Bob Weiner looked every bit the schoolmaster. He had taken to wearing spectacles, with the lens over his bad eye blacked out. "The fox is in the henhouse," Weiner observed dryly.

"All right, and what are we going to do about it?" Ross Hazard demanded. He stood from his desk, his hand shoved into his vest pocket. A gold chain with a dangling elk's tooth girded his now ample stomach. "I've heard of this Adrian Staughton. He's a damned thief, and a vicious one at that."

"The question is how do we get him out?" Charlie Peck said.

"Shoot the son-of-a-bitch," Cooms said, banging his

palm down on Hazard's desk. "I'll do it my own damn self!"

No one replied to Cooms' violent suggestion, and after a moment he calmed down. He sat stroking his huge yellow beard as Charlie Peck spoke.

"He's got the ore crushers locked up. He knows we're going to have to dig deeper to finance any further mining. And he damned well knows the richest ore is still down there. So the question is simply is it worth it to us to fight Staughton at all? We've come out sweet on this deal, boys."

"We've sweat and bled for it, six long years. What the hell has Staughton done? You know he's got our crews organized into some kind of miners' union?"

"They're under his thumb," Weiner agreed reluctantly. "And with the election coming up, guess who'll swing the votes and control the zoning, the safety standards, the law!"

"We've got Charlie up for mayor. If the miners have any sense . . ."

Hazard interrupted Weiner. "It's not going to be like that, Bob. It's a question of how much a vote is worth, who's willing to buy them. I can guarantee you Staughton is."

Weiner nodded wearily. From digging in a hole five years ago he had been pushed to managing a large mining company. At times it still seemed unreal. The problems were too large for any of them. There were situations they were not prepared to deal with arising each day.

"I have an estimate sheet," Charlie Peck said with a shrug which was almost apologetic. "It will cost Ross and me nearly a million and a half to go below the hundred foot level." Charlie put down the yellow-lined sheet. "Eighty per cent of what we've made to date."

"Plus the cost of ore crushers," Hazard put in. "Plus setting up a freight line. Guards . . ." Ross rumpled his hair nervously. "Hell, we've made a sweet score here, boys. The only way we can hold Staughton off is to pour every last cent back into the mines."

"Then, of course," Charlie reminded them, "the rough stuff will begin if Staughton follows his pattern. Flooding, cave-ins, intimidating our men.

"Ross and I have talked this over. We feel we have enough. We'll live out our lives in comfort. If Staughton makes a fortune after we've gone, well, let him have it. We can fight him," Charlie said, "but it's liable to leave us flat broke—right back where we started—or dead."

"No." It was Bob Weiner who said it, and there was steel in his tone. Cooms blinked at his partner. "I'll fight the man, fight for what's mine."

"Bob . . ." Cooms spread his hands in bewilderment. "You always wanted out. From the time we first struck it you said you'd had enough that you didn't give a damn about the money."

"That's right," Weiner said firmly. "I don't care about it that much. So why not develop Range West all the way? This territory is new, raw. There's men who will take what they can with a gun or with a bluff, knowing there's no law to shut them down. It's not right, boys. I don't want Colorado built by the likes of Adrian Staughton. I don't want him bluffing his way in where other men have built and struggled. Damn his capital, his influence.

"I won't run!"

Cooms smiled faintly, and Charlie Peck thought there was a touch of pride in that smile. "I'm standing with Bob. We're partners to the hilt. Ross?"

"All right." Hazard nodded slowly.

Charlie Peck took a slow, deep breath. "That doesn't seem to leave me much choice." A sickly smile crept over his lips. "I'm scared, and I don't mind admitting it. Scared—but I'm sticking too."

"All right." Ross Hazard nodded, "and I'm glad you are, Charlie. You've got the knack for organizing, and that's what we're going to need now. We need wagons, drivers, lumberjacks, steam drills."

"I'll get on it. I'll have the figures by Thursday and we can cut up the pie then. We're going to need several other things, Ross."

Hazard lifted an eyebrow. "I figured on finding the fighting men myself," Ross Hazard said coldly. "If we have to play it that way, we will."

"And you, Charlie," Bob Weiner said, peering through the one lens of his spectacles, "we've got to make sure you get elected mayor. I think that's as important as anything else."

"How about sheriff?" Cooms interrupted. "Staughton is running that miserable O'Reilly."

"What's Van der Walt doing these days?"

The Dutchman had had a rich strike, but it had petered out on him. The last any of them knew he was simply sitting on the porch of his big new house, soaking up sunshine. Maybe that was all Van der Walt wanted to do now.

"But I'll find out," Charlie Peck promised, jotting down a note. "The Dutchman is honest and experienced. I don't think he could be bought even if he needed money, and he doesn't."

"He doesn't need a job either," Hazard said candidly, "but maybe he's tired of that rocker."

There was nothing more to be done just then, so Cooms and Weiner left the Colleen office, leaving Hazard and Charlie Peck to their mine business. Cooms found his partner standing on the porch, hands in his pockets. Weiner surveyed the far mountains which appeared as majestic, atavistic as the day Mantaka had shown them Rose Canyon. Then his gaze swept down to the sprawling town below, to the tent city, the muddy river.

"We'll beat Staughton," Cooms said, slapping his partner on the shoulder. Bob Weiner turned slowly to him.

"That wasn't what I was thinking about. I was thinking about us, the wilderness. We'll be gone one day, this scar we've cut in the mountains healed by time, by rain and wind. So what have we done? Accomplished?"

"We've gotten bloody rich, Bob," Cooms said succinctly.

Bob Weiner nodded and the two men walked off uptown, Cooms' arm draped over the smaller man's shoulder.

By June the Rose Canyon Mine Owners Association was running its own ore through to Pueblo under heavy guard. Six other mines had joined the Range West-Colleen combine to pay freight through to the north, circumventing the Staughton ore crushers.

Staughton tried suddenly lowering his prices to almost nothing, but by then the freight line was well established and the mention of Staughton left a bad taste in the miners' mouths. A few wildcatters used the

Staughton crushers, but these few were barely enough to pay operating expenses.

It took nine months to get the first steam drills into Rose Canyon, but arrive they did, and Range West, shoring with box-like sections of buttressing, reached the two hundred foot depth, began using ore carts on iron rails drawn by mules and raised wages for the third time in a six-month period.

Peck was feeling good about things. Their plans were working out well, not without a hitch here and there, but overall things were smooth. The Range West and Colleen miners were drawing the best wages in Colorado, and that helped build Peck's confidence on election night.

It was raining hard, and now and then pitchfork lightning scoured the high peaks, leaving the scent of sulfur. The streets were little more than bogs, and Colleen Number One had been shut down temporarily. But all of that would pass soon enough. Peck was only concerned with the vote which would be cast this dark, storm swept night. A victory would effectively shut Adrian Staughton out of Rose Canyon politics as he had had the door closed on him with Rose Canyon commerce.

Charlie dressed and shaved carefully as befit a future mayor. The buckboard was waiting out in front, the horses standing miserably in the driving rain. Peck tugged down his hat, turned up the collar on his black slicker and tramped out onto the porch, surveying the dark night briefly, seeing no light except that from his own window. The rain slanted down.

Still he felt cheerful. Colleen was doing well, and he had decided that he wouldn't mind having a try at elected office. In the back of his mind was the growing thought that this office might even lead to another in the state capital. Peck whipped the standing water off the buckboard seat and clambered aboard, his hat dripping water, his face catching the breath of the cold wind. Stiffly Peck unwound the reins from the brake handle.

He walked the horses from his sodden yard and turned onto the main road just as a long chain of brilliant white lightning scored the wind swept skies. In that light Charlie Peck saw them coming, but there was absolutely nothing he could do about it. A bulky shadow stood in the roadway, blocking his progress, and a second man leaped onto the buckboard, ripping the reins from his hands. Peck's fist shot out, and his attacker grunted as the blow slammed against his jaw, but it was not enough. Peck felt a hand grip his shoulder and then he was yanked from the buckboard. He fell face down in the deep mud, tried to rise and was driven back by a kick in the face which snapped his head around and knocked him flat on his back. The rain was cold against his face, the mud cold beneath him. Blinking through the pain Charlie Peck saw the man raise the axe handle and drive it down against his skull.

O'Reilly hit him twice and then Sam Courtney, panting from the exertion, stopped him. "All right. He's dead. Give me a hand with the buckboard."

O'Reilly straightened up and picked up his hat which had fallen to the road. With Courtney he tipped the buckboard over on its side. Looking up and down the dark road they dragged Charlie Peck's body a little ways farther to where a boulder rested beside the road. They placed his head near the boulder. Then Courtney slapped the off horse on the rump and the two animals, startled by it, ran off down the road, dragging the overturned buckboard behind them.

The rain fell in constant sheets. Soon any trace of what had happened would be obliterated. Charlie Peck would simply be found beside the rock, his head caved in.

"There'll be suspicions," Sam Courtney said nervously as the two men stepped into the saddles of their hidden horses. O'Reilly looked at him, the rain streaming from his hat across his puffy face.

"They can suspect any damn thing they like, Sam. They'll not prove it. Unless one of us talks about it."

It was cold and Sam Courtney shivered. He said nothing more, understanding the implicit threat. He glanced at the bulky O'Reilly through the rain and shadows. The man was positively nerveless. O'Reilly glanced up suddenly himself, catching Sam Courtney's eyes on him, and Sam kneed his horse forward.

"Let's have us a drink," Courtney said.

He had no intention of crossing Michael O'Reilly. Ever.

Ross Hazard waited at the hotel where the election was being held. Cooms was out on the porch watching the storm tear the night apart. Outside of the thundering storm, the town was still—liquor sales had been cut off until midnight. The rain dripped from the eaves and the cold wind pressed Cooms' slicker against his body. Inside the hotel the band was playing a strident, brassy march. A miner from Range West slogged across the street and Cooms nodded to him.

"Seen Charlie yet?"

Weiner was at his partner's elbow. Cooms spat out

his tobacco and wagged his head. At the end of the street there was a sudden flurry of activity. Men with lanterns rushed out into the street. Someone shouted.

Bob Weiner glanced that way and then turned back toward the hotel. He was nearly to the door when a cold premonition stopped him in his tracks. His head snapped around and he took three quick steps up the hotel boardwalk, staring at the activity up the street. Now he could make out a team of horses and the buckboard. Cooms was beside him once more and they stepped down into the muddy, wind swept street. From there Cooms recognized the matched bays.

"Damn!" he breathed. "Get Ross," Cooms said. "Tell him Charlie Peck is dead."

Adrian Staughton was elected mayor of Rose Canyon. Staughton delivered a eulogy over Charlie Peck during a rain-swept funeral. It was a fine, flowery speech which Charlie would have liked.

There was a victory for the mine owners, tarnished as it was by Peck's death. Van der Walt was elected sheriff by a bare two votes which sent O'Reilly off into a drunken sulk but let Weiner, Cooms and Ross Hazard breathe a sigh of relief. Before a jail could even be built, however, Van der Walt was called out on the porch of his house one night and gunned down by a group of masked riders. Michael O'Reilly took his place, with Sam Courtney and his son Tim O'Reilly, a swaggering young buck, as deputies. It was on that day that Ross Hazard sold out his interest in the Colleen Mines to Staughton, saying he wanted to live to enjoy his wealth.

Cooms was gloomy, and he wasn't at all sure Hazard wasn't the smart one. "He'll kill us too, Bob," Cooms believed.

"Maybe." Bob Weiner was not pulling out, however. Never money hungry, he felt more of an obligation to the memory of Peck and Van der Walt than he did to his own skin. "If you want to pull your freight, I'll buy you out," Weiner told his partner.

Cooms could only shake his head. Maybe they were both fools. "I'll stick, Bob—as long as you do."

It was only the beginning. In late October with snows already heavy on the ground there was a blast deep in the bowels of Range West. Six men were killed. The cause of the blast was never discovered. A man Cooms suspected was turned over to the law, but that was a farcical gesture. Neither Cooms nor Bob Weiner went anywhere alone. Both men were always armed and Cooms had an entire retinue of highly paid gun toughs with him constantly. The ore wagons out of Rose Canyon were bedeviled by highwaymen. Three drivers were killed in the month of April alone. The wagons were generally found at the bottom of a deep gorge, ripped to splinters, the ore scattered across the mountainside.

Staughton seemed to have none of these problems. The Colleen Mines which he owned entirely were prospering. In addition he had purchased the Lame Duck and reopened Amsterdam, Van der Walt's old claim. His ore crushers were fed by the other mines—with the exception of Range West—to the tune of four dollars a ton. There was already talk—Staughton's talk—of running him for governor.

He had a new house built along the Fire Creek ranch road, a magnificent structure of brick and gingerbread-facing, three stories tall. Around that Staughton had planted cypress and cedar. His stables held twenty thoroughbred horses, his kennels the best bloodhounds in the territory. A designer was sent to Europe to purchase tapestries, Louis XIV furniture and the art of the Masters to decorate Staughton Hall. A balustrade of pure gold from Staughton's own mines was designed for his inside stairwell; the windows were stained glass obtained from some of the oldest cathedrals in Germany and France. When he had finally built what he considered a suitable house Staughton brought his wife and teenage daughter out from San Francisco.

The wife, Ella Staughton was a woman already wearied with Staughton and his ways. She had a pale complexion and tiny pinched features. Staughton's liquor bill skyrocketed after her arrival. Sarah Staughton was her father's pride and joy. A beautiful haughty young woman with ringlets of auburn hair and a stiff bearing, she rode with a flair and a heavy whip hand, hunted with the men and started the pulse of every young buck within a hundred miles racing.

The arrival of his family did nothing to slow Adrian Staughton's plans. There had been another cave-in at Range West, although this time the culprit—a nameless wanderer—was caught by the miners and beaten nearly to death. It was dangerous for any Range West man to go into Rose Canyon alone. A dozen men had been roughed up in the local saloons and Weiner and Cooms were paying off more and more miners who decided their health demanded a different climate. A torch was touched to Cooms' house but a sudden storm helped put it out before any serious damage could be done. After that Cooms' house was ringed with men day and night.

May brought rain, and Range West was flooded out. For weeks on end the skies were dark, filled with the hollow roar of thunder, the flaring lightning which arced from peak to peak. The rains came and it seemed they would never end.

Cooms had started to drink. He sat before the fire, brooding, wondering what in God's name he was doing. He could still get out. Now, while he still had his health, most of his bank account. The wind funneled down the chimney and churned up the fire. Cooms poured another drink and walked to the front door, glass in his hand.

Reaching the door Cooms turned down the lamp which burned there. *What was that?* His skin crawled. Taking a deep drink and then another he peered through the curtains, seeing nothing but the black night, the slanting rain.

*Something.* Cooms staggered and cursed himself for being so unsteady. He took another drink and reached for his rifle, lurching toward the door. His heart was pounding; the fire of the whisky was in his veins. He walked bareheaded, coatless out onto the porch, the rifle in his hands.

"Where are you?" he screamed. The wind was hard against him, the rain cold on his face. "I see you!" Cooms teetered unsteadily and walked half a step forward, leaning against the porch rail, his head hung down.

"Come on up here," he muttered. Then again he hollered. "Where are you!"

"Right here, boss," a voice from under the trees answered. Cooms' hands tensed on his rifle and he started to bring it up before finally recognizing his own guard. He lifted a hand to the puzzled watchman who faded back into the night and the shadows of the oaks.

Cooms clenched his fists and hung his head. His shirt was sopping wet, and his teeth chattered with the cold. His eyes lifted to the constant rain and then slowly he turned and walked back into his house, leaving his rifle lying on the porch.

He lay awake, blinking against the darkness, hearing a small, shuffling sound through the curtain of rain outside the cave. Mantaka did not move, but his hand tightened around the haft of his knife. His eyes were open, but against the overpowering darkness he could see nothing. He listened, hearing the dripping of rain from the lip of the cave mouth, the scuttling of a small creature farther back in the cave. But the sound he had heard was different. Different enough to awaken him on this miserable night.

Mantaka stared at the mouth of the cave, his heart inexorably beating faster. A trickle of moisture ran across his cheek. The knife was cool in his hand. Against the faint light of the cave opening a darker shadow moved and Mantaka came to his feet, naked, savage in the night.

He felt a body impact against his bare chest and he dug out, driving his knife home. The Ute howled and fell back as a second Indian struck Mantaka from behind, driving him to the floor of the cave.

"Now you die, child of the bear," the injured man grunted, and he leaped at Mantaka, his knife blade glittering. But Mantaka was able to roll aside and his powerful hand shot out, gripping the Ute's knife hand, forcing it back as he again brought his own razor sharp skinning knife into play.

He kneed the Ute in the groin and drove upward with

the knife, taking the jugular from the man. Hot blood spattered Mantaka's naked body as the Ute crumpled at his feet. The second Ute was on his knees, swaying in agony, a deep wound slashed across his abdomen.

"Leave me alone,' Mantaka said. He towered over the badly wounded Ute. "Leave me alone. I only want to live!"

The Ute glanced up with utter contempt. Blood flowed from between the fingers of the hand he had pressed to his wound.

"You will die! Die, savage. You are not Ute, you are half an animal, a soulless beast! You have killed me," he said in a softer voice. He looked in wonder at his bloody hand and pitched forward on his face, a terrible scream echoing through the cave.

From below Mantaka heard an answering yell and he ran to the rain-filled cave mouth. Yellow lightning formed a bridge across the black skies and in that light he saw a dozen more Ute warriors creeping up the narrow winding trail to his cave. Desperately Mantaka looked around, knowing that the precipice at his feet was sheer for five hundred feet. He was already cut off from his horse, which he had hidden in the aspen grove near where the trail began. The lightning flashed again and then returned the world to blackness, but in that flash the Utes had seen Mantaka, standing naked on the rim before his cave, and they came on now with a rush.

There was no time for gathering up his belongings, his rifle. True, he could get to the cave, stand the Utes off for a time with the Remington, but they would have him cornered, and it would only be a matter of time before they killed him, no matter how many of the Utes Mantaka took down first.

Above the cave the rotting roots of an ancient cedar protruded from crumbled rock, and taking a wild leap Mantaka caught the tangle of roots with his strong hands. The rain pounded against him, but he managed to swing up, catch another handhold and scramble on. If he could make it to the rocks above the cave. . . It was then that he felt the jagged pain course through his body, felt the burning impact of an arrow in his back and he went momentarily limp, the breath going from him.

A second arrow glanced off the rock near his hand, and another. Mantaka gathered himself and began climbing again, the wind against his naked, rain soaked body incredibly cold. His fingers clawed for a hold against the tangle of roots and rotten granite. A musket boomed loud in the night, filling the darkness with red fire, and Mantaka ducked as the musket ball powdered the granite near his head.

Frantically he climbed on, his breathing ragged, his back leaking hot blood. Pain flared up in his skull, filling his brain with brilliant flashes of light. His eyes blurred, and he felt his foot slipping as a volley of arrows struck the stone around him.

Glancing back Mantaka could see nothing but a black abyss. The rain howled around him, the wind pummeling his naked body. He reached out, drew himself up. Reached out again—and found the rimrock! He pulled himself up, panting like a wounded panther, and lay flat on his stomach, feeling the wash of cold rain. He struggled to his feet and ran on, into the deep forest, staggering flashes of pain racking his body. His bare feet were torn on unseen rocks, the brambles and boughs whipped his flesh. Twice he fell, twice rose to run on, dipping into the ravines which were now glutted with roaring white water.

Mantaka sagged to a rock, threw his head back in anguish, taking deep, icy breaths. He shivered uncontrollably for a moment and then fought to clear his head. Now what? Where could he go? No answer came to him. The rain poured through the dark ranks of pines. The white water gushed past, frothing up at the rocks at Mantaka's feet.

He knew he would bleed to death if something were not done. The wound in his back was deep, and frustrating because he could not reach it to treat it himself. Reaching back Mantaka found the shaft of the arrow which protruded from between the sixth and seventh ribs on the right side, near to his spine. Grimacing he snapped it off, angrily throwing the Ute arrow into the freshet at his feet. He sat there for a moment longer, his heart racing, the pain relentless.

Confusion spun cobwebs in his mind. *Where?* He had nowhere to go and never had. Yet now it was essential that he find help, warmth. He sat for a long hour fighting off the pain, the nausea, staring at the rain with pain-dulled vision, having no idea of what to do. And then he had a thought, a desperate inspiration, and Mantaka staggered to his feet and took his bearing through the dark, rainy night toward Rose Canyon.

# 10.

Sometime after midnight the rain stopped. A silver
half moon drifted eerily through a bank of sheer clouds.
Mantaka crept down the mountainside, fording the
quick running, icy Coscobo half a mile below the town
of Rose Canyon. Clambering up the muddy bank
beyond he darted toward the cover of the forest, ridden
by the driving pain. Cold water dripped from the pines,
stinging his bare flesh as he stood panting, head against
the pocked bark of a woodpecker-bedeviled pine.

Breathing heavily through his mouth, Mantaka
glanced first upriver and then down. Across the creek,
by the pale moon light, he could make out a thousand
tents. Here and there a light showed.

It was bewildering. How was he to find Weiner? Near
the mine site, he guessed. Hobbling over the broken
ground Mantaka moved that direction, seeing the town
itself emerge from the trees as he did so. There was a
barn just beyond the trees and then a house of some
size. Mantaka shuttled through the shadows, darting
behind the barn where he rested, gasping with the pain.
Slowly he eased toward the house, seeing a lighted window. Pressing against the wall he peered in. A man in

sock feet dozed before a fire, a book on his lap. It was not Weiner or Cooms.

Mantaka moved on, growing desperate. He tried three other houses. Two of them were dark, and he had no intention of getting shot and so he steered clear. The rain had begun to fall again, lightly, and Mantaka staggered on. He was nearly past the dark, impressive house when something pulled him up short—a sound.

There was a picket fence around the house and on the gate the symbols he had seen before, carved on a plank left at the original claim: "Weiner." Mantaka leaned against the gate, lifted his eyes to the rain and stumbled toward the door, his back on fire. And then he noticed that the door was open, although the house was dark. Frowning, Mantaka slipped up beside the house, again hearing a small scraping sound. Perhaps Weiner was awake, moving around the dark house.

Mantaka crept toward the door, his heart racing. He stepped onto the porch and pushed the door open with his foot, the pain spurring him to recklessness. The door swung open soundlessly and Mantaka stepped in out of the cold rain.

By the feeble light of the moon Mantaka could see the body sprawled against the floor. Suddenly the other men loomed up out of the shadows and they rushed past Mantaka, one man's shoulder striking Mantaka, knocking him aside.

Mantaka recovered and moved slowly forward, but already he knew it was Bob Weiner on the floor, already he knew that he was dead.

"Who the hell was that?" Stinger wanted to know. He and Tim O'Reilly rushed to their horses behind the barn, Stinger still carrying his knife in his hand.

"Prowling Ute, I guess. How the hell should I know!"

As tough as he was, or thought he was, Tim O'Reilly was shaken by what they had done.

Stinger stepped into the saddle, sheathing his bloody knife. He waited for the other deputy. "There was something about that Indian...." But Stinger could not put his finger on it. O'Reilly had a sudden inspiration.

"What the hell are we doing, riding off?"

Stinger didn't get it. "We just killed a man, that's what, Tim."

"Who says we did?" A sly smile spread across Tim O'Reilly's face. "I think that Ute did it. I think we just caught us a murderer."

Mantaka leaned over and listened for a heartbeat. There was none. His hand came away from Weiner's body, sticky with blood.

The wind rattled the oaks outside and Mantaka rose quickly, slipping Bob Weiner's clothes off. He stepped into the too-short trousers and pulled on the coat which was stained with blood but was warm. A hat he could not find, but going to the kitchen he found a long bladed bread knife which he thrust into his belt.

Food. He must find food, bandages if possible.... The front door burst open again and the two men stepped inside.

"Hold it!" Tim O'Reilly's gun came up even as he shouted his warning. "I'll shoot!"

Mantaka turned, dove through the window and landed roughly on the sodden earth outside as the blasts from the guns of O'Reilly and Stinger Matson tore the night apart, their bullets whining off into the trees. Mantaka struggled to his feet and began to run. The searing pain in his back had not ebbed in the slightest, but now he gave it no thought. A hail of bullets slammed into the trunks of the big oaks as Mantaka made the perimeter of the woods. O'Reilly was shouting excitedly behind him and a neighbor had been roused.

Mantaka ran on, slipping in the mud, the rocks bruising his feet. Finally he slowed, his eyes going back across his shoulder. He saw no pursuit, and after leaning against a tree, taking deep saving breaths, he plodded on.

Those men—they seemed to think he had killed Weiner. Yet Mantaka believed them to be the same men who had rushed out eariler. Perhaps they were the killers themselves... It did not matter. Only safety mattered, warmth, food.

The lights of a house blinked through the woods and Mantaka crept stealthily forward. He slipped into a gulley where a trickle of water flowed and he pressed himself flat, watching the house.

"I'll have wine too, please, Thorpe," Sarah Staughton said.

The butler turned his white head slowly to the young, blue-eyed woman and then to her father who sat at the far end of the table engrossed in an old Denver newspaper.

"No," Adrian Staughton said without lifting his eyes.

"You're too young, dear," Ella Staughton said. Her sad, prematurely lined face reflected her own drinking habits. Sarah was undaunted.

Seventeen, with a fully mature figure, Sarah held her

head haughtily, impatiently tapping a toe under the table as she snapped, "You seem to think I'm too young for everything!"

"You are," Adrian Staughton said. He turned a page of the newspaper and looked piercingly at his daughter. "Too young for the likes of Will Ford too."

"We were only riding," Sarah pouted. "And the way you talked, Daddy. I'm sure he'll never come around again."

"Small loss," Staughton grumbled, lifting his own wine glass. He shook his head, folding the paper.

"And who else is there?" Sarah implored. "Mother?"

"Your father does not like Will Ford, Sarah," her mother responded. Nervously she lifted her own wine goblet to her lips. Shakily Ella drank it down.

"But there's no men around here! Dirty miners, gamblers—clods like that Tim O'Reilly." She made a face. "He makes my skin crawl, the way he looks at me."

Adrian Staughton looked up at that. He would have to speak to O'Reilly. He would not have scum like that around his daughter. But he said nothing.

Ella Staughton, emboldened by the wine ventured a suggestion. "Sarah is right, Adrian. There are no suitable young men around Rose Canyon. Perhaps a year in the East...."

"No," Staughton said with finality.

Ella obediently shut up, but not Sarah, who was the only person within five hundred miles not afraid of Adrian Staughton. "I could stay with Aunt Elaine," she persisted.

"You'll stay here, child, men or none."

"It's not only that, Daddy," Sarah said petulantly. "Why, there's nothing at all to do in this town. No school."

"I would like to see Sarah in a good ladies' school," Ella dared again. "Why she hardly knows how to dine, to walk, but only how to ride around like a Red Indian."

Adrian Staughton left the door open saying, "We'll talk about it another time." Staughton was concerned with other matters just then. O'Reilly hadn't ridden by to report yet. Was Weiner out of the way or had they botched that up, perhaps even gotten caught? He was ready to pour himself another drink when he heard a horse in the yard. Staughton, in shirtsleeves went out onto the porch. Seeing it was Michael O'Reilly, he closed the door.

"Well?" he demanded as O'Reilly stepped onto the porch, brushing the water from the sleeves of his slicker.

"They just found Weiner—I was called out to investigate. He's dead," the sheriff assured Staughton.

"Was there any trouble?" Staughton wanted to know.

"Trouble?" O'Reilly scratched his head dully. "None that I know of."

"What did your boy tell you?" Staughton went on impatiently.

"Nothin' yet. Ain't seen Tim nor Stinger since this happened."

"You haven't seen him?" Staughton exploded.

"No. But it's all right. I figure him and Sting went off to get drunk."

"And that's *all right*," Staughton said in exasperation. "Can't you control that boy of yours, O'Reilly?"

"About as well as you control your daughter, I reckon," O'Reilly said testily.

Staughton's jaw tightened. No one was allowed to speak of his family. "What's that mean?"

"Just thought you'd like to know she's been riding with that Ford kid again, that's all."

"When?" Staughton demanded.

"Today, Mister Staughton. Tim saw them."

Staughton ran a harried hand across his brow. *That* was one little problem he could take care of. "When you see Tim and Stinger," Staughton said, taking O'Reilly's arm, speaking in a low voice, "tell them that I want them to become friends with Will Ford."

"That milksop! Why Tim would gobble him up before he'd shake his hand."

"This is for pay, O'Reilly. For pay. I'll fill you in later."

"All right," O'Reilly said with a slow, malicious grin. He was glad he was not standing in young Will Ford's boots right now.

"And find Tim—find out everything that happened tonight. Everything!"

"I will." O'Reilly stood there, hatless, the rain falling in lazy sheets behind him. Staughton watched, expecting the sheriff to leave.

Then it came to him. "Just a minute." Staughton re-entered the house and crossed to his safe, counting out a stack of coins. O'Reilly was waiting on the porch when he returned. Staughton slid the gold into the sheriff's hand.

"Don't forget what I've told you," Staughton said.

"I won't." O'Reilly stepped to his horse and

mounted, the rain swallowing him up. Adrian Staughton watched for a time, knowing that O'Reilly would first go and get drunk, then if the notion came to him, he might try to find Stinger and Tim. Adrian Staughton still counted himself a gentleman and there were times that working with sodden imbeciles like O'Reilly was enough to make him chuck it all in.

Yet now he felt relieved. Weiner was down. That left only Cooms, and the feeling was that Cooms would cut and run if left alone. Staughton went in, crossed to the mantle and poked at the fire as he finished his drink. "What was that?"

Staughton turned to see his wife standing on the staircase, clutching a wrapper around her narrow shoulders.

"Bad news, I'm afraid," Staughton said. He managed a worried little shake of his head. "Someone has killed Bob Weiner. The sheriff just informed me."

"He was a nice man." Ella Staughton looked at her husband with weary eyes, eyes which revealed little about her true thoughts. There was much she must have suspected, perhaps known, yet she never broached the subject, never pried. Now she only turned and dolefully climbed the staircase, going to her room where she would drink herself to sleep.

Adrian Staughton usually had no such problems. He fell off to sleep, utterly satisfied with himself and his place in the world, no matter what the day had brought. This night was no exception. He blew out the lamp and climbed to his own bedroom, opposite his wife's.

Still the rain drove down, and the house creaked in the wind. Sarah lay awake a long time, looking at the ceiling, watching the quicksilver of the raindrops racing down her windowpane. She tried to sleep, could not and tossed restlessly. Hours later she heard the sound. Sitting suddenly upright she peered quizzically into the darkness of her room. The rain was falling even harder now and she considered that the sound she had heard had been a branch falling from a tree or a shutter slapping open.

She listened, hearing it again. Groping for her wrapper Sarah slipped from her bed and went out into the dark hall, her feet silent against the carpet as she moved to the head of the stairs. It came from the kitchen. An odd, scuttling sound, perhaps a mouse.... Sarah looked back up the darkened hallway uncertainly and then quickly went down the stairs. She had never been faint-hearted, and although she was mildly apprehensive, she continued on, finding a lamp which she lit and carried with her to the kitchen door. Her hand stretched out and touched the door as the lamp cast wavering shadows against it. Sarah took a breath and walked through the door. He stood there and she screamed.

A tall, savage man with a tangle of black hair and beard, he carried a long knife in one hand, a sack full of pilfered food in the other. He was barefoot on this cold night, and the clothes he wore, torn and stained, were obviously not his. His strongly muscled chest showed in the lamplight. His eyes were black, steady as he watched back. Blood, Sarah now saw, leaked from his pant leg, spotting the hardwood floor.

There were rushing footsteps in the yard and others from upstairs. The savage didn't hesitate a second, but turned, clutching his knife and sack tightly, and burst through the back door into the cold and rain. Sarah's hand trembled and the lamp rattled as she put it down on the counter, leaning against the wall to steady herself.

Adrian Staughton, gun in hand, rushed into the kitchen. "What is it? Sarah!"

His daughter still trembled and he knew she was not easily frightened. A man in a raincoat peered in the back door and Staughton barked, "What the hell are you doing out there, Ben! Sleeping?"

"No, sir! We'll get him."

"Who was it?" Staughton asked his daughter. "What was he doing?"

"A wild man," Sarah said. Briefly she described him. "He wore a suit that only went to his ankles and wrists. He was carrying a knife, and..." she pointed to the floor where a smear of blood showed plainly. A bloody bare footprint led toward the back door.

"Damn that Ben. I'll have more men posted. You say, it seemed he only wanted food?" Sarah nodded. "But who can tell—a Ute, was it?"

Staughton's first thought had been of Cooms and his gang of toughs. Now he breathed a sigh of relief and held Sarah to him, feeling her pulse race.

"Get up to bed now," he said in a softened tone which he reserved only for Sarah.

She nodded dutifully and turned toward the stairs. Horrible—it had been horrible. The wild man splashed with blood, knife in hand. She lay awake a long while after that, thinking not of the blood, but of those black eyes which had not appeared savage at all. Only intelligent... and a little lonely. Fine eyes for a savage.

It was a paradox Sarah could not resolve, and so she pulled her comforter under her chin, stretched, and

112

curled up, listening to the constant rain.

Tim O'Reilly was more than half drunk before he and Stinger finally checked in with Michael O'Reilly. By that time the elder O'Reilly already had a good start on his own drunk. Before O'Reilly on the bare plank table of his ranch house were two neat stacks of gold eagles and the deputies wasted no time pocketing the money. O'Reilly shoved the half empty bottle across the table to his son and watched as the kid poured himself a drink.

"What happened?" the sheriff asked.

"We did the job." Stinger said. He patted the pocket of his leather vest, searching for the makings. He came up dry and O'Reilly tossed him his own tobacco.

"Yeah. But the boss wants to know the details."

Tim O'Reilly shrugged, studying his father's slack, beefy face by the lanternlight. He took another drink and told what had happened at Weiner's place.

". . . Then we went back in and that damned Ute had stripped off Weiner's clothes and put them on. We figured to catch him and lay it off on the Indians, but he made it to the woods."

"Anyone wants to look around out there," Stinger added, "they'll see the Ute was there. Bloody footprints on the floor. Weiner's clothes missing. Hell, it's a set-up."

"It looks good," the sheriff had to agree. "The boss'll be glad to find a scapegoat at hand. Otherwise folks are bound to be suspicious of him. You done good, boys," O'Reilly said with a heavy wink. "You done real good." He helped himself to another drink.

Adrian Staughton was not so pleased the next day

when O'Reilly reported and explained the plan to blame it on the Utes.

"No," he said flatly. "That's the best way to get the Federal authorities up here—to report Indian trouble at Rose Canyon. The last thing I want to see in my town is a United States Marshal!"

O'Reilly shrugged and got to his feet. It had sounded good to him. He was nearly to the door when Staughton called after him. "You didn't forget to tell Tim about Will Ford?"

O'Reilly turned dumbly, rubbing his whiskered jaw. "I guess that sort of slipped my mind, Mister Staughton."

Adrian flared up, "Damn it, O'Reilly, can't you be counted on for anything."

O'Reilly started to snap a response, but he calmed himself. "I'll tell him today for sure, Mister Staughton," the sheriff promised. He went out, closing the door, and it was then that his anger caught up with him. Damn that Staughton! Who the hell did he think he was?

"One day, Mister Staughton," O'Reilly muttered, "we'll meet up in a way you won't like at all. No one pushes Michael O'Reilly beyond a point." Staughton had damned near reached that point, the sheriff decided. Feeling the need suddenly, O'Reilly turned uptown toward the Single Jack Saloon.

From his upstairs window Adrian Staughton watched him go. It could be, he considered, that Sheriff O'Reilly was outliving his usefulness.

The man had always been a drunkard, a bully. Lately his drinking was getting out of hand. It was, Staughton supposed, because O'Reilly only drank when he had money. Before he had been broke at least half the time; now he was drawing steady wages, and a good wage at that. But O'Reilly was getting surly. His memory was slipping and he was starting to talk—that was a fatal offense.

One other item troubled Adrian Staughton as he stood, hands behind his back, looking out at the town, his town, and at the resolute high mountains beyond. This Ute. It was odd that a Ute should happen upon Weiner's place at the time of the murder, odd that the man would take Weiner's clothes or need them. And that very night this ... savage ... had appeared at his own house. Hadn't Sarah said he was wearing a suit which fit him poorly? But she had said the man was bearded. Bearded? A Ute? It puzzled and bothered Staughton that the man, whoever he was, had come from Weiner's house to his home.

There were several men in town who were intimate with the Utes. Wichita Jack was one, and Staughton resolved to inquire about this bearded Ute. On a sudden inspiration Staughton called in Sam Courtney. "Get over to Weiner's place, Sam. There should be footprints in the mud outside—bare footprints. Then hustle over to my place and see what you can find around the back door. If those tracks match, let me know."

And if they did—what did that mean? Staughton could make no connection, and so he sat to his desk taking the mine books from his drawer. It was then that the door burst open and the red-eyed, bulky man with wild blond hair entered Staughton's office. Adrian automatically came to his feet, but Cooms, brandishing a pistol knocked him down into his seat. There were six men with Cooms, all heavily armed, and they took up positions at the doors and windows as Cooms, trembling with anger hovered over Staughton.

"Damn you," Cooms growled, "you've killed Bob Weiner."

"I had nothing to do . . ."

"Shut up!" Cooms drew back the hammer on his revolver. "You did it or had it done. You know it and I know it. And now you'll pay for it, Staughton!"

"You wouldn't dare!" Staughton said coolly. Inside he was panicky. Cooms looked as if he hadn't slept in a week. His eyes were bleary, badly ringed. Staughton wondered if the man had gone overboard, his mind snapped.

"No," Cooms said and Staughton relaxed a hair. "I won't kill you here and now. That would mean a hanging and you're not worth me getting myself hung." Cooms was panting. He leaned far over across Staughton's desk, eyes wild. "But I'm declaring war. Get me? War! You'll not profit by Bob's death; you'll pay. Your mines are fair game as mine was. Your wagons are fair game. Your house and property."

Cooms stood, taking a deep slow breath. Only now, slowly, did his gun lower. "I'll not hang for the likes of you, Staughton. But by God, from this moment on, I'll only be living for the day I can see you hanging from a gallows. I'm going to burn you out, flood you out . . . and then I'm going to prove that *you*," a thick, menacing finger was shoved in Adrian Staughton's face, "that you killed Bob Weiner."

Then Cooms spun on his heel and stalked to the door, his armed retinue encircling him. Adrian Staughton leaned back, and reached for a cigar. His

116

hand, he found to his dismay, was shaking so much he could hardly cut the tip from the cigar and light it. *Prove it?* Could he? Could Cooms prove it? Only if someone talked, and talking would get the informer killed as well. . . . Unless. Staughton frowned deeply. Unless that damned savage Ute had actually seen the killing. If Cooms could find him . . .

Staughton stubbed out his cigar and rose unsteadily to his feet. It was a slim chance, he tried to convince himself. Yet he knew Cooms would be turning over every rock, searching for some evidence. But unless O'Reilly talked . . . There was another weak link. The man always talked. The difference was that talking this time could put a noose around both their necks.

# 11.

Tamany Wade had been trapping the Rockies for thirty years. He had lived with the Utes, the Pawnee and the Wind River Shoshoni, but very little among the whites. The furs were growing scarce now, and already that month, Wade had seen six white men—five of them digging for gold.

It was time to be moving north, he judged, into Canada perhaps. Wade was leading his pack mules up the south slope of Homestake where there was a good stand of pines. The air was cool, as he liked it, the day utterly clear. His feet were troubling him, and Tamany wondered just how many miles those feet had carried him. A tall, wiry man with a mass of gray whiskers, he decided he was not getting any younger. Finding a boulder alongside his winding trail, Wade sagged to it and took off his moccasins, rubbing his feet. It was then that he saw the man who, by the marks in the pine needle littered earth had dragged himself under the trees. Tamany, being a careful man, first picked up his Sharps rifle and then went to where the man lay.

"Funny," Tamany Wade said to himself. Dressed in a too-small suit, the man wore no shirt and no shoes.

Tamany looked around at the wilderness surrounding him, wondering how a man with no shoes and no gear had come to such a place.

"Alive or dead, are ye?" Tamany muttered. Touching a finger to the tall man's throat, he found a pulse. It was then that he saw the smear of blood soaking the old twill coat and gently removing it, prying it free of the scab, Tamany found the badly festered arrow wound.

"Ute?" Tamany could still see the distinctive bands on the broken shaft and he read it for a Ute arrow. "Damn me for a Yankee."

Tamany Wade sat back on his heels, pondering. No easy answer came to him, so he rose and went about the serious business of finding mistletoe to mix with rice for a cleansing poultice.

He also had a pint of store-bought whisky which he hated to use like this, but it might help cleanse the badly infected wound some. Throwing his hat aside so that his hair was blown across his craggy face, Tamany started a small fire with pine needles, and over that he turned the point of his bowie knife.

"I can't figure you, kid," Wade muttered to himself. "But I'd be almighty interested in finding out what you're doing here." He raised the sharp point of the bowie to Mantaka's back. "If you survive to tell me anything."

Sarah Staughton had her auburn curls pinned neatly in place atop her head. As she walked the ringlets at the back of her head bobbed. Before the mirror she turned appreciatively, studying the figure she cut in the floor length, powder blue gown. She wore pearl earrings and a pearl necklace, a touch of rouge and that constant, nearly impertinent smile. Her blue eyes looked back at her from the gilt framed mirror as she craned her neck, trying to see the hemline at the back of the gown.

"So lovely," Ella Staughton said.

Sarah's mother's face appeared beside her daughter's in the mirror. Her own eyes, Ella saw clearly, were watery. Her pasty complexion, a sign of her ill-health, was outshone by the radiance on Sarah's fresh countenance.

Unsteadily Ella Staughton turned and sat in Sarah's bedroom chair. "You'll outshine every other girl there," Ella said with evident pride.

"Betty Yount will be there," Sarah said with a shadow of jealousy. "The way she flaunts herself . . . Of course she is pretty. In that way . . ."

Ella believed the girl to be too wrapped up in herself, in her parties and flirting. But, she reflected, perhaps Sarah was happier that way. Happier than the real world could make her. The real world of the Staughtons.

"Is Father downstairs?" Sarah asked, turning around, flouncing to her mother's side.

"Yes, but he has a guest." Ella's trembling hand reached out and touched Sarah's curls for a brief moment. Then the girl turned and bounced away, saying over her shoulder.

"He won't mind an interruption."

Waving a goodbye, Sarah was gone, leaving Ella Staughton to sit in the late afternoon-shadowed room. Sarah was right, of course. Although Ella would never dare interrupt her husband at his work, Sarah had had that privilege since as a little girl she used to draw a

120

chair up to her father's desk as he bargained with Senators and railroad executives. Slowly Ella Staughton walked to the window of Sarah's bedroom and looked down at the grounds of the great estate Adrian Staughton had built in this wilderness. The great, empty estate grounds.

Sarah opened the massive door to her father's ornate office without knocking, and as she entered both men present rose. The stubby man in dirty buckskins was standing near the fireplace. Sarah glanced at him quizzically; he was a stranger to her.

"Here she is," Adrian Staughton said with a smile. "Jack and I were just talking about you. Wichita Jack, this is my daughter, Sarah."

"It's a pleasure, young lady," Jack said amiably.

"Wichita has spent a lot of time with the Utes. As a matter of fact he wintered with them last year. He knows all about this man you found in the kitchen the other night."

"The man with the knife?" Sarah sat down, smoothing her skirts, her blue eyes bright with interest.

"Yes. Tell her what you told me, would you, Jack?"

"Sure will. You see, Miss Staughton, this here man is a strange case. He ain't no Ute, that's for durn sure. They hate him with a passion, they do."

"Why?" Sarah asked. She rested her chin on her hands, watching curiously.

"Well it seems he's stolen a lot from the Utes—horses, weapons and such. And then, come a month ago, the Utes say they got into a tussle with him again and he ups and shoots one Ute, cutting another to mincemeat with a knife."

"If he's not an Indian," Sarah commented, "what is he? Who?"

"Well, he ain't Indian, but nobody knows who he is, or maybe they do, but they didn't tell me. Story they tell around them Ute fires at night is that this man is a savage whose father was a grizzly bear, his mother a princess . . . Now you can make what you can out of that. Like I say, maybe they know more than they told me."

"He was big enough to be a bear," Sarah said. "And hairy, not at all like any Indian I've seen."

"At any rate, he's a thief and a murderer," Adrian Staughton said. "I've a feeling that he murdered Bob Weiner the night he was here. The sheriff has evidence to indicate that it is certainly so."

Adrian was enjoying every bit of this. Now there was a scapegoat to hang that Weiner killing on without getting the Ute nation involved. Something he had been anxious to avoid. Perhaps, he thought, even Cooms could be made to believe it was the work of this savage, once the footprints were pointed out. They were still there to be seen. The warm sun had baked the clay where they were found after the rain.

As if to solidify this idea Staughton, rising, suddenly said, "You know, this savage should be hunted down. He's a menace to us as well as to the friendly Indians."

"Be tough to track that one," Jack believed.

"Yes." Staughton was thinking it mattered little if this savage was caught or not, it was the gesture which was important. "He frightened Sarah out of her wits and—I believe—killed Bob Weiner. I'm putting a thousand dollars on his head."

At that Wichita Jack got to his feet, put his beaded

hat on and turned toward the door. "Where are you going?"

"I'm gonna get a jump on the rest of them boys, Mister Staughton. You start talking money like that and they'll be combing those mountains fine enough to find a hop-flea."

When Jack was gone, Adrian Staughton stood before the fire, watching the golden sparks, blessing his good luck. It was a moment before he remembered Sarah was still there.

"What was it you wanted, Dear. You look so lovely." Staughton walked to his daughter and placed his hands on her shoulders, kissing her forehead lightly.

"It's seven o'clock," Sarah said with emphasis. Staughton had no idea in the world what that meant.

"Yes it is," he agreed, glancing at the clock on the mantle.

"Will Ford was supposed to call for me at six-thirty," Sarah said with exasperation. "I suppose he's not coming," she added.

"I can't imagine a young man standing you up," Staughton said convincingly. *So this too was working.* "I'll have Ben zip up into a suit and take you over in the buggy. He can wait there for you."

"I don't know if I shall even go," Sarah pouted. "I'm sure I shall be humiliated by having my father's foreman deliver me to the dance."

"Of course you'll go," Adrian Staughton said with a warm smile. "You can't waste that dress! And if Will Ford is boor enough, stupid enough to let this happen, I'm sure there are other young men who would fight to take his place."

"Well," she pondered, "I guess I shall go—but I

shan't forgive him. You were right about Will Ford too, Father." She got to tip-toes and kissed him, "as you are right about most things."

"Everything," he teased.

Sarah laughed. "Everything," she agreed.

"Ben!" Staughton called and the foreman appeared in the kitchen door, a sandwich in his hand. "You still have your wedding suit? Put it on."

The foreman shrugged and disappeared. Sarah went up to get her wrap and Staughton stood silently before the fire, feeling utterly pleased with the course of the day's events. The matter of Weiner's murder was working toward a solution with this savage showing up. Now this Will Ford matter had found a resolution. Staughton wondered idly how Tim O'Reilly had managed it. But he did not dwell on that question. It had as little importance to him as the fate of the savage.


Will Ford had been watching the clock in his father's general store all afternoon. Now it showed six, and Will hurriedly slipped off his apron and locked up the store. He had brought his good suit to the shop and was already wearing it; his father's surrey was hitched at the rail. Will was taking no chances on being late—not with Sarah Staughton waiting.

Locking the front door Ford went to the surrey, surveying the main street of Rose Canyon briefly. All of the businesses on the east side of the street with the sole exception of the Ford Store belonged to Adrian Staughton. Perhaps that was what Will's father had against Staughton, at any rate John Ford had a low opinion of Staughton. None of that mattered to Will Ford. His thoughts were only on Sarah Staughton's big blue eyes, those full lips which always wore half a pout.

"Where ya going?"

Will Ford had one boot up on the surrey. Now he turned back to see Tim O'Reilly and Stinger lounging in the saddles of their ponies. The late sun glinted on the badge Tim O'Reilly wore.

"This official?" Will asked, his broad face serious.

"No!" O'Reilly laughed and Stinger smirked. "Just conversation."

"That box social at the school," Will Ford said openly.

"Favor that sort of galavantin' do ya?" Stinger asked. "High steppin' and tight collars?"

"Sure . . ." Ford looked at Stinger. The deputy had a cigarette, unlighted, dangling from his lips. His cheeks were spotted with beard. "What's wrong with that?"

"Nothin'!" Tim said, holding up his hands. He swung down from the saddle and walked to where Will Ford stood, running his hand along the sleek flank of the sorrel. Tim propped his boot up on the yellow spoke of the front wheel. "Keep busy, don't you?" O'Reilly's eyes lifted to the general store.

"Sure do," Ford laughed, but it was a dry laugh. Just what did these two want? "Why?"

"Well," Tim drawled, scratching his chin, "it's just that we hardly see you around, Will. The boys get to thinkin' a man's uppity, you know?"

"Uppity?"

"Yeah, that's right," Stinger put in. He was playing his part to the hilt. He tipped his hat back off his lumpy forehead, letting a strand of rust-colored hair escape, and he leaned far forward, hands crossed on his pommel. "Like you're too good for ordinary folks."

There was a gleam in Stinger's eyes that Will Ford did not like. He knew about Stinger Matson, everyone did. As young as Will himself, Stinger had already been involved in four gunfights. He was said to have a hair trigger temper.

"It's not like that, Sting," Tim O'Reilly said, putting a hand on Will's shoulder as if to defuse the situation. "Look," he suggested to Will Ford, "you've got a few minutes, don't you? How about stepping to the Red River and having a drink with me and Stinger?"

"I really have to be going . . ." Will began, but Tim O'Reilly caught his eye and shook his head slightly, imperceptibly nodding at Stinger.

"I think you should, just one," O'Reilly encouraged him in a low voice. "Stinger's . . . well, he's Stinger."

Will Ford swallowed and took a deep breath. Glancing at Stinger Matson who still wore a fierce scowl, he answered, "Why sure, I guess I've got five minutes for a drink."

"Good." O'Reilly squeezed Ford's shoulder, meantime winking broadly at Stinger who pushed his hat down over his eyes, and grinning crookedly followed Tim and Will Ford to the Red River Saloon across the street.

"But I've really only got time for one drink," Will said.

"Sure." Tim O'Reilly grinned and slapped Ford's back again, pushing through the batwing doors of the Red River. Now, of course, they had young Will Ford roped in, and Ford was prodded and finally bullied into having a second and a third drink. By the time he reached the box social his coat and trousers were torn

126

and he was stinking drunk. Ben Chalmers was sitting on the porch railing. The Staughton foreman glanced up from his whittling to see Will trip and fall out of his surrey. With a glance behind him where the girls in party dresses spun past under the eye of the school teacher and the parson, Ben walked to where Will Ford was struggling to his feet.

Ben helped him up. "Boy," he advised, "best just clamber back aboard. The horse knows the way home."

" 'S all right. Be all right. Just need to . . ." Ben shrugged and let the kid go past him to the water trough where he soaked his head and shoulders, further ruining the coat. Then, taking a deep breath, Will Ford wound toward the door of the schoolhouse.

Sarah stood with Betty Yount, a perky, full figured blonde and Dana Kirsch, the school teacher's daughter. "It's too bad Will couldn't make it," Betty said, and Sarah thought she detected a note of triumph in her words. The two girls had been rivals and best friends for years.

"There are many things more important than frivolity to Will," Sarah said coolly. "He's helping his father with the bookkeeping. One day Will Ford will be a huge success in business while the boys who . . ."

Her words broke off and she gasped as Will Ford did appear. He opened the door, tripped across the threshold and went flat on his face. Rising he sat on the floor, shaking his head, blinking at the whirling mass of people surrounding him. He was trying to find Sarah Staughton, but he saw her only briefly as she rushed past him and out the door, her face flushed hot with embarrassment.

# 12.

The incident with Will Ford was not the sole cause, but it contributed to a decision. Sarah Staughton would go East at summer's end to stay with her aunt and attend a Pennsylvania finishing school. Ella Staughton was anxious to see her daughter receive the polish she lacked, and perhaps meet a young gentleman.

Sarah still acutely felt the embarrassment of the box social, but the smug satisfaction it had given Betty Yount and the other girls to see Sarah Staughton so embarrassed had quickly given way to envy. Sarah was going East, away from this awful town.

Adrian Staughton, who had been reluctant to consent to this journey, now approved. Two considerations had swayed him. Firstly he wanted to make sure that Will Ford and his daughter remained separated. There was a second matter. Cooms had never totally accepted the theory of the "savage" murdering his partner. Each day more Staughton wagons were burned, more Staughton miners harassed. It looked like the situation might develop into a full scale shooting war. Staughton wanted his daughter out of the way when it exploded.

And so she left, riding out of Rose Canyon that

August day on the eastbound Wells Fargo coach, and if Sarah saw the storekeeper's young son standing beneath the oaks at the roadside, waving, she never showed it. If Sarah had severed her ties with Rose Canyon and its intrigues, the savage, on the other hand was being more strongly bound to them.

A wanted poster of Mantaka, wildly imaginative, depicting him as a cross between a grizzly and a wild man from Borneo was made up and posted along the roadsides from Rose Canyon to Pueblo. That thousand dollar reward, as Wichita Jack had foreseen, drew half of the gunhands and toughs in Colorado into the mountains, though most of them gave it up after a week or so in that rugged country. Two Utes and an irate trapper named George Murdock were brought in mistakenly for the reward, and a fourth man had been shot by an over-eager bounty hunter. No one had yet come within ten miles of Tamany Wade's rough log cabin.

It was there that Mantaka lay—as he would lie for a long while longer. The fever had come, gone and come again. Tamany Wade had done all he knew how to do. Now it was up to nature, and so Mantaka lay up in the cabin, hobbling to the stove and out to the well while Tamany ranged farther into the mountains sometimes for weeks on end, setting his traps.

Mantaka felt secure in the cabin, as secure as he had ever felt. It was a sturdy and secluded hideaway. Set back against the face of a bluff, surrounded by willows and cottonwood, it was difficult to find until a man was right on top of it. Tamany had left a spare rifle, a Spencer .56, and Mantaka went no farther than the front porch without it. He felt much stronger, but Tamany was still forced to observe, "You ain't fit for travellin', boy. You'd best plan on winterin' up in the cabin."

Using the smattering of Ute he knew, Tamany was able to communicate with Mantaka clumsily. Yet Mantaka had never volunteered, nor had the hugely built young man ever responded, to questions about his past.

"I will winter with you. In the spring we will trap together," Mantaka offered.

But Tamany Wade shook his head. "Me, I'm travellin' now before the snows fall. Headin' north." He pointed toward Canada. "Better furs, fewer folks. But you're welcome to the cabin."

"I should not stay," Mantaka said, frowning.

"You damn well better stay, boy," Tamany advised him. "You ain't got your strength back and you'll not be outrunning any Ute war party up and down these mountains just yet."

Reluctantly Mantaka agreed. Tamany gave him the rifle and some cartridges, refusing any thanks. "They's only one more thing you should know," Tamany Wade told the savage on the day he was to leave. Wade was tightening the straps on his mule pack as he spoke. "Some of the boys use this cabin too, time to time."

"Other trappers?" Mantaka asked. He centered the pack on the mule's back while Wade drew the straps down tight.

"That's right. If you can't put up with them, well best try it on your own."

"They are your friends?"

"Yeah." Tamany straightened up, holding his back. "Ben Forge, Joe Winkles and them—old mountain men. They might not show up, but then again they might if they're in the area when the weather gets hard."

"They would hunt me?" Mantaka wanted to know.

"Them old coons?" Tamany shook his head. "No. They're free-livin' men, got no use for what goes on down below, and besides they've each got somethin' a might shady in their way-back past anyway. They ain't that sort. Rough men, yes, but they won't bother you, I don't reckon. So you stay or go as you like, boy." Tamany Wade stuck out a gnarled hand and Mantaka took it uncertainly. "Me, I'm walking the ridge north. Luck to you, boy."

Tamany turned and led off, with that mule trailing, and he never turned back to look at Mantaka, the cabin or Colorado. Mantaka watched him until he could no longer see the moving patch against the timbered slopes, then with a cold wind rising he hobbled back to the cabin, building a small fire against the coming of night.

Mantaka lived well at Tamany's cabin. Carrying his rifle everywhere he went, he gathered wild plums along the creek bottoms, found a tangle of raspberries which the bears had not discovered, and fished for brown trout in the cold creek beyond the cedar studded ridge to the south. He had seen no sign of the Utes, nor of any white man.

Winter would come in early, as the southward winging geese and the frantically working squirrels indicated, and Mantaka too began preparing for the snows. He smoked the meat of two elks and three dozen trout, gathered wild potatoes and sego lily bulbs. It was difficult still for him to chop firewood, but he had a cord stacked and ready. Climbing to the cabin roof, which he knew leaked when it rained, Mantaka went to work there to make it tight against the cold blasts of winter. He was unfamiliar with carpentry, but after spending most of the morning examining the roof and analyzing what he found, he began methodically tightening the planks, chinking the gaps he could not mend with pitch.

He was there, working on the roof, when they rode up.

"Howdy!" a voice boomed and Mantaka, rifle in hand, turned to see three men bundled in layers of furs watching from the yard. They all wore massive, tangled beards and carried fine rifles.

Mantaka eyed them closely, his thumb on the hammer of his Spencer repeater.

"Don't you speak?" the red-bearded man shouted hoarsely. "Where's Tamany Wade?"

"Forge?" Mantaka asked. "Joe Winkles?"

"I'm Winkles, all right," the red-beard answered. "Where the hell's Wade."

Mantaka pointed north. "Canada."

"Canada, is it? Well, maybe he's the smart one." Winkles leaned his rifle against the log box of the well and drew up a cool, sweet bucket of water.

They seemed little disturbed by Tamany's absence, or by the presence of the tall, hugely muscled savage. Perhaps in these men's wild lives there had been much sudden disappearing, many encounters so that it troubled them not at all.

Wes Torkleson was not so sure. He was the new man among them, running to the mountains to avoid a Texas murder warrant. "How the hell we know he didn't kill Tamany? He's got his gun."

"Takes a lot of brass to hang around patching a roof after a killing," Joe Winkles shrugged, wiping the water from his beard. "Besides, he knew our names. Don't figure Tamany would think to mention me while he was getting his throat cut."

Winkles laughed at his own joke and Ben Forge, a squat, rock-hard man joined him. Torkleson was not so sure, but he said nothing else, finishing his own drink of the water, so cold that it hurt his teeth when he swallowed it.

The three mountain men lost no time in making themselves at home. They entered the cabin and stowed their gear, and finding Mantaka's store of smoked trout they sat to the table and devoured three each.

After eating they took a nap, stretched out on the floor snoring before the small fire. An hour before sundown Joe Winkles got up, stretched his massive arms and went out with his rifle. He was back before nightfall with a mule deer he had killed. Conversation was basic. Only Winkles knew enough Ute to speak very well. Forge knew some phrases, and Torkleson's vocabulary was restricted to "How far?" and "How many?"

Still Mantaka did not mind them being there. The Utes, if they could find Mantaka, would not come lightly against him with three armed whites around him. And they did their share of the hunting and foraging.

Mantaka felt stronger with each passing day. By the time the first snows fell he felt that he could have travelled if need be. But there was no need, and Mantaka relaxed for the first time in memory. He watched the trappers play at cards, picking up a word now and then. He knew their supplies were adequate and so even the sight of twelve feet of new snow drifted up against the windward side of the cabin could not depress him. It did not bother the mountain men either. They had seen their hard winters too, and in shabbier places than Tamany Wade's cabin.

The days drifted past in dark, dreary progression as the long high country winter settled in. There was no sound but the singing of the wind in the trees, the slapping of cards against the table and the snoring—always the snoring. These men slept as if they had been awake all summer long.

"Want a haircut, Mantaka?"

Mantaka looked up from the buckskin shirt he was making to see Joe Winkles brandishing a pair of scissors.

"No."

"Well—think it over. Wait till you see how purty old Ben's goin' to be when I'm done."

This was something worth watching. Curiously Mantaka looked as Winkles put a towel around Ben Forge's neck, lifting his beard to spread it over the cloth. Then, with gusto Winkles went to work, chopping foot long sections of Forge's black hair free at a time.

When he had it trimmed to an inelegant fringe, Winkles went to work on the beard, lifting Ben's chin to hack away at the tangled mass sprouting there.

When he had the beard down to a three-inch length, Winkles put the scissors down on the table behind him and, reaching inside his coat, he gleefully produced a razor. Stropping the razor while Ben worked at his beard with soap and water to soften it, Joe Winkles spared a wink for Mantaka who was astonished by it all.

Already Ben Forge scarcely resembled the wild-haired man who had arrived with the other two, and by the time Winkles was through scraping the whisker from Ben's face he was an utter stranger. Ben Forge's face was utterly white under the stubble and he rubbed his smooth chin thoughtfully. "I guess it was about time," he commented, eyeing the pile of black hair on the cabin floor.

"Now them fleas are going to have to find a new home," Wes Torkleson chided him.

"And I know where they'll be headed," Winkles answered, rubbing his own massive red beard. "What about you, Wes? Want a haircut and a shave?"

"You can take a little hair," Torkleson agreed. "But this beard stays. Ain't no way I want to go back to lookin' like them wanted posters."

Joe Winkles was eager to play barber, but he declined to let anyone touch his jungle of red hair and beard. Perhaps he had simply grown accustomed to peering at the world from out of his underbrush. The excuse he gave was, "Winter ain't over yet. I need sumpin to keep my head warm."

Ben was pleased with his haircut and shave and spent quite a time examining himself in the chip of mirror which Tamany had tacked on the wall.

"My face itches like the devil, though," he complained. "Don't have any bay rum up your sleeve, do you?"

"Maybe Tamany had somethin'," Wes suggested.

"I never seen that old coon shaved," Joe Winkles said.

"I didn't mean bay rum," Wes explained. "Maybe he had some alcohol around, though. That would do the trick." Torkleson glanced around the dim cabin, his eyes settling on some boxes stacked on a high shelf.

"We ain't looked up there."

"What's up there, Mantaka?"

Mantaka glanced up and shrugged; he hadn't poked around that much either.

"Could be he's even got a magazine, an old newspaper up there," Joe Winkles conjectured. "I'd read anything just now. Even poetry!" he laughed.

Ben Forge was still scratching at his raw throat. "Let's have a look." They pulled the table over and climbed up, Forge handing the two boxes down to the others.

Eagerly they opened the crates, but their expectations were dashed. "Nothin' much," Ben Forge said, emptying the first box. "Nails, wire, an old harness . . ."

"How 'bout this?"

Torkleson had opened the other crate and when they turned toward him he was hefting a two gallon jug. He had already removed the cork and sniffed it. "Whisky, by God!"

"Let me see that." Ben Forge took it, sniffed it and took a swallow which set his eyes to watering. "Home-grown," he gasped.

"That damned old fox," Winkles said affectionately. "And him knowin' we'd likely be snowed in." He took a deep drink which scorched his tongue and cauterized his stomach. "Mother's milk," he declared.

He handed it back to Torkleson who took another drink and shuddered as it hit bottom. Ben Forge was sitting in his chair, a dull warmth already spreading through him.

"There's two gallons," Forge observed. "Enough for three light days."

"Or one big night," Joe Winkles said, taking a deep gulp. "Want some, Mantaka?"

Mantaka took the jug curiously, and frowned as the whisky fumes burned his nostrils. Shaking his head he handed the jug back. Winkles laughed.

"The kid's right. It's pure poison." So saying, he tipped the jug up again. Grimacing he sagged into the chair beside Forge whose formerly pasty cheeks were now flushed red.

"Break the cards out," Wes Torkleson said, sitting to the table. "We'll play for whisky cups."

"Winner or loser drinks?" Forge asked wryly.

Mantaka sat watching them, not completely understanding. The drink they had was enough to stop your breath and turn the stomach over, and yet they coveted it.

Having finished his shirt he turned it over, examining it, then he walked behind Forge who was holding his cards loosely.

"Three kings," Winkles said and Torkleson swore. "What's the matter, can't take it?"

"I'm through playin'," Wes snapped. "Can't play cards with a deck of forty-eight. That's all there is, you know? I counted 'em."

"What's the difference," Ben Forge asked, and Mantaka noticed that his words too were slurred now. "Wanna play cards, Mantaka?"

"No."

"Hell, he don't wanna play," Torkleson said. "He won't even have a drink with us."

"Settle down, Wes," Joe Winkles drawled. This was a repetition of other scenes he had seen in a winter with

137

pent-up emotions, and savage men, and he wanted none of it.

"Well he won't. Will ya, Chief?" Torkleson pushed it.

"I don't care." Mantaka shrugged. If it would make the man happy... He lifted the jug and filled his cheeks with the fiery corn liquor. He grinned triumphantly as he managed to swallow it, and showed the jug to Torkleson.

"That don't mean nothin'," Torkleson muttered.

He turned away to sulk drunkenly. Forge and Winkles had fallen to a two-handed game of solitaire and Mantaka sat beside Forge, trying to figure it out.

His stomach was warm now, his vision slightly blurred. Forge turned up a red six and frustrated, threw it down. It struck Mantaka as funny and so he laughed.

He shrugged apologetically to Joe Winkles who was pouring another tin cup full of whisky for himself. He shoved the jug toward Mantaka who took another deep drink.

"Ain't bad after you get the taste buds burned off your tongue, is it?" Winkles asked.

Mantaka shook his head and took another drink. Winkles looked funny now and the cards on the table were spinning in a red and black, patterned pinwheel. Mantaka laughed again.

"What's so goddamned funny?" Torkleson wanted to know.

Wes Torkleson had taken up throwing his bowie knife into the log walls of the cabin. "Wasn't that an ace?" Forge muttered. Mantaka hefted the jug and Torkleson suddenly whirled around, knife in his hand.

"I said have a drink with us, not drink the whole damned jug!"

"Settle down, Wes. Take a nap," Winkles suggested.

Mantaka took a seat next to Torkleson whose eyes were red blurs, watching as the bearded mountain man hefted his bowie knife, feeling the weight of it against his palm, watching the bright glitter of the steel in the dull lamplight. Then suddenly Torkleson would lift his hand and the knife would flicker toward the wall, sticking with a quiver.

At least this was a game Mantaka understood. He walked to the wall and cut a spot into the wall for a target. Returning he sat beside Torkleson, drawing his own knife from its sheath.

"I'm good, you hear?" Wes said.

"I hear."

Wes Torkleson took a little more time on this throw. He stuck his knife point not three inches from the tiny target Mantaka had drawn on the wall.

"Beat that," Wes said. Now, when he looked at Mantaka Winkles noticed that there was an ugliness in his eyes. A meanness brought on by drink.

Mantaka peered at the target, at Torkleson's knife and then he threw his own knife, his motions as fluid as a cat's, and the knife stuck dead center. Mantaka grinned and slapped Wes on the shoulder. Mantaka crossed the room and recovered the knives while Torkleson took another drink.

Why Torkleson was angry he could not have said himself. But it had happened before—leaving a man dead. He jerked his knife from Mantaka's hand and threw again, but this throw was even farther off. Mantaka flipped his own knife, again finding dead center. Walking to the wall to recover their knives Mantaka saw a flash of silver, heard a thunk and glanced beside his ear to see a third knife still quivering there. Torkleson laughed uproariously—he had missed Mantaka's ear by no more than an inch.

Mantaka laughed in return and nodded, acknowledging a good throw. Then, with a single, exact motion he took the knife Torkleson had just thrown and let it fly. The knife zipped past Torkleson's ear and stuck deeply in the opposite wall. With a roar of rage Torkleson lunged to his feet.

The mountain man grabbed a chair and winged it at Mantaka; nicking Mantaka's shoulder it crashed into the table, scattering cards and players. Mantaka rubbed his shoulder, but managed a grin, sticking out his hand to Torkleson. But it had gone too far. Torkleson, in a drunken fury, pulled his knife from the wall and leaped at Mantaka, who side-stepped and tripped the onrushing trapper. Joe Winkles, unsteady on his feet, tried to grab Torkleson and spin him around, but his partner shook him off. Instead Wes brought his knife around viciously in a low arc, and as Mantaka drew away he felt the knife point score him, saw the thin trickle of blood running from his abdomen.

Still Mantaka backed away and Forge hollered at the pursuing Torkleson, "Leave it be, Wes!"

Mantaka came up short, his back against the wall of the log cabin. He watched as Torkleson grinned, stepped in and drove his knife at Mantaka. The savage was too quick, however. Turning his torso to one side just enough to cause Torkleson to miss, Mantaka slapped the mountain man's knife aside and with a stiff right hand blow to Torkleson's jaw, he slammed him to

140

the floor. Mantaka picked up the knife quickly.

Seeing Mantaka hovering over his fallen partner, Ben Forge hurled himself through the air, slamming a shoulder into Mantaka, driving them both to the floor. "Ben, stay out of it," Joe Winkles shouted, but Forge was already in it. Mantaka got to his feet in a crouch, but he was a hair slower than Ben Forge, who swung a kick at Mantaka's jaw. Forge's boot caught the savage flush and he was driven back against the wall, nearly on top of Torkleson, who was only now getting to his feet.

Torkleson, in a wild attempt at retaliation, swung out at Mantaka who swiped the blow aside and landed a left of his own on Wes' jaw. Torkleson, falling back, grabbed for Mantaka's hand, which still held the knife. Striking back angrily, Mantaka cut Torkleson's shoulder and the man screamed out in pain.

Now deadly sober, Mantaka got to his feet, his back to the wall. Torkleson lay bleeding on the floor and Forge, a hatchet in his hand faced Mantaka.

"I did not mean it," Mantaka said softly, but Forge stepped in anyway, driving down with the hatchet. Mantaka retaliated, driving his knife upward. It caught Forge at the base of the throat and ripped open his jugular.

Torkleson stammered something and crawled away as Mantaka turned back toward him.

"Mantaka!" Joe Winkles cried out. Mantaka turned to face the big red-bearded mountain man. There was a rifle in his hands.

Joe hadn't known Torkleson all that long, but he was Winkles' partner—that meant something and Winkles cocked his rifle, levelling the bead on Mantaka's head.

The savage dove to the floor as Winkles' gun erupted with flame and a bullet slammed into the wall. The close room was filled with rolling black powder smoke.

Winkles hurriedly reloaded, the smoke burning his eyes, the roar of the explosion ringing in his ears. Where was the man!

He could make out nothing, and when he did it was too late. Mantaka leaped across the table and as Joe Winkles' rifle exploded at the ceiling, Mantaka's deadly knife slashed down and buried itself in the big man's bearded throat.

Winkles collapsed with a gurgling moan and Mantaka backed away, his heart pounding. Forge also lay dead on the floor in a pool of his own blood. Torkleson crouched, whimpering in the corner, blood staining his shirt.

Mantaka turned, snatched up a burlap sack and stuffed it full of what foodstuffs he could find. Then he went to the door where the snow lay drifted ten feet high. With a last look at Torkleson, whose face was ashen, frightened, Mantaka tunneled up until he found the iron gray day, the icy cold freedom of the out of doors.

# 13.

That was a hard winter, the worst Mantaka could remember. He moved from shelter to shelter—lean-tos or hollows found in the great jumbles of rocks along the southern flank of Homestake—always one step ahead of the Utes who hunted him despite the thirty foot drifts and hundred mile an hour winds which raked the peaks, bending the timber to their will.

During one three-week stretch Mantaka ate nothing but roots and jerky. The appearance of a snow hare was a magical apparition and Mantaka killed it, stretching the meat over three days. On another winter-swept day he fought with the Utes again. He believed he had killed one, but the sheets of swirling snow made it uncertain. He had fled into the wilderness, searching for a new shelter. A pile of rocks, a blown down tree ... anything to keep the icy razors of the wind off of him. Anything only to survive.

When spring did arrive it arrived tentatively. Clear days, brilliant, sunny alternated with days as cold as those in the dark depths of winter. Yet Mantaka hardly minded. The long winter was over and once again he could walk the long mountain slopes rich with new grass, spattered with wildflowers, hunting meat, fishing in the icy rills.

Once, following a herd of elk, he caught a glimpse of the far distant town of Rose Canyon, a postage stamp scene at his altitude, and he spared a thought for Weiner, who had been his only friend.

Adrian Staughton hardly gave Weiner a thought any longer, nor did he think of Cooms, who had sold out, worn to bare nerves by the constant danger. Michael O'Reilly had finally succeeded in drinking himself to death and his son Tim had ascended to the sheriff's position. Perhaps learning something from his father's death, Tim O'Reilly had nearly stopped drinking. He now sported black broadcloth suits and string ties. Yet he was utterly ruthless in enforcing Adrian Staughton's town law. That had not changed in the least.

Wes Torkleson had managed to survive the winter and he dragged himself into Rose Canyon to luridly tell his tale of the cabin fight. Belatedly, Tim O'Reilly had a recollection of Mantaka from Deep Water, and it was O'Reilly rather than Staughton who had lost all interest in the matter who kept the reward posted for the savage. Slowly a distorted legend had grown concerning Mantaka. Raised by a brutal French mountain man, the tale went, he was taught to hate the Utes and Americans alike. He had grown up, surviving by theft and murder, it was also said, and had a savage hate of all mankind.

He had been responsible for the deaths of half a dozen friendly Utes, a miner in Rose Canyon and the slaughter of two trusting trappers who had shared a winter cabin with him. There were further embellishments. Mantaka killed wild animals with his

144

bare hands, tearing their throats out and sucking their blood as he crouched, grunting with pleasure. No woman was safe, nor was any lone man. Tales of Mantaka who was known only as The Savage, were used to frighten children.

Oblivious to all of this Mantaka roamed the sun warmed meadows, scaled the high peaks and grew strong again. A massive young man of twenty, he still wore a full beard and buckskin clothes he made himself. He moved so silently that the Utes could not find him, flitting like a cloud shadow over the high mountain meadows.

It was already May, but still in this high country it occasionally snowed. This time it had snowed for two days and Mantaka was hardly surprised when he spotted the stagecoach bogged down by an avalanche.

He sat down on a rocky outcropping, studying their predicament, curious as a wild animal. The trail snaked up along the side of the mountain, far above the roaring river below. The late storm had blocked the trail with snow and boulders. The driver apparently had lost control of his horses—or perhaps the trail was too slick. The stagecoach rested on its axle, hanging over the brink of the precipice. Below white water raced and above the black rolling clouds threatened more snow.

The passengers huddled dismally against the bluff while the driver and another man tried to right the coach. They were only bits of color against the mountain from where Mantaka sat.

The wind was cold in his face from off the north. Bunched thunderheads smothered the high peaks. Soon it would storm again. The stagecoach would be in serious trouble. Mantaka still watched impassively, holding his rifle across his lap. It was only ten miles to Rose Canyon. Let these people learn to use their legs.

The horses, he saw, were balky. They should be cut free, Mantaka thought. Apparently the driver felt that would only delay him more. But the road ahead was blocked. That frightened the animals. The rear wheel of the stage hung into space. If they backed up the entire coach and team would be lost.

Mantaka rested his chin on his forearms, wanting to see what these men would try next. He felt a cold spatter of rain against his face and looking up he saw a curtain of rain farther up the valley. Whatever the driver was going to do he had better do it quickly. Watching them a minute longer, watching the storm gather as the men fought the horses and the trail, awash with slush and mud as the coach teetered on the trail's edge, Mantaka knew they would not make it.

The rear of the stage coach was slipping inexorably over. All of it—horses, coach, baggage would be spilled across the flank of the mountain. The rain was a steadily falling gray wash now, with only here and there the bright green of the spruce showing through the low clouds. Frantically the men tried to manhandle the coach, but it was useless. Mantaka frowned, arguing with himself. It was no good to simply watch them lose their possessions, the animals. Yet he was reluctant to go down. The decision was not an easy one, yet it had to be made soon obviously.

With a sigh, mentally scourging himself for this foolishness, Mantaka slipped down into the deep rocky ravine beneath his feet and worked through the brush which was still heavy with snow where the rain had not melted it. He worked his way toward the trail, all the time telling himself that he was a fool. They did not see him coming through the rain, with their attention on the wagon. He suddenly appeared out of the gray mist, jogging toward them with a rifle in his hands, his wild hair, damp with the rain streaming across his shoulders.

Mantaka saw the wagon slip. From the corner of his eye he saw the passengers standing up against the face of the cliff. He nearly stopped in his tracks. There were two older men and a woman—the most beautiful creature he had ever seen, and she looked back at him with wide, startled blue eyes.

"Hey!" Mantaka hollered and the stage driver turned his head. A man of medium height with a drooping mustache, he panicked at the appearance of this wild-haired phantom.

The man grabbed for his holstered gun. The second man, the shotgun rider screamed loudly, "The Savage!" and he too went for his gun.

The driver's pistol came up first and Mantaka, seeing it was shoot or die, touched off a shot from his Spencer rifle. The driver whirled around and slammed against the coach, sagging to his knees as the shotgun rider raised his weapon.

"No!"

"God, don't!" the woman yelled, but it was too late and Mantaka fired again, hitting the shotgun in the middle of the chest. He clutched at his shirt front and toppled back, disappearing over the lip of the cliff.

In a fury, Mantaka turned. Wild ideas, emotions collided inside his mind: anger, frustration, guilt, and he turned in a wild-eyed circle, staring at the passengers through the sweep of the rain.

"What can I do?" he shouted at them, his hand

147

pleading for their understanding. But there was no reasoning in their eyes, only stark fear, and Mantaka could only stand there, shaking his head slowly. Alone—always alone in every thought and action. Always failing to find a glimmer of understanding.

Always the blood.

He threw back his head and released an animal growl to the savage skies. The wind was wild in his hair; his face streamed with rain.

The driver, wounded but alive watched back in mortal terror. Mantaka turned, hesitated, stopped. He looked again at the young woman who stood there in the rain, at those blue eyes, the womanly figure beneath her red silk dress.

"No!" she screamed. But Mantaka was to her in a single step and no one tried to stop him then as he hefted her with one massive arm and threw her across his shoulder, striding away with the woman kicking, screaming as the other passengers watched. Soon they heard nothing more, saw nothing but the driving rain. They stood gaping a moment longer before a man spoke.

"My God! He's taken Sarah Staughton."

Higher the beast climbed, through the gray mist and falling rain, striding through the tall timber as if his strength were limitless.

Sarah had kicked and screamed, pounding on his massive back until her own strength had waned. It had done no good, any of it. Still he walked on, crossing a fallen pine log over a quick running creek, walking a narrow eyebrow of a trail which hung out into space. Below Sarah could see the rain drifting through a canyon hundreds of feet deep and she simply closed her eyes.

It was as if her nightmare had come to life—for that was what the savage was. Since the night nearly a year ago when he had appeared in her father's kitchen, she had dreamed intermittently of the bloody, wild creature. Those dreams had always been shockingly real, and she had awakened in fright many times.

Now, with her dress soaked through, with his massive arm locked around her, the icy wind off the peaks, it was no longer a dream, but still a nightmare.

"Why won't you let me go!" she cried.

"No."

His voice was firm, and he trudged on—toward what goal only he knew. They were among the trees again and the rain was blunted by the thick boughs overhead. Mantaka put Sarah down on a flat rock and she instantly tried to bolt. His hand shot out and he shoved her down once more.

"No."

He hovered over her, his great black mane dripping with rain, his black eyes deep, set.

"Eat," he advised her, and Sarah took a strip of dry jerky from him, attempting it. Her auburn curls which had been so neatly done up in Denver now hung in dismal strands. She shivered with the cold and flinched when a large hand stretched out and offered her a drink from his water skin. She shook her head nervously and her lips formed into a bewildered pout. Mantaka liked that expression and he grinned. In fact, he decided, he liked everything about this strange, soft creature. Her smooth skin and tapering, unblistered hands, those eyes which were the color of the sky.

He was right to have taken her. She was a fine prize. Sarah shivered. Huddled on the rock under the dense pines the wind still reached her and this man, this savage, simply crouched there grinning at her.

"You'll be exceedingly sorry you started this, sir," she told him. "My father is Adrian Staughton, and you can be sure he will not rest until you have been hunted down and hung!"

"Yes," Mantaka replied. The woman's eyes flashed when she was angry—that was a good sign.

"I am not joking! For God's sake," Sarah wiped a strand of hair from her eyes. "You have abducted me, murdered a man ... what is it you want? Is it ransom? My father will give you gold if you return me forthwith."

"Gold?" That was a word which Mantaka did not care for. The gold he had seen had only brought pain and death. Whatever the girl was getting at he did not understand. His English was simply not that good, and she spoke so rapidly.

But that too Mantaka liked. Her words bubbled through her lips like a brook over rocks. If she was a little angry, well she would get over it. Po-Ta-Liki had gotten over it, and Mantaka would be a different sort of man than Lacroix had been to Timid Morning Light. He would not leave this soft creature alone all winter.

"Don't you understand any of this?" Sarah asked miserably. "Don't you speak English at all?"

"I speak." Mantaka nodded.

"Then you do understand the wickedness you have accomplished ... oh!" He simply sat there grinning and nodding his head. It was hopeless, simply hopeless.

There was nothing to do but wait until the man

slept—he must sleep—and then flee. But in which direction? She glanced uncertainly at the wooded hillsides. At any rate, she told herself, it won't be long until Father finds me. If only in the meantime the creature doesn't take some animal notion into his skull . . .

She tried reading his expression, but had no luck. The man seemed a simpleton, a hulking idiot. He only grinned, and Sarah felt her strength ebbing as the rain continued to fall and lightning crackled across the iron gray skies. She placed her head in her hands and cried, the warm tears mingling with the cold rain on her cheeks.

She felt his hand again then, a rough clumsy hand as it brushed a tear away. Now he was no longer grinning, but only watching her tenderly. It was a moment before Sarah composed herself enough to draw away from the hand.

Then what was he, after all? A simpleton? It seemed intelligence flashed in those dark eyes. For a savage killer it seemed he had a deal of compassion. How tender his rugged face had been when he touched her tear.

"Will you let me go?" Sarah asked again, her voice soft, pleading. Stoically he watched her in return, and if there was compassion in those eyes still, it did not affect his flat response.

"No."

The rain still fell. Huge drops falling from the trees overhead pocked the earth at Sarah's feet. Above, beyond the deep forest, a gray, tumbling storm capped the earth. Sarah Staughton closed her eyes and leaned

151

her head forward again, waiting for the dream which would not end to dissipate before the storm.

# 14.

The storm had broken and a last silver ray of sunset pierced the high, jumbled clouds. Adrian Staughton sat before his cold dinner plate. Ella, at the far end of the table, was ready to fall apart. She had been drinking again, and as was her habit, not discreetly. Her eyes were blood red, ringed with dark circles. The stage was long overdue.

When the tap at the door did come Staughton nearly leaped from his seat. Striding to the door he opened it and found Tim O'Reilly on his porch.

"Well?"

"The passengers off that Denver stage just straggled into town, Mister Staughton. They was broke down up on Cheney Grade. . ."

"Where's Sarah?" Staughton demanded impatiently.

"She didn't come in with the others . . ."

"Then where the hell is she," Staughton interrupted again.

"I'm trying to tell you," O'Reilly said.

"All right—" Staughton noticed Ella beside him "—go ahead."

"The stage dumped a wheel over the rim up on

Cheney. The driver got shot during an attack . . ."

"Shot!"

"Yes, sir. While they were trying to right the stage they were attacked. That wild man who prowls up there came right up to 'em and shot Bill Brewster dead, wounded Hank Earnshaw. . ."

"But my daughter!" Ella Staughton said, no longer able to control herself. She held a hand to her breast as she leaned far forward, awaiting the answer.

"Savage up and took her, Mrs. Staughton. I'm sorry, but it's so."

Ella Staughton screamed and Adrian cursed deeply, profusely. "You're sure?" Staughton wanted to know.

"Sure. I'm damned sorry, but it's true."

O'Reilly didn't look in the least sorry, and Staughton was sure the sheriff was half-enjoying this. However, that didn't matter just now. Sarah did.

"I want you to find him," Adrian Staughton said. He was breathing irregularly, and he jabbed at O'Reilly with his finger as he spoke. "I want you on your way tonight. Now! Take Stinger, Wichita Jack . . . Go to the mine shacks. Tell every man of mine you see that I'll pay double wages to any volunteer. But find that savage. . .

"And when you do," Adrian Staughton said, his voice a hoarse hiss, "I don't want him *arrested*. You get me!"

"I get you, Mister Staughton. Don't worry about that."

Then Tim O'Reilly tipped his hat and stepped into the saddle of the big black gelding he rode now. Staughton watched him ride out of the yard, and then he stood for a long minute watching the empty skies go

154

dark. Morning dawned clear, with a pale flush against the eastern skies followed by a brilliant sunrise. The golden fingers of the sun stretched out and touched the forests, lighting the water-heavy trees with a thousand brilliant prisms. The creek, sunbright, danced by, gurgling over the stones. In the trees birds called to each other merrily.

Sarah, after a damp and miserable night, could not enjoy the sunrise. Not so Mantaka who had risen early, fished the brook which ran beside their camp, and was now cooking two large trout on a stick he turned over a low fire. This is a morning! he thought.

The first with his new woman. Certainly she would have much to learn, but she would in time. For now it was pleasant enough to look at her, to forage for her while she slept. That dress she wore was ridiculous—it was already coming apart, and obviously was no good for climbing. It was pretty, a deep red with black lace, but totally useless. And the Utes would spot the color miles away.

Sarah watched dismally as the savage picked a bit of meat from one of the trout, tasted it and nodded with satisfaction. Mantaka brought the fish to her and she took it absently. The meat was sweet, succulent, but she had no taste for it.

"Thank you," she said wearily.

"*Il n'y a pas de quoi*," Mantaka shrugged and Sarah nearly dropped the fish.

"You speak French! I know it from school."

"It was my father's language," Mantaka said. "I speak some, but not too well, I think."

Sarah answered him in French. "But that's wonderful! Now we can reach an understanding. You see, I

155

must get to Rose Canyon. My father will reward you handsomely." She paused, trying to recall her French. "Do you understand me?" she asked.

"Quite well," Mantaka nodded. He was packing his sack. "I am glad you speak French too. It will help me to teach you things."

"I am saying," Sarah said with slow exasperation, "that you must let me go. If you do not want money, why then are you doing this?"

"Why?" Mantaka thought that a curious question. Could the woman be so stupid? "I have found you. I am keeping you for my woman. I think you shall mother a fine son for me."

"I . . . !" She could find no words either French or English to express her total frustration, the rising anger, and she simply clenched her fists, biting at her lip as the tears began to trickle down her cheek. The black-bearded savage simply watched her curiously.

Sarah tried again, slowly. "I will *not* be your woman. I will *not* be mother to your child. I will not stay with you. If you try to keep me I shall run away. I will starve myself to death. One night I shall stick a knife in your ribs!"

Mantaka nodded. "You will learn," he said confidently. Then he shouldered his sack, and with his rifle in his other hand he turned to Sarah. "Will you walk or be carried?"

"I'll walk," Sarah answered. At least then there would be the chance to make an escape. If she should see a cabin or a hunter she would make a dash toward freedom. Even the Utes. Everyone said the Utes were friendly, and they would surely welcome the chance to

156

win a reward for her return. She would bide her time. And it would come.

Mantaka led off quickly, striding into the deep timber, and Sarah thought then about making a run for it. But the wilderness was vast, rugged, and she had no doubt Mantaka could run her down quite quickly. She followed after him feeling utterly helpless, stupid for following him like this. But she knew as well that he would not hesitate to pick her up and throw her over his shoulder like a sack of potatoes again. Already, she knew, rescue parties would be searching the mountains; her father would not waste a moment. It was simply a matter of staying alive, or staying alert.

Mantaka scaled a rocky bench and continued on. Sarah climbed up after him, tearing her fingers on the rocks. He was waiting for her when she slid exhausted up onto the top of the rocks. She was breathing hard, already dirty and her feet were hot. She sat in the shade of a massive pine for a long while, recapturing her breath. Mantaka watched.

"You are frail; you have not walked much."

"Not like this!" Sarah said angrily.

"You will grow strong. I will help you." Then Mantaka placed a hand on her ankle and Sarah recoiled at the touch. "These boots are no good." Mantaka reached behind his back and drew his bowie from the sheath. With it he pried the boot heels off of Sarah's boots.

"Your dress," he went on, his eyes sweeping her figure. "It is too ... fat. What makes it fat?"

"The bustle, my petticoats," she explained, but Mantaka did not follow her.

"They keep you warm?"

"No. They're just . . . to make it prettier, you see."

"You are pretty enough. But your dress is too fat. Take off these petticoats."

"I will not! You have bullied me enough. I won't undress for you!" Still seated on the ground, Sarah crossed her arms and stared defiantly at Mantaka.

"Very well. Then I will do it."

"You . . . !" She knew he would do it, and so feeling humiliated, she rose and stepped behind the trunk of the pine, throwing out her petticoats and bustle which Mantaka frowned at.

What were these people who dressed like that thinking of? These bits of cloth could not keep a woman warm, nor would they wear well. As for making her look pretty. . . Mantaka looked admiringly at Sarah as she stepped from behind the pine tree. The silk of her skirt now revealed the natural curves of her hips and thighs. "*That* is pretty," he said softly. "It delights my eyes."

"And that is all it will delight," Sarah said, tossing her head.

"For now," Mantaka agreed. "But you will learn."

They walked another mile through deep timber, the sun flashing in golden, brief moments as they moved across the soft, deep pine needles. The scent of the pines was everywhere, and the damp richness of the earth beneath their feet. A jay sang in the treetops, bouncing from bough to bough, following them a ways. They dipped through a vine-clotted hollow and up the far slope where rife green fern grew and then suddenly they were facing a high country meadow. Deep grass stretched away for half a mile, broken only by a huge, dead cottonwood tree and a pair of twin, wind-stunted cedars growing on a low knoll.

Mantaka put a finger to his lips and then Sarah saw the elk. There were six of them, grazing in the high grass, a bull elk and three of his harem plus two fawns. Slowly Mantaka lowered his sack and he went to his belly, crawling forward with incredible stealth and quickness, his rifle cradled in his arms. He wriggled a hundred feet nearer through the long grass and then Sarah saw his rifle come up. Mantaka snuggled up to the rifle, his cheek against the stock. He took an incredibly long time sighting, or at least it seemed so to Sarah.

The report of the rifle was unexpected, loud. Smoke curled into the crystal skies and the bull elk lay thrashing on the ground as the others rushed toward the forest beyond the clearing. Mantaka stood, grinning, and he waved an arm.

"Come on!"

Sarah took a hesitant step forward and then walked to where the savage stood waiting for her. She looked toward the magnificently racked bull elk which in its death throes still pawed at the ground. A beautiful creature, its silver and white coat now stained with hot crimson.

"God! It is such a shame to see it die," she said quietly.

"A shame? It is good," Mantaka said proudly. "It has lived, had its young. Now it has died for one reason—so that we may live! It is good meat, and much of it. What do you eat at home, foolish woman?"

"Meat—but I'm not sure I shall again." The elk lifted its head pathetically, yet it obviously was dying.

"Yes," Mantaka said, slightly puzzled. "I can live on roots and berries, but not for long, and not well. I have to have meat or I will die. Have you never hunted? Have you not seen your father hunt?"

"My father does not hunt," Sarah answered.

"I see." Mantaka frowned. "Then he must not be a good hunter. He must exchange his gold for meat. And what will become of him when there is no gold? It is a foolish way to live."

"You would know nothing of it," Sarah said proudly.

"No," Mantaka admitted. "But none of that matters now. To me or to you. This is now your world, and I must hunt for us. Now I will show you how to butcher this fine elk. How to skin it, and when we have found a place to stay, I will show you how to make a useful dress from his hide."

"I shan't wear squaw clothes!" Sarah snapped.

"No?" Mantaka fixed those deep dark eyes on Sarah. "Then what will you wear? You see we have no shops in which to buy dresses of silk." He waved a hand around at the empty mountains and Sarah felt her blood rising again. The savage actually believed that she would willingly become a squaw, an animal. A caustic reply surged to her lips, but she smothered it.

"And now," Mantaka said, "I shall show you how to do this work. Watch closely so that you will remember."

Then, approaching the downed elk with his skinning knife, Mantaka stuck the jugular, bleeding the animal. Then, working swiftly he skinned it out, scraping the hide roughly. Sarah watched with disgust as he worked, his arms bloodied to the elbows, scraping out the entrails. Mantaka had shed his shirt and the muscles of his back and shoulders rippled as he worked. The whiteness of his skin amazed Sarah.

Mantaka held up a trophy, a steaming raw liver. "This is the hunter's portion among the Utes. The best meat. Best eaten raw." With his knife he cut off a chunk of the purplish meat and began chewing on it. Sarah's stomach turned over and she was only able to shake her head when Mantaka offered her some of the meat.

"Here is another treat," Mantaka told her. He held up a section of intestine, slitting it he revealed a mass of green pulp in a colorless enzyme. "It is the forage the elk had digested—the juices of the stomach make a fine salad dressing."

Mantaka scooped out a handful of the half-digested grass and tasted it with a satisfied grunt. Then Sarah had to turn away, as she tasted the bile rising to her lips. She tried to fight it back but could not, and her own stomach gave up its contents.

She felt his arm around her shoulders. "Are you ill?" Mantaka asked with genuine concern.

"No." Sarah hid her face in her hands.

"Don't worry. I will work when you are ill. The high mountains will soon make you strong. You only need to eat."

"Yes," she agreed only to end the conversation. "But not now."

Mantaka returned to his work, butchering out large chunks of meat which he packed in the elk's skin. Shouldering this bundle too he walked to where Sarah stood unsteadily. The shadows were creeping out from beneath the trees, and a cool breeze was rising. The days can be short in the high country, and already the sun was sinking behind a distant peak, spattering the few high clouds with crimson and gold.

"Come. We must find a place to spend the night," Mantaka urged.

Sarah took a deep breath, sniffed and nodded her head obediently. "All right."

Mantaka carried the meat, his rifle and the sack of utensils now and they trudged a way toward the eastern hills before Sarah said finally, "Give me the sack. I will carry it."

"If you are not ill . . ." He searched her eyes.

"I'm not ill."

"All right." He unshouldered the burlap sack and gave it to Sarah who turned and walked out ahead of him. Mantaka watched her for a moment, her erect, proud carriage, the bundle across her shoulder, and he smiled.

It was good for a woman to help her man. She was a good choice. She would learn.

Their shelter for that night was a lean-to which Mantaka hastily built in a wedge formed by two massive boulders. He chopped pine boughs from the trees nearby and wove them together, overlapping them as he went up. "You see. This way the water will run off." Sarah was sitting on a fallen pine log, tired, disinterested in all of it. The evening was already growing cold. Long, flame colored pennants of cloud scarred the deep blue skies above the snow-clad peaks.

"You must pay attention," Mantaka said seriously. "One day you will wish to have a warm, tight shelter."

Her eyes lifted. "I will have again—my home."

Mantaka's mouth turned down slightly, but he said nothing. He continued to work on his lean-to, and at nightfall when the first star had already appeared in the western sky he built a small fire to roast the elk meat over. Sarah sat across from him, watching the firelight haunt the hollows of his bearded cheeks, flicker in his dark eyes. He was an enigma—a killer? If she had not been told so, if she had not seen him shoot the stage driver, she would not have believed it. She asked him about it.

"Why did you shoot those men?"

"Why?" Mantaka's mouth was filled with elk meat. "They wanted to shoot me. I did not wish to die."

Maybe it had been that way, it had happened so fast. So startling was the savage in his appearance that it had only been a blur to Sarah. She tried to recall exactly how it had happened, but could not.

"You are quick to kill. Animals or men."

"No." Mantaka shook his head, and he seemed hurt by the remark. "I kill animals to live. I kill men for the same reason."

"Then you must be filled with hate ... or fear," Sarah suggested. The wind twisted the red flames of their cooking fire. The mountains had gone dark. An owl spoke from the forest.

"Sometimes ... sometimes I fear," Mantaka admitted. "But I hate no one."

"Not even the Utes?"

"No. They killed my father, my mother, but I do not hate the Utes." Mantaka lifted his eyes to Sarah, choosing his words carefully. "The Utes, to survive, must have their tribe. The tribe is the unit, and an offense against the tribe is much more serious than an offense against an individual. My father, Lacroix, committed an offense against the tribe. The tribal memory is long, their need to avenge the tribe, to prove allegiance, is strong. Without the tribe the people have

163

nothing. And so through my father's act I have become an enemy of the tribe.

"But I do not hate them. We live as wild creatures in opposition, as the wolf and the cougar." He shrugged. "It is the way of the world to struggle."

"And to kill?" Sarah suggested.

"When it must be—it has always been so. A bear will kill to defend its cubs; a cougar will kill to gain freedom."

"No animal kills wantonly."

"No?" Mantaka's eyebrows lifted. "That is a pretty notion, but it is not so. I have seen a cougar kill when it did not need meat. A pack of wolves. At times it is a sport."

"As it is with you, undoubtedly."

Mantaka did not answer, and Sarah was ashamed of having said it. Yet she was far from convinced. "What about Weiner? But then, you probably didn't even know his name, the man in Rose Canyon. Why did you kill him? Not to eat, not for defense!" she said triumphantly.

Mantaka was silent. He peered into the pot he had boiling over the fire and then poured a cup of tea for Sarah. Sycamore tea, made from the inner bark of the tree, it was reddish in color and had a mild, pleasant taste.

"I knew Weiner by name," Mantaka said finally. "He was an old friend of mine. He and Cooms—I showed them where gold could be found."

"And later you wanted some gold for yourself."

"No." Mantaka laughed out loud, shaking his head. "I was hurt. I needed help and so I went to see Bob Weiner, my childhood friend. He had been killed. Two men—I saw them."

"You knew them too?" Sarah asked with sarcasm.

"Yes." Mantaka answered simply. "Two young men from long ago. Both with red hair. Now they wear silver stars on their shirts."

Sarah was dumbfounded. He obviously meant O'Reilly and Stinger. "You saw them there?"

"Oh, yes. They killed Weiner."

Sarah was silent. The idea was not inconceivable, knowing these two men. Mantaka finished his tea and kicked dirt onto his fire, plunging them both into momentary darkness. Then Sarah's eyes adjusted to the night and she lay there, watching the dark ranks of pines, the thousands of stars spattered across the black sky above.

Along the creek frogs croaked and crickets sang a frenetic tune somewhere. The big man, the bear, the savage, breathed deeply, evenly in his sleep and Sarah lay back wearily, watching the distant stars for long hours.

# 15.

The sun awakened Mantaka. He had slept late and the sun had been late in arriving deep in the secluded canyon. He rolled over and sat up—the woman was gone.

Yawning, stretching his arm, Mantaka climbed from his bed and went to the fire. He cut an elk steak which he broiled and ate slowly, washing it down with more sycamore tea. There was no sense in wasting the fire and so Mantaka took the time to construct a cone of twigs over the fire and on this cone he hung strips of elk venison to smoke. A jay boldly fluttered into the camp and Mantaka, smiling, fed it small bits of meat. Then, stretching again, he walked to where his rifle leaned up against the lean-to, and he picked it up.

Slowly then, his gait long and fluid, he began an easy jog across the meadow, his crooked shadow racing before him.

Sarah dipped down into the ravine, slipped on a rock and landed hard on her rump. Clawing to her feet she rushed on through the deep brush. Blackthorn ripped at her flesh and tore her dress and her lungs were on fire. Slipping again, Sarah slashed her hand on a rock. Rising she struggled on, trapped in a tangle of manzanita which grew so closely together it could not be breached. The only way up the hillside was to get to her belly and slither up along a game trail beneath the brush.

It was already noon and she had had nothing to drink since scooping up a patch of dirty snow hours ago. The air was cold on the crests, but hot in the breathless ravines. Deerflies swarmed around her, inflicting painful bites as she fought her way up the slope, struggling for breath as the brush scored her face, snagging her dress. How far had she come? A mile, two? Ten . . . She could not guess, nor was she sure how much farther she must go. She only followed the sun toward the west where Rose Canyon must lie.

Finally, emerging from the tangle of manzanita, she breathed in the cool air, sagging wearily to the earth, rubbing bruised knees and elbows, trying to pick a huge thorn from the heel of her hand with her teeth. If only she could find water, find a sanctuary until night fell . . . He sat there, watching her.

"You . . ." Sharah's eyes flooded with tears. Mantaka had been seated on the ridge, waiting for half an hour. Incredibly composed, comfortable, he studied her. "You damned criminal!" she shouted.

"Would you like me to get the thorn for you?"

"No," she spat. Dismally she looked at her hand which ached and burned. "Yes," she said meekly.

"That was a long climb," Mantaka said as he examined the thorn. Then he put his teeth to her hand and withdrew it. "You are very strong to make such a climb." He held out the thorn to Sarah who threw it aside with disgust.

167

"You—you sat watching me. Knowing I was trying to run!"

"Oh, yes." Mantaka handed his water skin to Sarah and her thirst overwhelmed her pride and she drank deeply. Mantaka added, "I let you run for a long way. I knew you must run eventually. It is good for you to have done it now, so that you know you cannot outrun Mantaka."

"I could kill you!" Sarah said hotly, her eyes sweeping his rugged face.

"For sport?" Mantaka asked wryly.

"To live!"

"No," Mantaka replied. "For you to live, I must live. There is no other way for you to survive in this wilderness."

"I do not want to survive in this wilderness—not with you!" Sarah fell silent. This was the point on which the savage would not yield. He had her, he would keep her. "Soon my father will find you. You will be killed. Despite my remarks, I do not want you killed. Please leave me alone. Run!"

"No. There is no need. No one can find Mantaka in these mountains. No man, white or red."

"Are you so sure?"

"Yes." He took her torn hands and turned them over. "I will make a salve for you. Agave is very good, mixed with elk fat."

Sarah tried to be angry, to curse, to yell, but instead a fit of laughter overtook her and she found it uncontrollable. "You will . . . take care of me?" She had to hold her stomach, so deep was her hysterical laughter. "After you have abducted me, after you rape me, after you hold me slave . . ." Tears of laughter rolled from her eyes. Mantaka only nodded.

"Yes. Come now. I do not want you to be hurt. Let me see to your hands." Perhaps he had been right before, perhaps the woman was ill—the way she laughed. He should not have let her run so far.

"Come on now, we have wasted the morning," Mantaka said. Sarah took his hand and let him lift her to her feet. Together they strode a high trail which had been invisible to Sarah's eyes. A mule deer doe stood in the path and her head came up nervously. Then she bolted, a wobbly-legged fawn appearing behind her moments later, its huge brown eyes and outsized ears producing a laugh of pleasure from Mantaka's lips.

Twice they stopped on their return, once only so that Mantaka could show Sarah a trapdoor spider's cleverly constructed web tunnel. "Small creatures like that," Mantaka said, "I need not know their ways to eat, but I like to know, to see, to enjoy. Some men walk these mountains like blind men, seeing nothing, knowing nothing. That is a sin."

Crossing a ridge they descended to a teacup valley where snow still lay. Yet Sarah noticed steam rising into the air and soon she saw its source.

"This water," Mantaka said, showing her a limestone tank "comes up from very deep. How it is warmed, I do not know. But there are minerals in the water, and it is soothing. Only do not stay in it long, it can be dangerous."

Then, pulling off his shirt as Sarah watched in amazement, Mantaka sat on a log, removing his boots. Then he stood and before she could turn away he stepped from his buckskin trousers and Mantaka stood there, a colossal, naked savage.

Sarah flushed hotly, and she could only gape at him. His stomach rippled with muscles, his thighs had great hard muscles where Sarah hadn't even known there were muscles.

"What is the matter?" Mantaka asked innocently. "Oh—you are embarrassed. But you need not be embarrassed. You are my woman, I your man."

Before Sarah could sputter an answer the savage had dived into the warm basin, and vanishing underwater for nearly half a minute, he appeared suddenly on the opposite side of the pond where fern and brilliant red monkey flowers grew in a sort of hanging garden against the cliff face.

"Come in!" Mantaka waved his hand. Sarah just shook her head. Fascinated, amazed at Mantaka's naked body, she was appalled at his lack of inhibition.

He swam toward her, his hard-muscled shoulders cutting through the water with long even strokes. He pulled himself from the pond and stood before her. Sarah could not take her eyes off him, nor could she look at him without shame.

"I will lie on the rock to dry. You should bathe now too. It may be a time before we can again."

"I . . . I do not want to," she said.

"It is not good to go about dirty when there is no need," Mantaka said as if to a child.

"Of course not, but . . . oh!" Sarah waved her arms in frustration. How does one communicate with a savage? He stood there as naked as the day he was born, a great hairy bear, lecturing her on hygiene.

"Do not be embarrassed. I am your man. I will see you undressed anyway." Mantaka blinked in puzzlement.

"You will not . . . !" She took a deep breath. "Let me slip behind a tree."

"Yes. Do what you will." Mantaka himself stretched out on a huge, flat rock, drying himself in the sun. He heard a splash sometime later and he opened an eye to see Sarah's white shoulders, her head bobbing in the pond. She was truly beautiful, and as he studied her, he felt a stirring in himself. Such a shy, beautiful bird. She seemed to be looking at him and so Mantaka stood and waved, grinning happily. Sarah immediately turned and swam away and Mantaka caught a glimpse of her long legs, her softly curving buttocks and he sat again, simply watching, blessing his good fortune.

She swam toward him and she called out, "I want to get out now!"

"Yes."

"I mean, I am coming out," Sarah repeated. The savage still sitting on that rock, his head bobbing said again, "Yes. You had better come out."

How long, Sarah wondered, would it take to explain to the man that she at least wanted him to turn his head? He sat there watching her, himself naked, his eyes utterly innocent. Was it worth it? Taking a deep breath, half-closing her eyes Sarah stepped from the pool and walked deliberately to where her clothing lay.

Mantaka felt his heart racing. Those wonderful long legs, broad hips and pendulous breasts. He had never seen a naked woman before, except once when he had surprised a heavy Ute squaw bathing. He watched Sarah, who snatched up her clothes and stepped quickly behind the tree with hungry curiosity. The blood pulsed in Mantaka's veins and he felt light-headed. An insistent urge surged in his loins. If he had been the least

171

bit uncertain before, he no longer was. Everything about this woman was delightful. The moment he had taken her was the finest in his life. They would have to kill him to take her from him.

Wichita was puzzled. He looked at the high, gray and purple peaks. A vast, upthrust landscape stretched out in all directions, a land broken by plunging canyons and sheer precipices, it was a challenge for a tracker, and a challenge he was not quite up to, it seemed.

"Well?" Tim O'Reilly was irritable. His suit itched, his face was streaked with perspiration. He waved his hat trying to keep the persistent deerflies away. He had grown used to town life, he supposed, to the comfort of a bed every night, the company of women.

But then he had never been a true mountain man like Wichita Jack—Jack was supposed to be able to track a mountain goat.

"Which way?" the sheriff demanded.

"I don't know," Wichita answered honestly. "Too much rain, too much hard rock. Even totin' the woman he knows what he's doin', how to cover his sign. Look at that shale out there."

Wichita Jack's gnarled hand waved, indicating the long slopes which were littered with slabs of slippery, iron-hard shale. "You couldn't track an army over that."

"I'm not askin' you to track an army. But I want this man. I want him bad."

For more than one reason—there was the reward of course—but too, if the savage were captured and brought in, it was possible someone might ask him the wrong questions. Questions about the night he was in

Bob Weiner's house, for instance. Tim O'Reilly wanted to make sure personally that no one ever got to the point of asking questions.

"My guess is he's gone up," Wichita Jack said.

"Up?" They were at nine thousand feet already. Higher up the mountains cut savage silhouettes against the cloudless sky.

"The Ute camp is south, down around that bend," Wichita explained. "To the west there's mostly hard rock and deep timber—nothin' to forage off of. He'd likely be headin' toward them high meadows, needin' elk or deer meat, good water."

"How is it up there?" Stinger wanted to know. He lifted his eyes to the cold, high mountains.

"Tight, son. Mighty tight. It's a land of hard winds and cliff hanging trails that don't lead nowhere. There's food, water for the man who knows what he's doin'. For others it's a fierce redoubt, impregnable. Even this time of year it snows up high, and that northwind can drop the temperature fifty degrees in an hour.

"Likely we'll have to abandon the ponies along the way and pack it in."

"Sounds to me like you're scared of these mountains, Wichita," O'Reilly said sharply.

"Me? Yeah," the mountain man agreed. "I got a healthy respect for raw nature. Mostly," he went on, peering from beneath the shadow the brim of his hat cast across his craggy face, "I was worried about you fellows. Them mountains can gobble a man up and spit out his bones. And they can't be bluffed nor bullied nor pistol-whipped."

"What's that mean!" O'Reilly snapped back.

"I guess you'll find out, son, if you want to go on."

"Of course I want to go on." Stinger was not so sure. He twisted in his saddle, searching the jagged mountains.

"We'd best drop back down to town and get us some pack animals and some supplies then," Jack suggested.

"That would take another week! He'll be long gone by then. Whose side are you on, Wichita?"

"Yours son, I'm on your side."

"Then lead off. We're going after him now."

Wichita Jack nodded and kneed his mule forward up a winding mountain trail, leading O'Reilly and Stinger and the dozen miners who had volunteered, looking for easy wages. Above them the shadowed peaks loomed and a frail screen of cloud. Up there, where winter never ended, Wichita Jack supposed the savage had made his stand. But Jack didn't figure on ever seeing him. Not that one.

# 16.

Sarah's eyes blinked open with a start, and then she slowly closed them again, for a moment, remembering. She was alone in the warm, dry cave. Alone but for the mockingbird which sat at the entrance and scolded her. Just beyond the mouth of the cave a pencil thin waterfall fell past the opening, jewels of moving sunlight sparkling in the water as it fell into a shallow pond before beginning a long, winding descent to the distant valleys. Sarah rose, stretching her weary muscles, and she walked to the mouth of the cave. From there she could overlook the wide expanse of grassy meadow which was dotted with the brilliant red of rosecrown, the electric yellow of yarrow, the lavender-blue of columbine.

Beyond the meadow where the grass turned silver before a gentle breeze, the blue spruce rose in majestic ranks toward a chalky high ridge where cedar grew among the pines. Above it all the high mountains where nothing grew rose up; a cawing lone crow wheeled through the empty sky, a black dot against the infinite reaches.

Such a prison! And yet that was what it was. She

could run but she could not hide. All escape was senseless endeavor. He had taught her that, and she hated him for it. She did not find it difficult to hate the savage, yet she did find it difficult to keep her hatred from faltering before his utterly ingenuous grin, his soft gaze.

"If only," Sarah thought at times, "he had been a civilized man ..." The thought was ridiculous, her mingled feelings difficult to untangle, and yet at times a comparison between this utterly self-confident giant and the other men she had known presented itself to her thoughts.

A boy like Will Ford—whom she still occasionally thought of—would break and run before this savage. "Savage" they called him, yet she saw no such oily, barely camouflaged savagery in his eyes as she saw quite clearly in the eyes of a man like Sheriff O'Reilly, whose eyes seemed to strip her naked in a way quite obscene. More obscene, it seemed than the actual stripping she had done before the savage.

It was all too much to consider on this warm, sunny morning, and so Sarah put those thoughts aside and she washed in the crystalline pool, eating the fresh trout which had been left on a wooden plate for her. *Where had he gone?* She wondered only idly, since it made no real difference to her situation. He would return, and if Sarah was not there, he would find her and bring her back. It was frustrating, maddening, but it must be accepted.

After breakfast Sarah went for a stroll, following a line of rocks along the low bluff for a way before descending to the broad valley. Grass there was knee high and she walked through it, breathing in the rich

176

scent of the sun-warmed grass.

She picked some yarrow and carried it with her; with annoyance she found that her eyes lifted anxiously toward the timber from time to time, searching for the savage. And if something had happened to him? She stopped suddenly, realizing for the first time that if that were to occur it would not mean liberation, but only possible starvation and death. A fuzzy, amusing distraction broke off that line of thought. A bear cub weighing no more than thirty pounds walked toward Sarah, its furry head bobbing, its pink tongue dangling. It growled—a sound more like a hoarse bleat—and the sound was so appealing that Sarah laughed out loud, going to her knees to call the cub.

"Come here," she coaxed and the cub ambled forward, turned tail and bounded off a ways, then turned and came toward her again, moving in a clumsy gait which made it seem back and front legs were not synchronized.

"Come here." She put out her hand and the cub, peering from its thick, luxuriant facial fur with tiny brown eyes cocked its head.

"I won't hurt you." Sarah was on her knees and she moved her hand slowly toward the cub which was even smaller than she had thought. Its fluffy, light brown coat was all of six inches long. "There." She pet it and then picked the cub up, laughing again as a long tongue flickered out and touched her cheek.

"You're something," Sarah said. She let the cub down and scratched its soft underbelly and the cub accepted it, staring dreamily into space as Sarah found the itch. "But what are you doing all alone out here?"

It was then the deep growl echoed across the

meadow, striking terror in Sarah's breast. She knew instantly what she had done, and looking up she saw a silvertip grizzly running through the tall grass.

The bear's loose skin rippled as it ran—it was the largest creature Sarah had ever seen. Nearly a thousand pounds of fur and claw, and the bear was fighting mad. She got to her feet, tripped, scrambled up and ran off, the cub, maddeningly, following as the she-bear bore down on them.

Now she could actually hear the grizzly panting. There was nowhere to run, to hide in that open meadow. Then the shout echoed across the meadow. A whistle, another shout. Across her shoulder Sarah glimpsed the savage, running toward her for all he was worth, his rifle flashing silver in the sunlight.

"Bear! Bear!" Mantaka yelled. The great she-bear had nearly run the girl down. The cub, taking it all for a frolic, loped along behind. "Bear!"

Sarah ran in a half circle, trying to get back toward Mantaka, who was also circling. Suddenly he appeared in the she-bear's vision and it startled her. Uncertainly the bear wheeled toward Mantaka, then back toward Sarah.

"Bear!" Mantaka actually pursued the bear now, screaming at it until the grizzly turned in earnest and charged at him. Then Mantaka put on a burst of speed. A grizzly charges at terrible speed, but it is not a long running animal. She pursued Mantaka toward the perimeter of the meadow. With long strides he raced ahead of the bear, clambering up a jumble of boulders and into the branches of a white, long dead pine. Mantaka climbed higher as the bear struggled over the jumble of rocks. Standing at the base of the tree the grizzly bawled and paced nervously from side to side. Then she stood up, her huge claws digging the wood from the tree. Would she climb...? Mantaka held his breath as the grizzly decided. Across the meadow he saw a flash of red. The girl stood watching.

With a last threatening growl the bear finally shuffled off, glancing back over her shoulder once. The cub bounded alongside, quite content with the outcome of the game. Mantaka waited a time, then he shinnied down, and he walked slowly across the high grassy meadow to where the auburn-haired woman waited. He came before her and her lip was trembling.

"I..." Then Sarah threw her arms around him, not drawing back for a long moment. She was still trembling.

"I thought you knew better than that," Mantaka chided her lightly.

"I did... I don't know why I took that chance. Perhaps because I am alone."

"We will find a safer pet for you," Mantaka said. Sarah's hands had been resting on his shoulders, and now with nervous confusion she withdrew them as if they had been burned. She turned her eyes from Mantaka's.

"You are all right?" Mantaka inquired.

"Yes. Oh, yes," she answered. Now her blue eyes lifted to his and there was a question in them. "You had your rifle. You could have simply killed the mother bear rather than risk your life."

"Yes. But I would never do that. Not unless it seemed she would kill you. Then," he shrugged, "I would have no choice. Despite what you may believe," Mantaka said, "I do not like to see blood. I only want

179

to live." They were walking back toward the cave, and as they came to the spot where Sarah had found the cub, Mantaka picked up the yarrow she had collected.

"A beautiful flower. Everything that grows is beautiful," he commented. Sarah took the yarrow flowers and carried them.

Sarah suddenly stopped. The wind played in her hair as they stood in the center of that broad meadow. She realized she did not know his name; suddenly she wanted to know.

"My name is Mantaka," he told her. "My mother named me. She was a Ute. She also loved beautiful things, all of nature."

"What happened to her?" Sarah asked, reading the melancholy in the savage's eyes.

"The Utes killed her. She had disgraced the tribe by not destroying me. Or so I think their reasoning goes. They are a superstitious people," Mantaka observed, "nearly so superstitious as the Americans, I think."

Sarah began to angrily retort, but there seemed no malice in Mantaka's observation, and the longer she herself thought of it, the more accurate his statement seemed.

"I have a few delicacies for your dinner," Mantaka said. "I thought you might be tired of fish and elk meat." At the cave he showed her what he had scrounged.

"Gooseberries—very tart, but juicy. And this. It is honey. I know where a bee tree is, but I take only a little at a time."

"They don't sting you?" Sarah asked in wonder.

"I speak softly to them. Now they know I will not destroy their hive." He shrugged as if it were perfectly common. "And," he said unwrapping a cloth, "I have brought some quail eggs. Small, but very tasty. These foods," he asked with genuine concern, "they do not make you ill?"

"No," Sarah laughed, and it was the first time he had heard her laughter. Mantaka's head lifted slowly and he told her quite sincerely.

"I would give everything to always hear you laugh like that."

"Then let me go!"

"Then I could not hear your laughter," Mantaka replied logically. "No." His eyes were determined when he told her, "I will not let you go. Not ever. And so you must determine whether you will be happy or sad with me, woman."

"My name is Sarah!"

"Your name is beautiful too," Mantaka said, ignoring her angry expression.

They ate in silence; the food was surprisingly good. Mantaka boiled the eggs and mixed the honey with the gooseberries. Obviously he had gone to a lot of trouble to procure these items, yet Sarah could not find gratitude in her heart. He was, after all, still a criminal. He was, after all, but a savage . . . Yet, an odd savage who spoke so softly and when, occasionally, he touched her, his hand was gentle.

What sort of man, she wondered, would Mantaka have been with an education, a polish . . . Sarah sat at the cave mouth, her knees drawn up, arms clasped around them. Mantaka had taken the cured elkskin from its drying rack and now he was cutting it with experienced hands, industriously making a dress—for Sarah.

"There is no way to get through to you, is there?" Sarah said quietly. Her chin rested on her knees now and Mantaka glanced up, a faint smile on his lips. He did not answer.

"I wish," Sarah said softly, and in English, "that I knew the French word to describe the savage man I see. Perhaps they have none. Right now," she said tiredly, "I am not even sure if it would be a damning word or a title of awe."

They walked the high country together. The weather held mild for a week. Sarah tried the buckskin dress which Mantaka had made reluctantly. Surprisingly, it fit, and surprisingly it was attractive, besides being absolutely functional. Mantaka had decorated the nearly white elkskin dress with long fringes, which he hastened to explain were not merely decorative, but which helped to drain water off. From somewhere he had gotten numbers of tiny beads—red and blue mostly—and these he had patiently sewn on.

"I feel like an Indian princess," Sarah said. She had taken to wearing her hair down, there being little choice about it, and Mantaka appraised his own work with satisfaction.

"Yes, you are a princess."

"But not forever, Mantaka. This cannot last forever, you must understand."

"I do not understand that . . . perhaps I do not want to."

Sarah did not argue. She followed him on his explorations, living each day now as a holiday rather than a day of captivity.

But she was not lulled into a sense of endless joy as Mantaka appeared to be. Although there was joy in the high mountains where the wild wind blew free, and their only considerations were food and amusement. Still her eyes went to the low valleys, to the passes, searching for her rescuers. Mantaka did not know Adrian Staughton as Sarah did. Her father would no more give up than the Utes had. If the Ute tribal memory was long, Staughton's was longer. And if theirs demanded retribution, she had no doubt her father's demanded it equally.

"Look there!" Mantaka lifted a finger to a high out-cropping where a family of mountain sheep stood watching warily. The big buck had awesome, curled horns. He was wary, but haughty, it seemed, knowing that nothing could climb to his perch but one of his kind.

"In his moment of existence he knows dignity," Mantaka said. "That all men could . . ."

"You have your dignity," Sarah responded. The wind was in Mantaka's long hair as he turned to Sarah.

"While I have you. Before they called me beast, and I was. You lend me your own dignity."

He took a step forward and she half-responded. His arms lifted but Sarah was unable to step into them. *Not as a slave*, she thought proudly.

Mantaka must have read that spark of pride in her eyes, for his arms lowered slowly and he turned away, his head slightly bowed. A tiny mountain sheep peered over the outcropping at them, and then the entire family, urged by some atavistic impulse, bounded away, scaling incredible escarpments agilely before they disappeared, leaving the day empty.

"I cannot give you enough," Mantaka said. But before Sarah could respond he was walking away in long strides, toward the timbered hillside beyond. He never again made such a remark, but the thought stayed in his heart.

They sat on the hillside where the wind played among the pines. Gray squirrels chattered in the tree tops. Below the land spread out in incredible grandeur. Awesome peaks crumbled away to beautiful green valleys, and a lake sparkled off to the north through a light haze. But there was no sign of human habitation, of man's incursion. "So this is how you have lived your life," Sarah said.

"Yes." But Mantaka's thoughts were elsewhere. "We shall have to move higher," he announced.

"Higher?"

There was still snow on the high peaks—snow which never melted. Naked, ice-streaked slopes unbroken by timber scraped at the belly of the sky. Sarah shivered.

"Nothing can live there."

"The eagle lives there, the grizzly . . ."

"I am neither," Sarah reminded him.

"I am half a grizzly," Mantaka said with a smile which would not come. He knew far better than Sarah the hardships of the high country. "There is no choice," he said, but Sarah did not answer.

He did not tell her the reason for his decision. He had seen them yesterday—sixteen white men climbing the rugged South Pass, coming to take his woman from him, to kill the bear. They would do neither. Not unless they were stronger men than Mantaka marked them for. Not up there. His own eyes lifted to the heights where sunlight blinked brilliantly on the ice and snow. He stretched out a hand, started to stroke Sarah's soft, sun-warmed hair, then let it fall without attempting it. Her blue eyes gazed out at the distances, searching the valleys below for her past, for her future, and for a moment Mantaka felt shame. Rising to escape from it he said sharply, "Come, Sarah, we will return to the cave."

Mantaka was silent, curiously so as they ate and watched sunset flood the western skies. Silently he unrolled his bed and undressed, climbing in as the fire burned itself to embers. Hours later Sarah was awakened by some distant sound, and looking toward Mantaka's bed she saw his dark eyes on her across the dully glowing embers. There was such incredible tenderness, such longing in those eyes that Sarah could not bear to watch him, and she quickly shut her own eyes again, frightened at the depth of the emotions she had seen.

Before the sunrise they were up and moving. Fog hung in the valleys, the grass was heavy with dew as Mantaka, with Sarah following, forded the gravelly stream bed and found the trail toward the high pass. With the sunrise, a brilliant brief flash of crimson, the wind began to blow, and hard. It pressed against them, making the going even harder as they scaled a difficult ledge and crept around a precipitous mountain trail where a stone kicked off the path fell straight down for a thousand feet.

Mantaka held Sarah's hand as they inched along the path, their faces pressed against the wall of the cliff. Twice the trail was broken by slides and they had to work their way over loose rock and earth which was given to fall at any whim of gravity. A foot had to be gently placed, the footing tested and judged before their weight could be transferred. Against the face of the mountain the sun was warm, but the wind was cold, gusting with enough force to knock a man down.

It was not until afternoon that they found the cut-off and ascended into a high, narrow valley where the grass was sparse, the rock clad peaks harsh-appearing, forbidding. Sarah was breathing hard as they struggled up a final grade to a grassy bench which overlooked the valley and the trail up. Sarah was ravenously hungry, thirsty. Her hands had been scraped and she was breathing raggedly, but she did not complain—what was the point in that? Mantaka had found the spot where he expected to make his camp but something was wrong. His dark face was lined with concern.

"What is it?"

"This." He crouched and showed Sarah the ashes of a previous campfire. "Not many days old—the Utes have been prowling here."

"But they're not here now!"

"No. But perhaps they will return. If they do," he reminded her evenly, "they will scalp me. We will climb higher."

Sarah lifted her eyes to where Mantaka was looking. Gray, convoluted rock rose another thousand feet through sparse timber, of a path she saw nothing. "I can't go on . . ."

"We must. The Utes will kill me. You know that."

"And you, Mantaka," Sarah asked bitterly, "will you kill me? I am no mountain goat, no grizzly. I am a simple town woman. This—this is beyond me!"

"No. It is simple, you will see. Do not make me carry you, Sarah. *That* would be dangerous indeed."

"So that is the choice again. None. Still you treat me

like baggage, a slave, a pet!"

"I will not lose you."

"But can't you let me make a choice?"

"You do not know enough yet to make a choice, Sarah. When you know more, we will consult, I promise." His words were sincere, infuriating.

"If I live that long. Yours is a strange love, Mantaka," Sarah said and she fell abruptly silent. Never before had one of them used that word. But it was true, he did love her. What else could one call what Sarah had read in his eyes last night? "Show me the way," she added quickly.

The path, true to Mantaka's promise was not so difficult as it looked. Only at one point, where there was no trail and he had to climb a sheer face for thirty feet, finding handholds Sarah could not even see, was she deathly afraid. Swinging a leg up onto the ridge, Mantaka sat back for a moment, breathing hard. Then he uncoiled the rope from his sack and dropped the end to Sarah who tied it around her. Slowly, strongly he pulled her up and they sat together on that ledge which hung out into cold space, breathing deeply.

"The trail from here is easier," Mantaka said. For a long moment he looked out over the vast, raw land below them and he said, without looking at Sarah, "I am sorry. Sorry that you must travel with a criminal, learn the hard ways of an outlaw. We should be free, walking the long valleys in the warm sun. It is something . . . I do not even understand what . . . carved into my fate to live like this. It is hard, brutal. Only you are good in my world, Sarah. And so I selfishly cling to you, make you wander my dangerous paths with me. I am sorry."

She looked at him, studying his massive neck, the black-maned head of this wild creature. What *had* he done to deserve this fate? Sorting it out, Sarah was uncertain. The crimes committed around him had not been his, and yet the guilt was his, it seemed, the burden and blame.

Slowly her hand reached out and touched his and she said quietly, "I am sorry too."

# 17.

The high valley where Mantaka had led them was a dreamland where silver waterfalls plummeted through the reaches to fern-clotted pools. The hidden park where they built their shelter was small but grassy. Great cedars grew toward the sky, their scent everywhere in the soft breezes. Summer had filled the meadows with wildflowers of every imaginable hue and variety. There were friends to be made. A docile doe and her spotted fawn, a grumpy badger which favored Sarah yet waddled away from Mantaka. A tremendous horned owl which waited patiently for the leftovers from the evening meal, blinking with its great yellow eyes into the fire from its low perch.

The nights were cold. The wind which never totally ceased to work against the mountains built to an icy rage at times, and then there was nothing to do but build the fire and pull up another fur. Their shelter, of woven pine boughs, was nearly water tight, as they discovered when the night skies coalesced into great bulky thunderheads and poured down a rain which lasted for three long days.

Now Sarah too could be proud of that fact. She had

worked nearly as hard as Mantaka on the shelter. With satisfaction she looked through the doorway at the washes of silver rain which blotted out the surrounding hills, then back to the interior of the shelter where hardly a drop leaked.

"You see," she said proudly, "I *have* learned."

Mantaka glanced at the roof and nodded. "You have," he smiled. He was bare-chested, working on a new belt beside the low fire which was enough to warm their hut. The smoke lifted through a cleverly-constructed vent which angled to prevent the rain from falling through. Outside lightning flashed, illuminating the meadow brilliantly; a thunderous boom followed. The rain continued to fall.

"I'm worried about Oswald," Sarah said.

"The owl!" Mantaka laughed. The great bird was docile enough now to take bits of meat from Sarah's hand without so much as scratching her. "He and his kind have survived the eons in such weather and worse," Mantaka assured her. "Like us, Oswald is snuggled up somewhere awaiting the sunshine which he knows somehow will always follow the storms of his existence."

"*He* knows. . ." Sarah sat cross-legged on an elkskin which had been placed over a mat of pine boughs, watching the powerful, gentle man opposite her. One day they would kill him . . . It could end no other way. The Utes, the whites, some stronger savage. . . Tears were in her eyes and she fought them back angrily. Somehow, slowly, Sarah had crossed a bridge. This had become her reality, as hard as she fought against letting it become so. She could now scarcely remember Pennsylvania, her school friends, let alone Rose Canyon and her friends there. Try as she might she could not determine whether something had been taken from her life, or if despite her protestations much had been added.

At any rate, this seemed natural now. She scooted closer to Mantaka, watching his thick fingers dexterously stitching the elkskin belt. It was warm in the lean-to. Outside the storm raged. Sarah began to sing. It was a simple song, a song from school, only half-remembered. Her humming filled the gaps for forgotten words as she poked at the fire, watching it dance and sway. But when she looked up Mantaka had ceased his work and was watching her blissfully. Sarah stopped abruptly.

"Do not stop, Sarah," Mantaka said. "I have never heard anything so beautiful. Your voice so soft. To hear a woman singing in my shelter . . . it is like an angel has descended. Please, sing."

And so she continued, with embarrassment at first, but seeing that Mantaka did not care whether she knew the words or not, that whatever note she hit was music to him, she went on more freely.

Fair Jenny's soul that morn was winging
   up above,
And by her bier he cried,
Yet for me the saddest death
   is never knowing love. . .

Sarah fell silent and again went to the door of their shelter, watching the brilliant display of chain lightning, the iron-gray wash of rain. The wind howled down the canyons. Gently she shut the door.

"It's grown dark," Sarah said. Her head was bowed. Her hands were held clasped before her.

191

"So soon?" Mantaka said with mild surprise.

"We shouldn't waste our firewood," she said, but her eyes did not meet his.

"No," he agreed. "Not while we have plenty of warm furs." Mantaka stood slowly, putting his work aside. "When you are in bed I will put the fire out."

"Put it out now," Sarah replied. Mantaka looked at her curiously, but he nodded, tossing a handful of sand on the fire. Then, in the darkness, with the thunder echoing up the valley, he undressed and crossed to his bed, rolling in between the piles of furs as the rains drummed against the roof of the hut. Rolling over, his leg grazed something warm and yielding. In disbelief his hand shakily stretched out and found Sarah's bare shoulder. She trembled beneath his touch but did not move away.

They lay side by side in the warmth of their bed a long while, neither moving, making a sound. There was only the rain, the night, the warmth. Sarah, who had never even slept naked before, let alone with another human being, moved closer to Mantaka, feeling his thigh against hers, his deep chest against her breasts, and she laid her head on his arm, kissing his chest once lightly. His arm went around her and Mantaka held her there. Such a massive, capable arm, it shielded her from the night. Her heart was drumming and she felt light-headed. With her ear next to Mantaka's chest Sarah could hear a responsive pounding of his heart.

They lay that way a long while, the warmth of Mantaka's body, the strength of his arms being all she needed. Gently he kissed her forehead and wiped the hair from her face in the darkness and his hand traced patterns on her back.

"So soft," he whispered, "you are so incredibly soft, Sarah."

His hand had descended to her buttocks and he let it rest there a moment. Then she lifted her lips to him, and they kissed. As they did Sarah felt his hand drawing her to him. His heart still pulsed wildly, and now she was aware of an answering, entirely masculine throbbing against her thighs. They were together in the rain, in the night, clinging to need, and there was no wish to hold back anything.

"But you must be gentle, Mantaka," Sarah said into his ear. "I have never done such a thing before."

"Nor I," he said touching her lips. He rolled to her, and his mouth touched her ear, his breathing warm, moist, compelling. Sarah's head rolled back and she felt him kiss her throat, a tender kiss which sent a tingling across her abdomen, an electric spark down along her thighs.

His lips lowered to her breasts and Sarah put her hand on his head, running her fingers through his long, wild hair as his mouth searched her breasts, lingering on her nipples, which grew more sensitive, more demanding of his kisses with each lingering touch.

Slowly Mantaka's hand dropped to her thigh and she placed her hand on his, staying it for a moment in confusion. And then she lifted her hand, shifting to make it easier for him to explore her softness, and as he did touch her she felt that electric charge center there, felt the moist desire growing. Such a brute, such a bear, such a tender creature. He kissed her mouth, her throat, her closed eyes as he lifted himself to her, slowly entering as Sarah encouraged him.

"Yes, it's all right. Yes Mantaka." He was pressed

against her now, massive, hairy, strong, his touch sensitive and kind as he settled against Sarah, whose heart was racing, the slight discomfort she had felt at first giving way to a throbbing, dizzy need.

She lifted her mouth to his, taking his head in both hands drawing him to her, kissing him so that he understood her need. Her hips had begun to sway, to work against him and each movement sent a flash of unexpected joy through her. An incidental touch of his flesh against hers was a searing, summoning flame.

Then she felt him shudder, this massive savage, felt him release himself into her and Sarah smiled as her own body searched for and found an answering emotion. In the darkness she felt as if a wave of light had washed across her, and the drumming of the rain against the hut seemed to be within her.

He lay there, breathing more gently now, his hands and lips still touching her, and she in her amazement kissed his savage breast, his lips. Then she drew his head to her breast and as Mantaka listened to her heart, she held his great shaggy head, the warmth lingering on to warm a cold and rainy night.

It rained for another day and another night before the sun, itself miraculous after a long absence, dawned brightly, flooding the long meadows with golden sunshine.

They strode the cedar forest, watching shadow and sunlight merge, intermingle. Arm in arm they walked the meadows, together they discovered tiny secrets. A lark bunting's nest where six fuzzy hatchlings peeped insistently and a mound of rocks where golden marmots whistled to them, turning tail and taking flight before Sarah could blink. They bathed in a hidden pond, no more than ten feet across, where the water was cool, but the warm sun shielded from the wind as they were. Vines climbed the cedar and magpies sang in the rocks.

Now it was Sarah who was totally fascinated, entranced by Mantaka's body as they bathed. That deep, dark-haired chest where those booming laughs were born. Massive shoulders, deeply muscled thighs. "Kiss me," she demanded with playful petulance, and he took her into those arms, standing waist deep in the water. His body was warm, slippery against hers, and her breath would quicken as she felt his pulse rising. And then they would make love, sometimes in the pond itself, sometimes on the soft, sweet grass in a secluded nearby cove where they could hear the water trickling, feel the warm sun on their bodies as they clung together.

Mantaka sat up, his fingers tracing patterns on Sarah's naked flesh, his lips emphasizing his remarks with tiny kisses. "You are so perfect, Sarah. Your legs so long and slender." His rough hand ran up along her thigh and paused as his lips brushed Sarah there.

"Your breasts, which all of nature, all of time has intended for me. Smooth, begging my lips . . ." Mantaka kissed her sun-warmed breasts and then his head lifted. He smiled, looking into her blue eyes. "You see fate which has denied me so much has nullified every deprivation with one moment, one taste of your lips. Inevitable love . . . Nature does have its incredible ways. For what are you, my Sarah, if not incredible?"

Sarah answered with a smile and a tear. As deep as her love was, she had never learned to put things into words. Mantaka, it seemed, should have been some thundering Welsh poet, a ballad smith. Such a savage hiding place God had chosen for his poet's heart...

"I love you," Sarah said simply. Her fingers touched his bearded cheeks, his thick eyebrows, those lips which were filled with magic. She wondered what a shaven Mantaka would look like, and she mentioned it.

"Would you like me to shave? To put on a town suit?" he asked with willingness. "I would cut off my arm for you, Sarah. The beard on my chin means nothing."

"No. You would not be Mantaka. Not without your mountains, your wild aspect. Mantaka smoking a pipe in an easy chair?" she laughed helplessly. "These things are an integral part of you, I think," she added more seriously.

"No," Mantaka answered thoughtfully. "These are only the trappings, my legacy from circumstance. You, Sarah. You are a necessary part of me, the missing part for which I have searched. The rest means nothing."

She kissed him and held him tightly, her heart racing. She did love him. Love him so... Tears began to trickle down her cheek and Mantaka, noticing, kissed her cheek and asked, "Why are you crying?"

"Everything you have said is true. I have needed you as well, never knowing it, fighting against my fate. And now... Don't you realize this cannot last?"

"It can last! I will not let it end," Mantaka said strongly. "What can separate us?"

"Time. We have our single moment, our spark in the darkness. But time... it is not benevolent."

She searched his dark eyes, his rugged face, but he did not seem to understand. Perhaps he simply would not admit it. He was too strong to bow to defeat easily.

"They will come. Who, I don't know," Sarah went

on. "My father's men. The Utes. Perhaps only winter will separate us. Only time."

"Nothing, Sarah," he said passionately. "Nothing will separate us."

"I don't know," she replied, "how fast I will be able to run, how well I will be able to climb with your baby growing within me."

"Baby?" He blinked in astonishment as if such a thought had never occurred to him. "A little baby?" He scratched his head.

"I have felt it stirring already, Mantaka. Your child."

"My . . . baby."

As Sarah watched he stood, turning in a slow circle. His black eyes were damp when he turned back to her. "A little child . . ." He raised his arms then to the sky and shouted, a roar like the thunder and he began a crazy, impromptu naked dance. "I shall have a child!" Suddenly he stopped, and grinning madly, his eyes filled with tears, he came back to where Sarah lay, crouching beside her.

"And so you see, Sarah. Everything is right! Nothing now can harm us. We are not two strangers, but the heart of a family. You . . ." he kissed her lips. "I . . ." Mantaka touched his own broad chest. "Nothing can harm me!" Mantaka shouted. "I have Sarah. And she has my baby! It is magic against all harm." He lay beside her, and he whispered, "We are safe."

He took Sarah's hand in his own and they lay watching the sunlight stream through the towering cedars, listening to the quiet, distant sounds of the birds, the trickling waterfall.

Sarah turned her head and looked at Mantaka, whose

face was bright with joy. She took his hand and placed it to her abdomen, and beneath his palm Mantaka felt the faint stirring of new life. He smiled and let his hand linger there. An innocent peace smoothed his features, causing his own rugged face to appear childlike. Sarah squeezed his hand.

Then she turned her head, letting the hot tears run from her eyes. She was no innocent; the end would come, and quickly. But Mantaka did not understand. He lay there happily, as oblivious to the future as the sunlit cedars bright with shifting sunlight and shadow.

# 18.

The rains came again, and early snow. Then sometime in September, the Utes returned. With winter coming on Sarah and Mantaka had been preparing their stores. Sarah had been making pemmican which she had learned to like, crushing the fruit which would be mixed with meat. Blueberries they were, the last of the crop, rich and juicy. Mantaka was cutting the meat of a deer into strips for smoking when the door to the hut burst open and Sarah heard a savage howl.

She had hardly time to react, to move. The door to the shelter stood open and a painted Ute, dressed in furs, his knife in his bronze hand was rushing toward them.

The Ute knocked Sarah aside and dove toward Mantaka, who turned at the sound of Sarah's scream. The Ute brave drove his knife against Mantaka, but Mantaka caught his wrist, and with his incredible strength held it. The Ute howled again with pain, and Sarah distinctly heard the bone in the man's wrist crack. Driving a knee at Mantaka's groin, the Ute fought back. The knife clattered to the floor of the hut as Mantaka evaded the Ute's knee and ducked a wild, driving blow aimed at his face.

They fell apart then, circling, the Ute panting heavily. The Indian said something to Mantaka which Sarah could not understand, then he dove for his knife, coming up with it in his good hand. He lunged again, but Mantaka had snatched up his rifle and the gun exploded in the close confines of the hut, the Ute falling back, blood smearing his chest and face. Mantaka hovered over the Ute, his face expressionless.

Sarah put her hands to her head and screamed. Mantaka's face slowly turned toward her.

"Is he dead?"

"Yes."

"Couldn't you have . . .?"

"I could have done nothing else. Pack your belongings, Sarah. We will be travelling."

"Perhaps there was only this one," she replied, groping for comfort. Her eyes strayed again to the bloody brave. A young man, perhaps twenty, his life leaked from him.

"No. There will be more. Pack now."

Shakily Sarah did as she was told. Outside it was raining. A hard wind followed them up the trail to the western slope. That small hut had already seemed like home. Sarah looked at Mantaka's broad back, realizing fully for the first time how it had always been for him. He had never had a home, a safe refuge.

The wind twisted in her hair and she started to speak, but Mantaka put his finger to his lips. He stood looking back into the valley, and then Sarah saw them too, six more Utes stealthily approaching the lean-to.

"Quickly now," he urged her, "we must move higher."

The path was treacherous, the day cold. Sarah moved slower now, her stomach already showing signs of roundness. In the mornings her legs were sometimes swollen. She tired more easily. Near nightfall the temperature dropped and the rain turned to damp snow, drifting through a somber sky. They had come upon no good shelter and so they huddled together beneath a tangle of roots from a toppled tree, Mantaka's arm around Sarah's shoulder as the wind howled and the snow twisted through the sky. He held his rifle in his hand and stared up the backtrail until darkness fell and then he dozed, the rifle still firmly in his grip as the falling snow built up cold layers of camouflage, burying their tracks.

Morning dawned coldly. The sun showed briefly, flooding the snowy forest with orange and pink light, then was screened off behind a new curtain of storm clouds. They were up and moving with first light, chewing on their jerky as they walked. The temperature had dropped incredibly. Balls of ice hung from trees, icicles from the low brush as they tramped through two feet of new snow. All above was black, empty, and all of the earth beneath was white, shrouded in snow. It crackled beneath their feet and gathered on Sarah's collar, dripping down her neck as she followed Mantaka with their breath steaming from their lips as they sketched tracks in the snow beneath the high timber.

They forded what had been a lazy stream, but which now, flooded with snowmelt, was a raging freshet. Mantaka inched from rock to rock as the water surged all around them. Sarah followed, felt her foot slip and instantly a strong hand gripped her wrist. Only that had prevented her being swept away by the current.

They walked on for another mile and then Mantaka stopped. "Your feet—we must warm them," he said. Scraping dry tinder from the underside of some pine bark he built a small fire. Removing Sarah's moccasins he rubbed her feet gently, and only after a minute's good rub did he allow her to move them nearer the fire. Her teeth chattered and Mantaka gave her his own bearskin coat, standing watch as she warmed her feet, her moccasins which steamed against the cold air. The snow still fell, and the wind was cold, although they had momentarily lost the edge of it in this depression.

"Are you all right?" he asked with concern.

"I'm all right. I got dizzy for a moment. It happens when. . ."

"When you are with child?" Mantaka frowned. "I did not know that."

"Your child will be a mountaineer, Mantaka. But it is not ready yet for such exertions." Sarah attempted a smile; it was not a successful attempt. Mantaka's face was serious. He was not climbing because he wished to, but because somewhere behind the Utes hunted him. "I think," she said, "I can go on now." She stood and leaned dizzily against a tree, but Mantaka seemed not to notice.

"Are you sure you can travel?" he asked, his eyes still on the trail behind them where the snow funneled down the long, sheer-sided canyon.

"Yes."

"Then let us go. They are coming."

They struggled, on, moving across a steep, snowy slope. Mantaka looked continually back across his shoulder. Desperately Sarah followed, twice she fell. Without her, she knew, he would be running, each stride lengthening the distance between himself and the Utes.

The wind now shrieked across the barren slope, whipping up the snow which had already fallen. New snow drove down, pelting Sarah's face, stinging her eyes. Mantaka kept a firm grip on her hand. Now they could barely see one another. Climbing higher yet they worked their way into a stand of pine. Scraggly, wind-flagged trees, they were heavy with snow and scant protection against the gusting wind which roared up the slopes. Mantaka's beard and hair were hoary with frost, his eyebrows white. He carried his rifle inside his furs now to keep the mechanism from freezing.

Sarah's legs were wooden, her blood cold, her breath coming in steaming gasps. She was towed along by the hand through this bitter icy world, this endless wilderness as the wild man before her climbed higher yet. Endlessly upward, into the teeth of the storm.

Darkness began to fall and they forged on, each step an agony, an impossible task which once accomplished had to be forgotten immediately and repeated. Endlessly. Sarah could see nothing any longer. There was no reality but the cold, the blackness of night and the strong hand which held hers.

Finally they stopped—somewhere. Sarah could see nothing, hear nothing but the howl of the angry wind. She buried her head in Mantaka's shoulder and he placed his arm around her. Dawn offered a brief promise of clearing, but farther to the north, drifting toward them like a black, threatening armada new storms were visible.

"Eat now," Mantaka said, offering her jerky. "We will find a new place before this storm hits."

"You surely don't think the Utes are still coming?" Sarah asked hopefully.

"Yes. I know they are coming. And so we must move."

They trudged upslope again, always upward, crossing a snowbound landslide which had uprooted an entire forest, hurling it into the canyon below. The clouds now were below them and only the tips of the peaks flashed in the sunlight. Sarah walked on, slipping, fighting for breath at this altitude.

Mantaka had stopped. Knee-deep in snow he was gazing off toward the west, his face etched with sorrow. She came up beside him and took his arm.

"What is it?"

"They are coming. They have seen us."

"But we knew they would follow." Sarah shielded her eyes against the glare of the snow, seeing nothing.

"Not the Utes," Mantaka said firmly. He turned those dark eyes toward Sarah. "Your father's men. White men." He lifted a pointing finger and now, far below along a snaking gorge she could see a patch of color, a moving black dot . . . and another.

"It might not be them," Sarah offered.

"It is them," Mantaka said with certainty.

The woman was cold, weary, he saw. Where now? Higher, of course, still higher, where only the eagle and the grizzly ranged. Suddenly he knew where he would go.

"There is a stone house far above us. Beyond the timberline where the wind howls constantly, where no man will come." His eyes lifted to the jagged peak where the heavy winds still drifted powdery snow.

"The house of Lacroix?" Sarah asked.

"Yes. That house. I complete the cycle," he said slowly. Mantaka took a deep breath, his mighty chest rising and falling evenly. "Come."

The wind grew colder, and Sarah's legs felt dead beneath her. Each breath was icy, jagged like broken glass in her lungs. Mantaka walked ahead and then stopped to wait for her, his eyes sweeping the distances.

They had breached the timberline now. No trees could survive at this altitude but for a few scattered bristlecone pines, ancient, gnarled, appearing dead themselves. Ahead stretched only fields of gray stone, mortared with snow and ice. The footing was icy, and three times in rapid succession Sarah slipped down.

She rose and struggled toward Mantaka, who waited, his eyes concerned. The wind was in his beard and he stood like some Mosaic figure against the wilderness and danger. But Sarah suddenly knew. As she fought against the wind, her plodding legs mechanically carrying her after the man she loved, she knew. She reached him, fell into his arms and held him tightly, feeling his hand on her shoulder, his warm kiss on her forehead.

"We must hurry now," Mantaka said.

"No."

Mantaka had half turned away, now he turned back slowly, his eyes piercing. "But we must."

"I can't, Mantaka."

"I will carry you," he offered.

Sarah refused his hand, and shaking her head in anguish, she repeated, "No. It won't work, Mantaka! We can't escape them. You *know* that!"

"If we can get to Lacroix's house . . ." It was then that the memory flared up. The fire, the blood. His mother dead on the floor of that cabin . . . Mantaka's eyes lifted in bitter frustration. Across the vast field of snow and rock he could see the bits of color which were the hunting party drawing nearer. "We must go! I won't lose you. You are my life!"

"You are my life." Sarah stood in his arms, fingering the shoulders of his badgerskin coat. Her eyes pleaded with his. "You will die if you take me with you. They will run you down. Go now. Alone!"

"No! Never. I will not be alone again." He held her, his mind turning over frantically. What she said was true, but what was there for him if he left Sarah? Again, vividly, he saw his mother dead on the floor of that house. And Sarah. . . . What if the Utes found her.

"They will kill you," Sarah insisted. "Run."

"They will kill me if you are taken from me."

"I won't see you die!" Sarah screamed. She trembled, kissed his arm, shook her head. "Mantaka . . . And what of the baby?"

The hunters drew nearer. Now across the slope a shout echoed. In confusion Mantaka shook his head, kissed Sarah's tears and dropped his arms. Tears now streamed from his own eyes. Tears which the wind touched with icy fingers and turned cold.

"Mantaka . . ." Sarah touched his tear, his cheek. Another shout sounded across the slope and now, higher up, to the north, Mantaka could see the Ute party dog-trotting through the boulders.

"There must be a way."

"Run. They will kill you." Sarah held him. "I can run no farther, and you know it. And so," she sniffed, "I cannot go and you cannot stay."

A piercing Ute cry reached their ears, twisted by the

wind and Mantaka put his arms around Sarah, holding her gently, at length, as men advanced from above and below. The dark clouds had drifted over and the wind had increased. The hunters shouted all around them. The world had been reduced to chaos. There was only a moment longer and then he was gone.

Mantaka lumbered off upslope, his long legs as fresh as they had been at sunrise and the woman stood alone.

"There she is!"

Sarah head the cry, filled with triumph. A mock triumph and she stood, a slender woman dressed in buckskin and fur, watching her life rush away from her as Mantaka disappeared into the shadows of the clouds, the fresh wash of snow. With a faint smile playing on her lips she turned to watch her rescuers struggle up the slope. The snow began in earnest and the day grew darker yet. Slowly Sarah walked forward to meet them.

# 19.

The frail, gray-haired woman stood at the upstairs window, watching the snow bound valley, the trees which were cold, black as iron. Ella Staughton turned from the window and closed the curtain. Slowly she walked to his room and tapped on the door. After a moment Adrian called her in.

He was behind his desk, busy with his papers as always, and yet something was gone from his eyes. A drive, a fire. He had aged, she thought with sudden surprise.

"Well?" he asked impatiently.

"She's pregnant," Ella said. She sat, smoothing her skirts, watching the fury redden her husband's cheeks.

"That wildman assaulted her! Have you checked with the doctor?"

"There's no need to ask a doctor. I've seen her undressed. It shows plainly already," Ella answered.

"How is she doing?"

"Well enough," Ella said with a nod. "But she refuses to leave her room, to see any friends. She only lies there, watching the ceiling. Yet when I ask her, she says, 'Mother, I'm all right.' "

"There's nothing to be done about it." Adrian sighed, leaning back in his chair, running his fingers lightly across his temple. "Sarah's strong, she'll weather this. When the child is born we'll find someone to take it."

"Yes. That's all there is to be done," Ella agreed wearily. Then she stood and with a curt nod turned toward the door. Only belatedly did she think to inquire, "How are the mines?"

"Worse and worse. Range West has hit pockets of steam. It costs more to take a ton of ore from Colleen than it returns. I don't think I will be getting more credit from Denver."

Ella had hardly been listening. None of it mattered, never had. She muttered something sympathetic and walked from his office, closing the door quietly.

"Mrs. Staughton?"

Ben Chalmers in shirtsleeves stood there. "Yes, Ben?"

"Company calling, Ma'am."

"In this weather?"

"He's waiting in the parlor," Ben said.

"Very well." Ella patted her hair briefly and walked downstairs. In the kitchen she could hear the talk between Tim O'Reilly and his deputy.

"Maybe if the youngun was defanged and declawed a man could raise it up like a puppy." Someone laughed harshly and Ella hurried on, her ears burning.

Will Ford sat uncomfortably in a parlor chair, his hat on his lap, and he rose as Ella entered the room.

"Why, Will!"

"Ma'am." The boy nodded. "I come to see Miss Sarah . . . if you think . . . if she would see me, if she's

209

strong enough."

"She hasn't wanted to see anyone, Will."

"No, Mrs. Staughton, I know . . . But I'd hoped. It's kind of important."

"I'll ask her, Will."

She smiled and the boy feigned a smile of his own. Nervously he sat again, his hat still showing dampness from the snow, his boots muddy. Ella started for the staircase, but spotting Ben Chalmers she halted.

"Ben?"

"Yes, Ma'am?"

"I want Sheriff O'Reilly out of my house. Now."

Ben blinked in puzzlement, "But, Ma'am, Mister Staughton . . ."

"I'll advise Mister Staughton what I have done and why," Ella said, and Ben Chalmers just nodded. He had been Staughton's foreman now for five years. This was the first time in those years Chalmers had ever seen a fire in Ella Staughton's eyes, and he knew she was deadly serious.

"Yes, Ma'am," he agreed hurriedly.

Sarah still lay in her bed in the darkened room, her arms inert on top of the coverlet, her hair brushed out, her eyes deep. "Someone's here to see you. I think you should."

"Who?"

"Will Ford."

It took a long moment, but Sarah finally answered, "All right."

Will was still holding his hat in his hand as he rapped lightly on the doorframe and was beckoned inside. It took a time before he could see her clearly in the darkness, and when he did he was surprised to find

210

he hardly recognized her.

Sarah's eyes were deeper, it seemed, her cheekbones more sharply defined. Her mouth was serious, not at all like the pouting, childish mouth he had known. When she spoke it was gently, as if her words were coming from a great distance.

"Sit down, Will. You look fine."

"And you, Sarah." His throat was dry. "Fine." He sat in a chair near the bed, nodding for a moment then staring away at the wall. "You're feeling well?"

"Yes, Will. Thank you."

"Yes. You look ... Sarah I've come for something important!" he said forcefully. Unfortunately his voice cracked and the forcefulness became a mockery.

"Have you?" Sarah smiled, distantly.

"Yes. I know you've had a rough time... That you *are* having a rough time, will have..."

Will Ford loosened his collar and cleared his throat. Sarah watched him patiently, amazed at how young he looked.

"Go on," she encouraged him.

"Well, I know you've had a rough time." He flushed. "My father ... I thought, Sarah Staughton, that you might do me the honor of becoming my wife," he said so quickly that the words trod on each other's heels. Having said it he sat rigidly in his chair, watching her expectantly. Sarah replied with a faint smile.

"I couldn't Will. You know it wouldn't be fair to either of us."

He seemed to relax a little at that reply, nevertheless Will Ford persisted, "I always did like you, Sarah, and what folks say ... it don't bother me. You know I work hard, Sarah." He lifted his eyes.

"You always have," Sarah acknowledged.

"And I reckon one day I'll have my own store and all. I'd be a good provider."

"I know that, Will. But it's not so simple, this marriage. I don't even believe you really want it. It's generous, kind, but you *would* mind what people said. It would be no good for you, for me, for my baby. I thank you, Will," Sarah went on, "and you are a fine young man. A courageous, upright man. One day you'll make a good husband, a provider for the right girl. But not me, Will, not me."

When Will had gone, greatly relieved, it seemed, Ella Staughton returned to her daughter's room. She sat on Sarah's bed, smoothing back her hair.

"Did he ask you?"

"He did."

"I thought so. Well, it would have been a solution, I suppose," Ella commented.

"But not a very good solution," Sarah replied.

"No." Ella smiled and brushed her daughter's hair back, kissing her forehead. "Not a very good one." Ella rose and started from the room. She stopped then, and with her back still to Sarah she asked, "Was it all so terrible—up there?"

"It was dreadfully cold."

"And that . . ?"

"Man, Mother. He was a man, and a kind man."

"But he. . ."

"He loved me, Mother. I loved him as well."

"Really!" Ella Staughton turned back, and a slow, sly smile crept across her tired mouth. "Then I expect it was not so bad at all."

"Some day I will tell you," Sarah responded. "One day."

# 20.

It was a joyless Christmas in the Staughton house. Festive bunting hung in the parlor and guests chattered over punch or stronger drink. The three-piece string band brought through the snow by sleigh all the way from Denver provided dance music for the young women and men. The tables were spread with roast goose and ham, plum pudding and crabapples.

Adrian Staughton smiled and nodded as he greeted his guests, yet everyone knew by now that it was only veneer. The mines were played out. Rose Canyon was dying and with it the fortunes of Staughton, who for the first time in his career had made the mistake of reinvesting too much capital.

Staughton owned blocks of empty buildings, flooded out mines and thousands of acres of denuded hillside. From time to time a word or disparaging glance could be caught directed at Staughton. Some of these people had gone down with him. Sarah sat in the corner near the band, her roundness obvious to all. She sometimes listened to the music or watched the dancers, but chiefly she sat looking out the window at the empty, snow clad mountains.

"Sarah! It's been so long."

"Hello, Betty."

"Why I haven't seen you since . . . you went away to school," Betty Yount said with hopelessly false sincerity. The corners of the blond woman's mouth twitched with barely subdued triumph. Sarah noticed this shallow mockery and then forgot it. She only smiled to Betty.

"Yes, it has been a long while."

"Perhaps we will be going East to school together next year. Assuming you can go."

"I don't think I shall be going back," Sarah said, feeding Betty Yount's victory still more. "If I do, I hope we shall travel together."

Sarah's composure slowly wilted Betty's smugness and almost in disappointment, she turned away, waving to a friend. "Oh, Danah!"

"She's become an irritating little thing," Ella said, handing her daughter a cup of punch.

"So was I," Sarah said frankly. "She'll grow out of it."

"Yes." Ella drew up a chair and sat down, watching the dancers, the mutton-chopped gentlemen, the young ladies speaking in whispers. "I never really noticed how they all felt about us before. Without money they would have ignored us entirely. Even the likes of him," Ella commented, nodding at Tim O'Reilly, who with a big red mustache and a gold watch chain across his stomach seemed to quite fancy himself.

"Him." Sarah nodded. "Why does he still have his job? Did you tell Father what Mantaka said—that O'Reilly and Stinger Matson killed Weiner."

"Yes." Ella turned her eyes down. "I believe I mentioned it." She smiled quickly; but not quickly enough. Sarah had read it in her eyes.

"He knew! He knew already that Mantaka had done nothing!" Sarah closed her eyes a moment. "Then why did he not . . . Father! He was involved, wasn't he?"

"Oh, no, I don't think so, Sarah."

"You *do* think so!" Sarah lowered her voice to a whisper as heads turned toward them. "You know it, don't you, Mother? He had to have Range West and so Weiner was killed!"

"I . . ." Ella could not even frame a new lie. She rose and walked away, Sarah watching her go, a sad, tired woman.

So that was how it had been. Mantaka had told only the truth. They had blamed him for their crimes and then hunted him down as if they believed their own accusations. All of the world had been massed against that one man, the white world, the red world. Yet with the Utes one could forgive it. They were a pagan people, living by their own code as their ancestors had done. She remembered something then and she smiled as she looked from the window toward the high mountains. What was it Mantaka believed, that the Utes were nearly as superstitious as the Americans. Certainly, it seemed, as savage and unforgiving.

Sarah rose and walked toward her mother, who stood with Judd Fitch and Adrian Staughton.

"I apologize," Sarah said. "Please enjoy yourself, Mister Fitch, but I really must turn in."

"Are you tired, Dear?" Adrian Staughton asked.

"Yes." With pain she met her father's eyes, studied the bitter lines around his mouth. "Quite tired."

Fitch watched her go, carefully, heavily climbing the

215

stairs to the second floor rooms. "Such a shame," he commented, "so young and so empty her life must be now."

"Not so empty as some," Ella Staughton said, and she walked away, leaving the two men to wonder what that remark could possibly have meant.

Spring arrived in Leadville, revealing a shabby, empty town beneath the snow. The water gushed off of the barren slopes, inundating the streets of Rose Canyon with mud. There was a fire in one of the two remaining saloons and it was simply allowed to burn itself out, leaving a scorched pile of wood and ash which stretched halfway into the street. Rose Canyon was dying. The town had been born of gold, and as the ore played out, the town died. Colleen Number Two was still active, but on half-crew. Range West had flooded out and been abandoned.

Only the mountains renewed themselves, and Sarah, gazing toward the far reaches, could see the grass greening the hillsides, and she knew that flowers were blooming already in the high valleys. She turned slowly from the window and walked to her mother's room, holding her abdomen. When the door did not open soon enough she swung it open herself, and stood there, panting.

"Sarah?" Ella did not have to ask any questions. Ben was sent on the run for the doctor.

It was a slow birth; perhaps Mantaka's child was reluctant to enter this world. It was two in the afternoon when Sarah first started having contractions. At midnight the baby still had not come. Sarah lay in her own bed, the doctor dozing, arms folded, in a nearby chair. Ella held her daughter's hand and mopped away the perspiration from her forehead. Outside it had begun to rain.

"It can't be long now," Sarah said. Her eyes were closed, her face drawn. "There's another one. Stronger. I'm sure it won't be long now."

"No, it won't be long," Ella agreed.

Sarah's hand squeezed hers tightly.

"I really think . . ." Sarah puffed, "that it's time to awaken the doctor. . . ." Then she cried out in pain and the doctor awakened himself. Crossing the room he nodded to Ella.

"Nearly time." His voice, utterly calm, was still not soothing, and Sarah felt a moment of stark panic, remembering old tales.

"Young lady," the doctor said, bending over so that the lamplight sparkled on his spectacles. "You're young, strong. The baby will also be strong and well. You do what I ask and we'll bring him into this world. Now," he said, rolling up his sleeves, "between those contractions I want you to relax, think of pleasant things."

Sarah nodded and closed her eyes, trying. Almost immediately an image came into her mind. A long grassy meadow, surrounded by lofty peaks. The grass swayed in the wind and she was running, laughing through the meadow. . . . A sharp, lengthy pain broke off. Sarah bit her lips and rolled her head. Ella's hand was still in hers, but it was distant, far distant.

*Then he came running toward her*, across the meadow and he was laughing, his arms out to her. He carried bundles of some kind with him, but he cast them away as he rushed toward Sarah. . . .

"Doctor!"

"It's all right. Fine." He positioned her legs. Sarah lifted her head but could not even see him.

*They fell together*. Mantaka and Sarah, rolling down the long slope, stopping finally with the sweet scent of new grass all around them . . . he smiled. . .

Sarah cried out.

"Now. Push," the doctor demanded, and she did. "Again!" he barked like a drill sergeant. Sarah panted, writhed, pushed when told to. . .

"*I love you*," he said and his lips came down to meet hers as the birds sang in the deep forest. . .

"Push!"

"*Yes, I love you*". . .

"Again! Sarah, again! That's it."

"*I do love you, Sarah* . . ." The summer breeze touched the tears on Sarah's cheeks. . .

"Now! Once more. Only once more!"

"*Mantaka*. . ."

"Now!"

"*I love you* . . ."

And then the cry broke the stillness, shattering the dream and the pain with one warbling note. Sarah's eyes were filled with tears, but through the tears she could see the doctor smile, holding something aloft. Something reddish, damp, protesting. And then it was bundled and placed beside her and Sarah suckled it as the doctor, still smiling, cleaned up.

"A boy or a girl?" Ella asked.

"Why, a boy," the doctor answered. "Sound of lungs—obviously. A sturdy baby boy."

The infant nursed and Sarah watched it in amazement, touching its tiny red fingers, watching the fine, long lashes and the unformed chin in amazement. Then again she was crying, and she could not even say why.

There was a sound, or perhaps it was not a sound, but only a knowledge, and Sarah's eyes lifted to the window. He was there, watching, his hair and beard damp with the rain and he was smiling, happy, well.

*Mantaka.*

He was there only for a moment and then he was gone. Had he really been there? In this rain, at her upstairs window? How could he have known when to come? Perhaps it was not really Mantaka, but a part of the dream. It did not matter, for his spirit was there. And his son. Sarah drew the baby closer to her and closed her eyes. The light was turned down and the voices of the doctor and her mother faded away into the night.

It rained for a day and a night, the storm finally breaking at dawn, a brilliant golden fan flashing through the dark, dissipating clouds. Adrian Staughton did not come to see the baby for three days and when he did it was a cursory glance, as if to check to assure himself the thing was human, not covered with fur or scales.

"We'll find a place for it," Sarah's father said.

"It has a place, his place is with me," Sarah answered.

She sat by the window, watching the sunlit hills, and at night she constantly awoke, glancing at her window. She told her father she had not named the baby, but when no one was around, she called him Mantaka and sang the songs that his father had loved.

Again Adrian Staughton mentioned adopting the baby out. "It's quite absurd, Sarah," he said patiently. "To keep this child, born out of a crime. You'll never

219

have a chance at happiness if you keep him."

"I don't see how I could be happy without him, Father," Sarah answered. "As for the people here who don't like the idea. . ."

"I wouldn't worry about anyone in Rose Canyon," he interrupted. "We're moving anyway."

"Moving!"

"The town's dead. Judd has a feeler out on some interests in Nevada."

"Nevada," Sarah repeated tonelessly. "I didn't think we'd ever leave Rose Canyon."

"Why not? Everyone else has. What is there to stay here for, Sarah?"

She answered with a wistful smile which caused Adrian Staughton to wonder if after all her abduction hadn't harmed his daughter's mind.

"I suppose I won't ever understand her again," he told Ella.

"No. Perhaps I won't either. She has changed. We are meant to change, Adrian. There's nothing to be discovered without it, is there?"

"That is what I tried to explain to Sarah just now."

"You told her we were leaving Rose Canyon!"

"Of course." Adrian frowned at his wife's discomposure. He supposed he would never understand women. "And when we do get to Nevada," he pronounced, "that . . ." his hand lifted . . . "infant will be given to the first squaw willing to take it."

"You told her that?"

"Not so strongly as I should have," Staughton snapped. Then he opened the portmanteau which rested on his cluttered desk and removed the reports from Judd Fitch, his mind already working on new accomplishments, richer claims. He barely lifted his eyes as Ella walked from his office.

Ella Staughton went to the linen closet and removed two warm blankets. In the kitchen she filled a small cotton sack with tinned goods, matches and sugar. She did not have to turn her head when the door opened behind her. "You'll need a few things."

Sarah nodded. The baby was silent, bundled in a thick blanket. The sunlight streamed through the high kitchen window. Ella could think of nothing else, and so she rose from her crouch, giving the sack to Sarah.

"One must live," Ella Staughton said. She clung to Sarah's arm and then lifted on tip-toes to kiss her. Slowly, with a shaking hand, she unwrapped the blanket to peek at the yawning baby. She smiled tenderly and covered him back up, her hand still trembling.

"Goodbye, Dear."

Ella Staughton hugged Sarah again, briefly, tightly, and then she walked with her to the open kitchen door, watching as her daughter strode across the open field toward the stand of sunbright oaks beyond the barn. Sarah heard the whistling of a lark bunting, but she ignored it. Then again the bird called, more insistently, and her head turned slowly toward the oaks.

He came from the shadows of the oaks, a dream, a wish—a great bearded man with deep eyes and a smile playing on his lips. He was to her in four strides and she clung to him, speaking his name over and over.

"Mantaka."

"I had hoped...how long I have waited here." Then his eyes brightened and he looked at the baby, throwing back his head and laughing with pride and pleasure at the tiny baby, his innocence and trust.

"Such a baby as only you could have given to me, Sarah. Only you...

"I have heard the furs are rich in Canada. There I could build my own stone house. I am not so clumsy . . ."

He was silent as Sarah's lips met his and he held her to him. "Wherever you go, Mantaka," she said simply, and they turned and walked toward the north. Behind lay only the empty, crumbling town. Ahead lay the far blue mountains, the high valleys, life. The day was warm and so Sarah unwrapped the baby, letting the sunlight fall on him.

# GREAT WESTERNS
## by Dan Parkinson

**GUNPOWDER GLORY** (1448, $2.50)

Jeremy Burke, breaking a deathbed promise to his pa, killed the lowdown Sutton boy who was the cause of his pa's death. But when the bullets started flying, he found there was more at stake than his own life as innocent people were caught in the crossfire of *Gunpowder Glory*.

**BLOOD ARROW** (1549, $2.50)

Randall Kerry returned to his camp to find his companion slaughtered and scalped. With a war cry as wild as the savages', the young scout raced forward with his pistol held high to meet them in battle.

**BROTHER WOLF** (1728, $2.95)

Only two men could help Lattimer run down the sheriff's killers—a stranger named Stillwell and an Apache who was as deadly with a Colt as he was with a knife. One of them would see justice done—from the muzzle of a six-gun.

**CALAMITY TRAIL** (1663, $2.95)

Charles Henry Clayton fled to the west to make his fortune, get married and settle down to a peaceful life. But the situation demanded that he strap on a six-gun and ride toward a showdown of gunpowder and blood that would send him galloping off to either death or glory on the . . . *Calamity Trail*.

**SUNDOWN BREED** (1860, $2.95)

The last thing Darby Curtis wanted was an Indian war. But a ruthless bunch of land-grabbers wanted the high plains to themselves, even if it meant flaming an Indian uprising. Darby found himself in a deadly crossfire of hot lead. The Kiowa were out for blood . . . and the blood they wanted was his.

---

# TALES OF THE OLD WEST

**SPIRIT WARRIOR** (1795, $2.50)
by G. Clifton Wisler
The only settler to survive the savage indian attack was a little boy. Although raised as a red man, every man was his enemy when the two worlds clashed—but he vowed no man would be his equal.

**IRON HEART** (1736, $2.25)
by Walt Denver
Orphaned by an indian raid, Ben vowed he'd never rest until he'd brought death to the Arapahoes. And it wasn't long before they came to fear the rider of vengeance they called . . . Iron Heart.

**WEST OF THE CIMARRON** (1681, $2.50)
by G. Clifton Wisler
Eric didn't have a chance revenging his father's death against the Dunstan gang until a stranger with a fast draw and a dark past arrived from West of the Cimarron.

**HIGH LINE RIDER** (1615, $2.50)
by William A. Lucky
In Guffey Creek, you either lived by the rules made by Judge Breen and his hired guns—or you didn't live at all. So when Holly took sides against the Judge, it looked like there would be just one more body for the buzzards. But this time they were wrong.

**GUNSIGHT LODE** (1497, $2.25)
by Virgil Hart
When Ned Coffee cornered Glass and Corey in a mine shaft, the last thing Glass expected was for the kid to make a play for the gold. And in a blazing three-way shootout, both Corey and Coffee would discover how lightening quick Glass was with a gun.

*Available wherever paperbacks are sold, or order direct from the Publisher. Send cover price plus 50¢ per copy for mailing and handling to Zebra Books, Dept. 1957, 475 Park Avenue South, New York, N.Y. 10016. Residents of New York, New Jersey and Pennsylvania must include sales tax. DO NOT SEND CASH.*

# GHOSTWORLD™
## MIDNIGHT CHILL

**Barbara Siegel and Scott Siegel**

**AN ARCHWAY PAPERBACK**
Published by POCKET BOOKS

New York   London   Toronto   Sydney   Tokyo   Singapore

AN ARCHWAY PAPERBACK *Original*

An Archway Paperback published by
POCKET BOOKS, a division of Simon & Schuster Inc.
1230 Avenue of the Americas, New York, NY 10020

ISBN: 0-671-70905-4

First Archway Paperback printing October 1991

10  9  8  7  6  5  4  3  2  1

AN ARCHWAY PAPERBACK and colophon are registered
trademarks of Simon & Schuster Inc.

Cover art by Vince Natale

Printed in the U.S.A.

IL 6+

*For Greg Tobin—*

Good friends are a lot like good books: for both, a good character is key. Each must also have a unique and appealing style, worthy content, and, of course, you hope that neither the book nor the friendship will ever come to an end. Greg knows a good book when he sees one and, in Greg, we know a good friend when we have one.

Let this heartfelt dedication, in some small measure, suggest that a kindness done once many years ago has never been forgotten.

## Acknowledgments

The authors wish to thank Pat MacDonald for her editorial vision and unswerving support, Marjorie Hanlon for her thoroughness as well as her perceptive eye for detail, and Lisa Clancy for her warm-hearted professionalism. They are, as always, a pleasure to work with.

We also want to offer our appreciation to you, our readers. Though ghosts populate the book you now hold in your hands, it's only when you read about them that you give our characters life. And for that, these authors are eternally grateful.

# CHAPTER
## 1

THE DARK SILHOUETTE WAS HIDDEN BEHIND a tree, only its head jutting forward. The head had no eyes, no nose, no mouth—no features at all. Of course the details of a face in shadow are never visible. But this was more than the shadow of a being. This blackness was palpable—alive. And there was coldness and evil within the gloom of its black outline. . . .

Andy Moser shivered and his eyelids fluttered open. He was lying on his back, staring up at an ever yellow sky. He knitted his brows, wondering why the sky wasn't blue or even gray.

"Are you awake?" whispered a soft voice close to Andy's ear.

The sound of Elizabeth's question startled and then calmed him. She was close, and he could smell her hair. Knowing she was near made him feel safe until he remembered where he was. That filled him with a quiet dread.

Andy didn't answer Elizabeth. He was too tired. Turning his head to one side, he saw a small stand of trees and slowly his eyelids fell closed again. It was then, just before the final darkness, that he caught a glimpse of something hiding behind a tree.

He sensed the danger and tried to force his eyes open again, but his lids were too heavy. There was something terrible out there. He knew it by the fear that had welled up in him. Desperately, Andy tried to wake up, fighting an exhaustion that refused to lift. It scared him that he couldn't open his eyes. But what scared him even more was that with his eyes closed he *still* managed to see something coming for him from the trees.

Was it his imagination? Was he dreaming? Or was it real? He didn't know. All he knew was that the thing he was seeing was dark and shaped vaguely like a man. Despite its being lit by the perpetual bright yellow light of day, the figure coming toward him remained nothing more than a shadow. At most, its outer edges receded slightly under the glaring yellow sky.

The silhouette moved slowly but steadily

out from the shelter of the trees to enter the open meadow. Why didn't the light illuminate the being? Why didn't the darkness disappear when the figure came out of the shadows?

Andy could see the outline of the creature's feet, which seemed never to touch the ground. The silhouette floated toward them now. As it came closer Andy could smell the evil stench that wafted off its body. Yet he still could not understand how he was able to see all of this with his eyes closed.

Struggling somewhere in the depths between sleep and consciousness, Andy's mind swirled in confusion.

The shadow creature slipped closer.

Andy screamed to himself, *"Wake up!"*

Elizabeth gazed down upon Andy's sleeping face with concern in her warm brown eyes. She wondered if he was coming down with a fever. His handsome sixteen-year-old face was dripping with sweat. He groaned and thrashed as he lay on the soft grass of the meadow.

Andy watched as the shadow creature moved up close behind Elizabeth. It was coming for her to wrap its arms around her and pull her into its darkness. Andy saw it, sensed it, knew it, but he couldn't stop it because he was paralyzed with sleep.

*"Open your eyes!"* his mind thundered in warning.

Elizabeth leaned forward to tenderly wipe beads of perspiration off Andy's forehead. She remembered how her mother had kissed her forehead to see if she had a fever as a child. It had been such a loving, caring gesture; she smiled at the memory of it. And she leaned forward now to kiss Andy's forehead in the same way.

Andy watched the shadow creature directly behind Elizabeth. It was hovering there, its arms outstretched, reaching out to take her away.

*"Wake up! Now! Wake up!"*

Just as Elizabeth's lips touched his hot, sweat-drenched skin, Andy forced his eyes open. He saw two shadow hands on either side of Elizabeth's head, ready to encircle it.

Andy moved with the speed of the truly terrified. His hands whipped up and grabbed Elizabeth's shoulders as he rolled hard to his left, pulling her with him.

"What the—" was all she had time to say.

Andy and Elizabeth rolled over three times. When they stopped, she finally tore Andy's hands from her shoulders and shouted, "What's wrong with you? Didn't anyone ever kiss you on the forehead before?"

Andy didn't know what she was talking about. He shook his head and pointed at the shadow creature that was a few yards behind her. She turned to see what Andy was pointing to as he struggled to his feet.

A deep, impenetrable shadow reached out for Elizabeth. She flinched out of the way, falling into Andy and knocking him down. They both tumbled, their arms and legs entangling, while they frantically tried to get up and away from the fast-approaching creature.

"You were dreaming again!" Elizabeth accused him, trying to get her footing.

"I couldn't help it," Andy breathlessly replied, helping her up.

Running and stumbling over their own feet, they never turned their backs on the silent blackness that relentlessly pursued them. They made their way across what was left of the meadow, fleeing into a protected area full of heavy brush and broken boulders.

The shadow creature kept coming.

"What is it?" Elizabeth asked fearfully.

"I was dreaming about the unknown. That's the shape it took in my dream."

Elizabeth stared into the face of the unknown and shuddered. "We've got to get away from it; we've got to hide!"

Unable to tear their gazes from the creature, they didn't see where they were going.

Andy was the first to make contact; he slammed hard into something that wouldn't give. He reached back with his hand to find a way around the obstacle—and his fingers brushed something *hairy*.

Just then Elizabeth hooked her foot around something that felt heavy and thick, like a tree stump. She lost her balance and started spinning to the left. She flung herself forward to grab hold of what had tripped her. Her hands clamped upon something thick, hairy—*and warm*.

As the shadow creature closed in on them, Andy and Elizabeth were both startled by what blocked their path. It was a shortish, massive, hairy man with long, apelike arms, a jutting jaw, and long, sloping forehead. He wore nothing but a loincloth. In one hand he held a primitive stone ax.

That ax was raised in one quick motion and then suddenly came swinging down toward Elizabeth's head!

# CHAPTER
## 2

ELIZABETH WATCHED THE SHARP EDGE OF the ax as it swung downward. It was happening so fast she didn't have a chance to react. Andy saw the blade, too, but could only manage the beginnings of a scream.

The blade cut the air but did not land on Elizabeth. Instead, it chopped down onto the dark hand that was just beginning to wrap long, thin, black shadow fingers around Elizabeth's throat.

The shadow was more surprised than hurt. In fact, it didn't seem hurt at all. It did back away and withdraw its hand.

Elizabeth saw her chance and took it. She bolted, circling behind the huge, apelike man. Andy did the same.

When it realized it wasn't injured, the shadow creature surged forward again. The ape-man, however, stood his ground, swinging his ax again. This time the shadow creature was ready. After the ax whooshed through the air, aimed directly at the silhouette's chest, the blade simply passed through the darkness the way it would have passed through a cloud. It entered the chest on the right side and came out on the left, but it didn't do the slightest bit of damage.

The ape-man grunted something under his breath that neither Andy nor Elizabeth understood. However, they did understand the fear in the backward steps of the half-human who stood between them and the unknown.

They retreated as a group, the shadow creature floating toward them across the uneven ground, remaining fifteen yards away.

They kept bumping into and tripping over rocks, bushes, and small, stunted trees as they hurried backward, away from the horror that pursued them.

"You dreamed it up," Elizabeth shouted. "Can't you undream it?"

"Don't you think I would, if I could?"

"Well, we've got to do *something!*"

There was another grunt from the huge, hairy humanlike creature who had tried to rescue them. Then the ape-man clearly added,

"Methinks, fair lady, it be good plan to zap yonder dude."

"You think *what?*" Elizabeth asked incredulously.

"Me say we need bop that hockey puck."

"I like the way he thinks," Andy said. "Is he a friend of yours?"

"Nope. Nobody I know," Elizabeth replied, shaking her head.

"I am Makasha," the ape-man announced, glancing at the two young people for an instant before refocusing on the shadow monster that relentlessly followed their retreat.

"Well, Makasha," Andy said in a ragged voice, "I'm for bopping and zapping that hockey puck, too. But *how?*"

"Me caveman, not rocket scientist. You go figure."

"Great. You know—"

"Look out!" Elizabeth cried, spotting danger out of the corner of her eye.

Andy pulled up short and turned to see where he was going. A small fire burned right in front of him.

"My camp," announced Makasha. "I make fire to summon Guardian of Mist."

"We sure could use the Guardian right about now," Elizabeth said anxiously as she watched the shadow creature close the gap between them. The dark force was only ten yards away now.

9

"No can run forever," Makasha said stoutly. "Must show who is top dog, el primo, Mafia boss. All Makasha need is weapon for fight." He bent down and scooped up a long spear lying next to a leather bag on an animal skin beside his campfire. A two-sided, sharp-edged rock that came to a point was lashed to the end of the spear.

"You no more follow us, dark demon!" shouted Makasha, lunging forward with the spear. He plunged the long blade through the head of the shadow creature. It didn't seem to have the slightest effect. In fact, the evil silhouette reached out then and clutched Makasha, its long arms embracing him in a bear hug.

The huge, powerful caveman screamed as the shadow monster began enveloping him into its darkness. The unknown is the most terrifying horror, and Makasha was being absorbed into its depths!

This strange caveman had tried to help Andy and Elizabeth, and now he needed their help—they had to try to do something for him. Anything—because Makasha was fast disappearing into the shadow monster.

Andy reached for a rock at the edge of the campfire. When he touched it, though, he gasped in pain; the rock was burning hot.

Meanwhile, Elizabeth reached out to grab the safe end of a long tree branch, the other end of which was burning in the campfire. She whipped around with the stick in her hands, the air fanning the burning tip into bright flame. She jabbed the white-hot tip into the shadow creature's shoulder.

The shoulder vanished! And when the shoulder disappeared, so did one of the arms that held Makasha.

The shadow monster staggered back in shock.

Makasha, half swallowed by the darkness that was the creature, struggled to free himself, but he couldn't do it.

When the flame at the end of the tree branch flickered out, the evil silhouette began to grow another arm to replace the one it had lost. When Elizabeth jabbed at it again with the stick, the creature took no notice of it—it didn't seem to be hurt by it at all.

"It's got to be the flame!" Andy shouted. "Either that or the light. When it gets inside the thing, it destroys it. Put the stick back in the fire!"

Elizabeth started to do exactly that when Andy shouted for her to wait.

He dove for the animal skin on the ground, knocked the small leather bag off it, picked up the hide, and rolled over to where Elizabeth was standing. Then, breathlessly, he tied the dry, furry skin around the end of the tree branch. "Now put it in the fire!"

Elizabeth dipped the fur into the campfire, and a moment later it burst into bright white flame. She immediately spun back and stabbed her flaming torch into the right leg of the shadow creature.

The light from the fire illuminated the thigh from the inside out, and then the leg disappeared. The creature, unbalanced now, tumbled over and fell. Makasha fell with it, less than half his body left untouched by the darkness.

"Get him in the arm!" Andy said, pointing at the shadow monster.

Elizabeth maneuvered the still brightly glowing torch at the dark arm that held Makasha prisoner. And again it worked. The arm vanished.

Andy wrapped his hands around Makasha's legs and dragged the caveman's head, shoulders, and upper body out of the bleak darkness of the shadow creature's torso. That was when Elizabeth delivered the final blow to the monster, swinging her fiery torch into the top of the evil being's head and through the length of what remained of its body.

An instant later there was nothing there. Just a smoking stick with the ashes of an animal skin flaking off in a light breeze.

Makasha lay on the ground, stunned and disoriented.

"Are you all right?" Elizabeth asked the caveman.

"I survive," he weakly replied.

Andy crawled up close to Makasha's face. "What did you see in the unknown?" he asked.

The caveman stared back at him. It was a long time before he answered. "Nothing," he finally said. "And that scare Makasha worst."

"It's over now," Elizabeth said. "So I guess we should thank you. That's Andy," she said, gesturing with a smile in her eyes. "And you should also know that this was all his fault. You see," she explained, "Andy isn't a ghost. He's actually alive."

The caveman's mouth fell open. "Alive? You're pulling my foot."

Elizabeth laughed. "That's pulling your *leg.*"

"Right. Makasha gets confused. But still not believe this boy living in our ghost world. Gimme a fracture."

"You mean a *break,*" Andy corrected, grinning.

Makasha did not grin back.

Hastily, Andy added, "It's really true. Elizabeth saved me from getting murdered, except the only way she could do it was to bring me to her world. The problem is, I can't get back to my own. Your Guardian of the Mist promised to help, but he hasn't been around lately. So here I still am."

"Because he's alive," Elizabeth explained, "he needs to sleep. When he sleeps, he sometimes dreams. And when he dreams, what he imagines comes to life. Let me tell you, that's definitely not one of his most endearing qualities. I mean, why did he have to dream up a creature from the unknown? Why couldn't he have a normal nightmare like being sent to the vice-principal?"

"Oh, no," Andy cautioned. "Not the vice-principal. That'd be much worse."

"Yeah." She giggled. "Maybe you're right."

While the two teenagers talked, Makasha listened intently, nodding his head as if he understood what was being said. And maybe he did. As far as Andy was concerned, the caveman looked a bit like his high-school vice-principal. Makasha was only a bit hairier. Then it dawned on Andy that their introductions hadn't been completed. "Hey, buddy," he said. "Sorry, this is Elizabeth."

The caveman nodded his head. "Makasha delighted to meet you."

"Wow, a gentleman," Elizabeth said. "I guess they don't make guys like they used to, huh?"

"Makasha made almost one hundred thousand years ago. Been ghost long time."

Her gaze turned more serious. She wondered why he had been in the ghost world all those years. Why hadn't he found a way to his final peace? Surely, she thought, there must be a reason why he'd remained there so long. Had he done something so very wrong that he couldn't leave? She pushed that thought out of her head, unwilling to believe that someone who had so selflessly come to their aid could be that bad.

"Almost a hundred thousand years," Andy said softly. "You really are a caveman."

"Used to be," Makasha corrected. "Learn much in thousand centuries as ghost. Many to learn from. Speak eighteen languages. Know much slang. Do magic tricks. Bad with numbers, though. Someone from Athens try to teach me geometry, but it Greek to me."

Andy and Elizabeth burst out laughing.

"I can't believe it—a stand-up comedian caveman," Andy said.

"Why you surprised?" Makasha asked, perplexed. "No think prehistoric man like to laugh?"

"Sorry. I never really thought about it."

That seemed to satisfy the Neanderthal, who grunted and got to his feet. He walked barefoot back to the place where his animal skin had once lain. There, on the ground, he found his leather pouch. He picked it up and ambled over to a large boulder with a flat smooth surface. He opened his bag and took out some powders, which he mixed with water from a nearby stream. Then he began drawing

15

a frightening picture of their battle with the shadow monster.

In silent awe of his artistry, Andy and Elizabeth watched him. When he finished, Andy threw more wood on the fire because he was feeling cold.

The fire did little to warm Andy because his shivering came from the realization that, while Makasha could leave his legacy in paint, he might never be able to tell his own people—the living—about this ghost world. His greatest fear, the one that chilled him, was that he'd grow old and die before ever returning home.

"More wood on the fire?" Elizabeth asked, noticing Andy's trembling.

"I'm okay."

"You sure?"

He smiled at her. He couldn't think of anyone dead or alive that he cared for more than he did Elizabeth. Her dark curly hair framed a pale-skinned beauty that made him ache with longing. He shivered again.

Despite his protestations, Elizabeth tossed more wood onto the fire. The flames leapt up a few inches, as they should have, but then inexplicably they climbed higher!

Within seconds, a spire of bright red flame had shot at least a hundred feet into the air— and remained there.

"What kind of wood is that?" Andy asked anxiously.

He received no answer because neither Elizabeth nor Makasha knew more than Andy did.

At its peak, the fire spread open like a glorious umbrella and flowed down in a circular waterfall of flame. Andy, Elizabeth, and Makasha were surrounded now, boxed in, by the fire. The flames had a life of their own. And, seemingly, they had a will to destroy.

Makasha clutched his leather pouch and spear close to his chest and made no more movements.

Elizabeth's terror was obvious. She had died at the age of sixteen in a fire in 1966. Even though she couldn't die again, she could suffer the pain from the blaze and then be "transported"—the ghost equivalent of death. She'd be set down along the great river someplace far from where she'd always stayed, far from anyone or anything she knew. All alone to begin again.

Andy pulled Elizabeth close, hoping to protect her and to share his final moments with her. He knew there was nothing else he could do. There was nothing any of them could do.

# CHAPTER
## 3

THERE WAS NO PLACE TO RUN. NO PLACE TO hide. The fire made a perfect, impenetrable wall and burned with a terrible, steady fury.

Elizabeth closed her eyes tight, burying her head against Andy's chest. Her mind was full of images of her long-ago death and she cried without tears—for ghosts cannot weep—trying to forget the past while hoping to avoid a fiery future.

The flames rose even higher, the light grew even brighter. Something about this made no sense to Andy. He lifted his right hand from Elizabeth's trembling shoulder and ran it across his forehead. His hand came away dry. He wasn't sweating.

With all this fire, Andy thought, I should

feel hot and be sweating. Tentatively, he reached out a finger to touch one of the flames. Less than an inch away, he still didn't feel any heat. He closed the gap between his fingertip and the fire—*and screamed in pain!*

The fire was real. Yet not exactly real. Andy let go of Elizabeth, hoping to find a way out of their trap. He took hold of Makasha's spear, with the idea of ripping his way through one of the walls of flame.

Makasha, however, would not let go of his weapon.

"Give it to me!" Andy demanded, pulling on the shaft.

"No."

"Then use it yourself. Or use your ax. Slash through the fire."

"No."

"It's our only chance!"

"No!"

"Why won't—"

Makasha stopped Andy in midsentence with his, "Look!" and swung his pointed finger in a circle, gesturing to four images emerging along the wall of flame about ten feet above them.

It was the beginnings of a face. It was the same face displayed four times on the round wall of flame. Slowly, it formed and became clear. The skin was made of yellow fire, the bone structure outlined in orange, the eyes a bright blue.

When the features were fully formed, Makasha bowed, saying in a humble voice, "It is the Guardian—he has answered my signal."

Andy recognized him, also. Besides, not too many regular folks, ghosts or otherwise, make their appearance as four disembodied faces on a round-walled room of flames. "I don't know if he answered your signal, Makasha, or if he's finally come back to honor his promise."

Elizabeth elbowed him in the side. "Don't get the Guardian angry," she whispered. "We need his help."

"You do, indeed," intoned the Guardian, his mouth of orange and red flames flickering ever so faintly as he spoke. "I am pleased that you have met Makasha," he continued in his loud, commanding voice. "I have guided the great Neanderthal hunter to you in the hope that you would find common cause. It is good that you have so quickly become friends, for you will need Makasha's help, just as Makasha will need yours. You see, I am keeping my promise to help you find your way back to the living world. After all, Andy, it was your magic that saved us from the toxic waste that burned from your world into ours. Now I will do my part to help you."

"Andy, you're going home!" Elizabeth cried

out, hugging his arm from happiness and from the fear of letting him go.

"He may or may not go home," warned the Guardian. "I make no promises. I only announce that I will do what I can to help. The rest will be up to the three of you."

"Why should Makasha help me?" Andy asked, gazing at each of the four faces of the Guardian in turn. He didn't know which of them to address. "I mean, what's in it for him?"

Makasha stared at Andy with a look of awe-struck wonder on his face. Elizabeth saw it, but Andy was too busy talking to the Guardian to notice.

"Why does Elizabeth help you?" the Guardian answered.

"That's different," Andy said. "She brought me here. She wants to help me get home."

"Isn't there another reason?" probed the Guardian.

"We like each other," Elizabeth offered, glancing quickly at Andy and then down at her feet.

Andy blushed.

"Yes," said the Guardian. "And would not a simple man like Makasha, a man who has seen the sorry development of the human race throughout his years in our world, be mightily impressed with a human like you who cares first for Makasha and only second for himself?''

Andy blushed again.

"I go with them," Makasha announced. "They already save me once from dark monster. Good fighters. Good people."

"Are you sure?" Elizabeth questioned, making sure the caveman wasn't helping just because the Guardian wanted him to.

"I sure," Makasha said solemnly. "Maybe I do this thing and I go to final peace."

"Will he?" she demanded of the Guardian.

"As I said before, I make no promises," the face in the fire replied.

"But he's been here so long," Elizabeth said. "Can't you give him your word that he'll finally leave if he helps Andy?"

"What about you?" the Guardian said. "Don't you want to go to your final peace?"

"Of course."

"Then why don't you try to bargain for it, too?"

"I know the rules," she said humbly. "But Makasha has been here for almost a hundred thousand years!"

"He knows the rules, too."

Makasha gently took one of Elizabeth's small hands in one of his own huge ones and shook his head. "Say no more, fair lady. I go to final peace when time is right. Maybe soon. Maybe not. But first I help."

Andy placed his own hand over Makasha's. "You guys are something else."

"Something else? Is this good?" Makasha asked Elizabeth.

"It's good," she replied simply, in a quiet whisper.

Andy took a deep breath and turned back to one of the images of the Guardian. "What do we have to do?" he asked.

"There is only one way back," the Guardian said ominously. "And it will not be easy. You must travel to a place that is always close but far away, that is always in mind but not always in sight, that is at the center of everything yet is as ephemeral as the mist."

*"What are you talking about?"* Andy complained. "If there's someplace I have to go, give me a map, not a riddle."

The fiery images roared with laughter. "If I make no sense, then I'll tell you something that does. You cannot return to the living world until you are complete. Remember that, and remember that you must find someone from your past who is here. When you do, help that person, because he or she is the key to your escape. Don't forget this if you ever want to return to the living world."

"Where can I find this person?" Andy immediately asked.

"Close your eyes and spin around once."

"What?"

23

"Don't question the Guardian," Makasha whispered.

"Just do as I say," said the flaming images. "Whichever direction you end up facing will be the right one."

"Are you sure?"

The Guardian laughed as the flames turned into a cool white mist that floated off on the wind.

Before the mist was gone, Andy had done as he was told. He closed his eyes and spun around. When he came to a stop, he opened his eyes to see where he was destined to go.

# CHAPTER
## 4

"THAT'S THE WAY BACK TO THE RIVER," Andy said, noticing the mist rise from the broad waterway off in the distance.

"Every way leads back to river," Makasha explained. "No way you can go without finding it. I know such things."

"I'll bet you do," Elizabeth agreed. "You've been wandering around this world long enough to know how to find everything."

"Can find everything but final peace," the caveman said soberly. "But find that someday, too."

"What did you do to get stuck here so long?" Elizabeth asked.

Makasha sighed. "Have big problem," he began. "Guardian choose me to witness

25

changes in humans. He say I have perspective of time.''

"You mean you have to stay here forever?'' Andy interrupted, horrified.

"Here until Guardian release me from job. No get overtime, either.''

"I hope the Guardian releases you soon so you can go to your final peace.'' Elizabeth offered.

"Same here,'' Andy piped up.

"Kind friends,'' said Makasha. "But no more time for talk.'' He smiled. "Let's rock 'n' roll.''

Between them and the river lay sprawling country of barren, steep hills and lush valleys. The hills were not much more than bare rock, but the valleys were covered with deep undergrowth that was nearly jungle thick. Using his ax, Makasha led the way, cutting through the heavy foliage of the valley and creating a makeshift trail.

They journeyed for a long time, stopping occasionally to let Andy sleep. Happily, he had no more nightmares. As for food, there were countless bushes with ripe berries and other exotic fruits for the taking, so Andy didn't starve.

They saw no one. Andy had hoped they might quickly find the person from his past, the one whom the Guardian had mentioned.

No such luck. In fact, their progress through the brush was terribly slow—not to mention painful. There were thorns that tore at their skin, and branches that slapped at their faces, arms, and legs.

None of that was bothering Makasha. But something was. He kept a constant vigil, glancing over his shoulder every few feet.

"What is it?" Elizabeth asked more than once.

Every time the caveman would shake his head and say, "Can't see anything, but feel someone. Maybe I be foolish."

At first Andy and Elizabeth were worried. But then they asked themselves, Who would want to follow us through this mess? So they began making jokes about the phantoms who were supposedly behind them.

"Maybe they're exercise freaks who like chopping through this stuff," Andy suggested with a grin.

"No, I think they're a group of machete testers, trying out new equipment," Elizabeth offered.

Makasha took no offense at their gibes. He even laughed at their jokes. It didn't matter if they believed him or not because he knew he was right.

They traveled on. If anything, the undergrowth got thicker and the ground beneath their feet became more treacherous. They couldn't see anything except what was right in front of their faces. And they couldn't walk without stumbling over thick roots or slipping on moss-covered rocks.

It was on such a rock that Elizabeth lost her footing and was sent flying into a thicket. She gave out a muffled cry as the branches cracked and split, cutting at her skin. The force of her fall was so great she barreled right through the heavy growth and disappeared from view.

"Are you all right?" Andy cried out anxiously.

There was no answer.

"Elizabeth!"

"I'm okay," she finally answered in a low, hoarse voice. "But keep your voices down and come take a look at this."

"At what?"

"Just come and look. Crawl through slowly, so you don't roll down the hill. And make sure you aren't seen."

Andy and Makasha glanced at each other, each thinking his own thoughts. Andy was thinking that maybe she had spotted someone from his past. Makasha, on the other hand, was afraid she had seen whoever was following them. And maybe they had seen her as well.

Carefully, the caveman used his ax to cut a passage through the thicket low to the ground. Andy wiggled through easily. The broad-shouldered Makasha had a tougher time. When they were both through the hole, Andy and Makasha finally saw what Elizabeth had spotted. It was not at all what either of them had expected to see.

The undergrowth gave way to a steep, down-sloping hillside dotted with small patches of trees. At the bottom of the hill, nestled next to a lake and a towering butte, was a large village.

The three of them lay flat on their stomachs, looking down on the town. Even at their considerable distance, they could see large numbers of people walking on the streets. Outside the town, guards seemed to be patrolling the perimeter. One of them was leaning against a tree, just fifty yards down the hill.

"Did he see you?" asked Makasha, gesturing toward the closest guard.

"No," she replied. "He hasn't moved since I spotted him."

"There are an awful lot of ghosts down there," Andy said, marveling at the sight below. Then he studied the village a little more closely and slowly shook his head. "Am I crazy," Andy asked, "or does every single house in that village look exactly the same?"

"They're the same," Elizabeth said, nodding her head. "The houses are all the same drab gray, too. They're mirror images of one another. And get a load of the people," she added. "They're all dressed alike."

"Everything same," Makasha ventured. "Houses, clothes, everything. Makasha no like."

"Me neither," said Elizabeth.

"You guys sure have strong opinions," Andy countered. "Sure, I admit it looks a little boring, but what's so terrible about that? It's like all sorts of towns back home."

"I saw some of those towns in the sixties," Elizabeth said sadly. "I guess there are even more of them now, huh?"

"Probably. People seem to like them."

Elizabeth just shrugged.

"Let's go down there and check the place out," Andy said, starting to rise to his knees.

Makasha grabbed one of his arms and Elizabeth grabbed the other. They both tugged him down to the ground, hard. He hit the earth face first.

"What's the matter?" he angrily complained. "I think you broke my nose!"

"No can risk being seen," Makasha said. "Dangerous."

"Why?" Andy demanded, rubbing his nose and making sure it was still in the middle of his face.

"They are the Mediocrities."

"The what?"

"You heard him," Elizabeth said.

"I heard him, all right, but what does it mean?"

30

"They're the largest group of people in the ghost world," she patiently explained. "The Mediocrities live together and always conform to the same dull, boring rules. They like it that way because it's safe. The truth is, their land really is the safest place in all of the ghost world, but that's because nobody is willing to risk anything—good or bad. If you make your home here, you've got to be just like them. The Mediocrities are very prejudiced against anyone who isn't exactly the same. If you're found to be even a little bit different, they'll tear you apart and then you're transported. Isn't that right, Makasha?"

"She speaks truth."

"I believe you," Andy said. "But this is the direction the Guardian said would lead me to someone from my past. Down there are the only people we've seen. I've got to check that village out."

"It'll be risky," warned Elizabeth.

"With you and Makasha with me, how could that be possible?"

"You're sweet," Elizabeth said, impulsively kissing him on the cheek. "But then," she added, "sometimes you're pretty stupid, too. I just hope we're not as stupid for going along with you."

"We be just as stupid as him," Makasha volunteered. "Just hope Andy not soon be just as dead as us."

31

# CHAPTER 5

"THE ONLY WAY TO GET INTO THE VILLAGE IS to pretend to be one of them," Elizabeth said.

"Your shirt has to go," Andy noted, pointing at her sixties psychedelic tank top. "The cutoffs, too."

"Yeah, and my sandals," she added. "And let's not forget Makasha's loincloth."

"I no forget loincloth," the caveman said, bewildered. "See. I wear it now."

"No," Andy said, chuckling, "she means we shouldn't forget that you need to wear something over or *instead* of your loincloth. The fact is, we all need a set of their gray threads if we're going to get into that village."

"That's not all," cautioned Elizabeth. "They talk funny, too."

"Funnier than you? Funnier than Makasha?"

"Try to talk like they do," Elizabeth said seriously. "If you don't, they'll know we're imposters."

"I'll be careful."

"And you, Makasha, you had better not talk at all."

"Yabba dabba doo. You believe I do not speak tongue of Mediocre?"

Makasha had been a great hunter when he was alive. Since then, he had had almost a hundred thousand years to perfect his skills. Therefore, it was easy for him to sneak up behind the Mediocre guard, who was still leaning against a tree. He clamped one of his huge, meaty hands around the guard's mouth so he couldn't cry out. With his other hand he wrestled him to the ground.

Quickly Andy and Elizabeth crawled up to the guard and stripped him of his gray shirt and pants and his ordinary black shoes. After they had his clothes, they tied him up with strips of leather that Makasha supplied, stuffing the guard's mouth with his own socks so he couldn't cry out, and then they set out to find two more guards, carefully choosing their victims by size.

It wasn't hard finding guards whose clothes were reasonable fits for Andy and Elizabeth. It was nearly impossible, though, to find anyone whose clothes would cover the considerable bulk of Makasha. Eventually, they found someone who could have been a TV wrestler when he was alive. The caveman knocked him out easily. Unfortunately, even *his* clothes were terribly tight and ill-fitting on Makasha. The caveman's arms were much too long for the sleeves. At least the guard had had a hat, which, worn low, covered Makasha's apelike forehead and eyes. It would have to do.

Dressed like true Mediocrities, the three of them finally walked the rest of the way down the hill and into the village. When they reached a small, open gate that led to the main street, an old woman walked by them and nodded her head, saying, "Nice weather we're having."

The first thing that popped into Andy's head was to say, "What are you talking about? The weather is like this every single day and night. The sky is always flat and yellow. It never changes!" Before he could get that thought from his mind to his mouth, though, Elizabeth jumped in with "Yes, and there's a lovely breeze, too."

The old woman smiled. "Have a nice day," she said, waving her hand before ambling on.

"I thought you said they talk funny here," Andy whispered as they crossed the street to the other side and walked along its broad

34

expanse. "This is just how people talk back home."

"I know. But here, they never get past the clichés. It's all surface stuff. If you say anything the least bit controversial—what's that expression you use?—you're dead meat. In fact, if you say 'dead meat,' you'd be dead meat—if you catch my drift."

"Shhh," Makasha said under his breath as a crowd of people walked toward them. As the big group passed, they heard snatches of conversation with phrases like "You always have to look out for number one," "If I had had a nickel for every time . . ." and "Well, I'll be a monkey's uncle."

As the large group went by, one of their number took a long look at Makasha. Fortunately, he was distracted from the sight of the badly dressed caveman by one of his party, who said, "You know, people always talk about the weather but nobody ever does anything about it."

Elizabeth noticed how the man stared at Makasha. When the large group was out of earshot, she said, "We'd better avoid crowds. The Mediocrities have more courage in groups than they do when they're alone."

"You're making me nervous," Andy said.

"You should be nervous," Makasha said in a low voice. "This be bad place for 'free spirits.' "

When he got no reaction he huffed, " *'Free spirits'*. That be pun. Get it?"

"The humor is definitely primitive." Elizabeth giggled.

Makasha grinned. "I hear great joke four thousand years ago. A real knee breaker. Want to hear?"

"That's 'knee slapper,' " Andy corrected. "But remember what Elizabeth said about you—"

A voice behind them suddenly interrupted them. "I love a good laugh. Tell it to me."

They whirled around as one to face the villager who had overheard them. He was a pleasant-looking, if sad-faced, man who appeared to be middle aged. Slightly hunched over, with round shoulders, he gave the impression of someone holding up a world of problems. Nonetheless, he had clear, intensely blue eyes that peered at the trio with an expression of genuine interest. Fearful that his interest might be in turning them in, Makasha made a move to silence the eavesdropper.

Out of the corner of his eye, Andy noticed another group of villagers heading in their direction. Without a moment's hesitation, he quickly stepped between the caveman and his intended victim, saying, "Go ahead and tell him the joke. After all, laugh and the world laughs with you—cry and you cry alone." He glanced at Elizabeth to see if he was speaking the right way.

She gave a tiny but meaningful nod of her head.

"Joke goes like this," Makasha began nervously, remembering Elizabeth's warning that he shouldn't speak at all. "Knock, knock . . ."

The villager's eyes opened wide in surprise, but he played right along. "Who's there?"

"Wait a minute!" Andy immediately interrupted. "This is a knock-knock joke?"

"You know it?" Makasha innocently asked.

"*It?* There are a million of them. Do you mean to say that you heard a knock-knock joke four thousand years ago?"

"Uh, maybe I exaggerate?" offered Makasha soothingly, less alarmed by Andy's questions than the villager's reaction to Andy's unexpected outburst. The local was aghast.

Andy realized his mistake and immediately calmed down. "Oh, well," he said. "What does it matter anyway? After all, a joke, is a joke, is a joke. Right?"

"You know—I once wrote a play," said the villager furtively, glancing once over his shoulder. "It was actually called *Knock Knock,* and I was going to act in it, too. I should have tried harder to get it put on. I gave up too easily."

"Writing and acting in a play don't sound

like very Mediocre things to do," Andy boldly ventured.

"What? No. I'll deny I said it. I never said it. You misunderstood me. I—I—"

"Take it easy," Elizabeth said, touching the villager's arm. "We won't tell anyone."

"I admit I—I had hopes once. But that's all over now. I swear."

Andy shook his head. "Hey, everybody has hopes," he said. "I once hoped to be a writer—a novelist." He frowned at the painful memory.

"Sure," Elizabeth agreed. "I once hoped to be a doctor, but most people told me it was too hard for a girl—that I should be a nurse, instead. So, I forgot about medicine. But who knows what would have happened if I hadn't come here so soon? You know what I mean?"

"No," the villager protested. "You've got to give up your hopes, all of them, if you want to be like everyone else here. At least I try to be. Please—please don't tell anyone what I said before about my play."

"Elizabeth said she wouldn't tell," Andy gently reminded him. "None of us will. You have our word." He offered the villager his right hand. "I'm Andy."

Tentatively, the villager slowly raised his own right hand. "I'm Peter." They shook hands. Elizabeth and Makasha shook Peter's hand, too.

"I—I'm glad I met you folks. I was afraid to tell anyone here about my—my past," Peter said. "I didn't know if it was allowed. I—I just want to fit in. You know what I mean, don't you?"

"Know very well," Makasha said with a straight face.

*Booong! Booong!* A loud, angry bell had suddenly begun clanging. A cry went up in the streets and people started running and shouting.

"What is it?" Elizabeth wondered aloud.

It didn't take long to find out. Someone ran past them, crying out, "There are outsiders here. A guard was found tied up with his clothes stolen. Be on the lookout for an intruder!"

Andy and Elizabeth caught each other's eye, than glanced at Peter, grateful that the other two guards hadn't been found yet.

Peter turned beet red. "I—I hope you don't think they're—they're looking for me, do you?"

"No," Elizabeth said with total honesty. "But it might be a good idea if you stayed with us for a while; a person all alone might attract attention right now."

"You're very kind—thank you," Peter said gratefully.

While Elizabeth engaged Peter in conversation, Andy whispered to Makasha, "What's the best way out of here?"

"Head for lake outside of village. Travel on side closest to tall hill. Then hide in rocks beside it."

Andy put an arm around the villager's shoulder to ease him down a side street that would take them in the direction of the lake, which was still several blocks away.

*Booong! Boooong!* The warning bell rang even more insistently now. A new cry went up among the scurrying villagers. "Two more guards have been found. Three intruders are in the village. Beware!"

Peter blinked several times when he heard the news, then he gave Makasha a sidelong glance and quickly took in Andy and Elizabeth. The faintest trace of a smile formed on his lips. Clearing his throat, he suddenly announced, "I can only walk with you another block. I live in that hut over there—"

"Which?" Andy wondered aloud. "They all look the same."

"The third from the end, on the left side. I-I'd continue on with you, but there's something I have to do."

Elizabeth was afraid he knew who they were and wanted to break away so he could turn them in. Yet there was nothing they could do to stop him. With so many Mediocrities out on the street, they could hardly create a scene by attacking Peter. They had to let him go.

When they reached the front of his home, Peter smiled inscrutably at them. "Meeting the three of you has given me food for thought. Thank you."

He turned and went into his hut. As soon as he closed the door, Makasha said, "He'll go right to back, slip out, and rat on us."

"We've got to split up," Elizabeth said decisively. "They're looking for three people. Alone, each of us might have a chance. Let's each take a different street and meet at the edge of the lake outside the village. If one of us doesn't make it there in ten minutes, the other two go on anyway. Okay?"

Makasha nodded.

Andy swallowed hard. It had been his idea to enter the town. He was sorry he had opened his big mouth. "Okay," he answered finally. "See you in ten minutes."

They split up, each taking a separate street toward the lake. Then something happened that none of them could have predicted.

*Boooong! Boooong!* Another alarm rang out in the village. A vast mob of Mediocrities turned the corner in front of Elizabeth, racing in her direction. She thought they knew who she was and were coming for her. At the last moment, though, she saw the fear on their faces and realized that they weren't running

41

*toward* her—they were running *away* from something behind them. She knew she'd be trampled if she didn't get out of their way.

Elizabeth dove to the side of the street and rolled, slamming up against the side of an empty hut.

Stunned and dizzy, she lay there, counting herself lucky. She didn't feel nearly so lucky, though, when she saw what the Mediocrities had been fleeing. . . .

# CHAPTER

Two distorted and beastly creatures dragged their hideous bodies up the street toward Elizabeth. Though they each had a head, two arms, and two legs, they hardly appeared human. One of the invaders dripped acid from his fingers. When he put his hand on the flesh of a Mediocrity, it cut like a power saw through balsa wood. Elizabeth actually saw it happen to one hapless villager who had been knocked to the ground by the fleeing mob.

The other interloper appeared to be made of glass, but from the way the light caught each facet of his body, blinding anyone who looked at him, Elizabeth realized that his entire outer shell—including his face and limbs—must be made of diamonds. He walked a few steps ahead of his partner, blinding everyone with his brilliance, which allowed his acid-dripping compatriot to do his sizzling worst.

Elizabeth thought they might be nightmares created by Andy—except it didn't seem possible that Andy could have fallen asleep and dreamed these beasts in the short time they had been parted. But then where had they come from? These creatures had never lived on earth, so how could they exist in the ghost world?

Elizabeth had no idea how many Mediocrities had been "removed" or "transported" by these twin horrors. She just knew she didn't want to join them. Confused and frightened, she picked herself up at the last possible instant and did what the others were doing—she ran!

On a street parallel to the one Elizabeth was on, Makasha faced two other macabre creatures. One had a body with sharp spikes sticking out from it; he hugged his victims close. The other was a carrier of every disease ever known to devastate humans. He brought disease to those already dead with a mere breath.

A staggering number of Mediocrities fell before these two creatures and were transported to another place along the river in the ghost world. Makasha wondered if these beings were the ones he had sensed following them, the ones he thought were on their trail. But he didn't waste much time wondering. He took off with the fleeing Mediocrities.

One street over, Andy faced only a single strange being. Like a character from a horror movie, the corpselike man had bolts of lightning flying from his hands, mouth, and eyes. He lumbered steadily up the street, spewing sparks of destruction and sending a terrified horde of Mediocrities into flight, Andy with them.

Retracing their steps, Elizabeth, Makasha, and Andy met where they had parted. Together, they retreated up the street.

"And you're sure you didn't fall asleep, even for a second?" Elizabeth questioned Andy as they fled.

"Not a chance. I didn't even daydream."

"Then what are they?" she asked. "Where did they come from? And what do they want?"

"No matter now," Makasha said. "Must keep running."

The five gargoyles had met up also and converged behind them. One of them—the disease carrier—seemed to be pointing at Andy.

"What do they want with us?" Elizabeth asked anxiously.

Just then a bolt of lightning struck the

45

ground in front of Elizabeth's feet. It exploded there, sending a shower of dirt into the air. Andy and Makasha both grabbed Elizabeth by an arm and pulled her away from the smoldering crater.

An instant later, though, another bolt of lightning streaked at them, this one hitting a bush right next to Makasha. Splinters of wood ripped through the air, stinging and cutting the caveman's flesh.

"We've got to find shelter," Andy cried after they'd made it out of sight of the five monsters.

"Let's go in there!" Elizabeth shouted, pointing at Peter's hut. "Maybe they'll pass by if they don't know where we are."

They hurried to the door, which Makasha broke down with his shoulder. They were just about to rush inside when they heard the thunderous, deafening roar of a human voice. They paused to see who could have made such an incredible sound.

Scanning the streets, they saw nothing. That was because they were looking too low.

Andy caught on first and raised his eyes. Looking back the way they had come, Andy saw the giant head of a man come into view over a butte. And then with a lurch, the giant stepped around the butte, his entire body suddenly on display. Literally as tall as a mountain and dressed in a black eighteenth-century cutaway coat, he was a gargantuan figure who towered above everybody and everything.

"For the love of might, get me that boy!" bellowed the giant, his thirty-foot arm pointing down at Andy. "We need him!"

Elizabeth gasped. "It's—"

"Yeah," Andy said, pushing her into Peter's house. "It's Sir Aleck."

It wasn't long after Andy's arrival in the ghost world that he and Elizabeth had their first encounter with the then normal-size evil Englishman from the eighteenth century. He had captured and begun to torture Elizabeth, but she had been rescued by Andy. They didn't see Sir Aleck again until Andy dreamed up a mountain to plug the toxic-waste dump that had burned a hole between the living and the ghost worlds. Except before the mountain fell into place, Sir Aleck had entered the toxic tear, and when he stumbled out he was transfigured, transformed, and mutated. Sir Aleck, it seemed, blamed Andy for his misfortune and that of his men, who were also mutated.

The caveman did not know Sir Aleck, but he knew trouble when he saw it and dove into the house behind Andy and Elizabeth. A bolt of lightning exploding exactly at the spot where Makasha had just stood.

"Find a back door!" Elizabeth called out as soon as they were all inside.

"It's too dark," Andy complained. "I can't

see where I'm going." With that, he bumped into a chair, stumbled, and bounced off a wall, barely managing to stay on his feet.

"It's this way," offered a familiar but very nervous voice.

"Peter? Is that you?" Elizabeth asked.

A figure stepped out of the shadows, a sad face illuminated by the light streaming in through the window. "Yes, it's me," Peter sheepishly replied.

"What are you doing here?" Andy asked, surprised.

"I live here."

"Yeah, but I thought—"

"That I was going to report you?"

Andy hesitated.

"You don't have to say it," Peter said matter-of-factly. "I know it's true."

"No time talk now," Makasha said urgently as he peered out the window. "They come. The big one might step on house. Must go."

With Peter's help, they quickly slipped out the back door, running beside a tall ridge of bushes that temporarily hid them from sight. At least it hid them until they had to seek shelter across the street.

"There!" boomed Sir Aleck, stepping forward and pointing his huge forefinger in their direction. "The rapscallions are moving to your left. Don't lose them!" he yelled to his men.

Andy was the only one huffing and puffing when they stopped to see if they were being followed. The first thing they noticed, though, was that they were now four instead of three. Peter had come with them.

"What are you doing?" Elizabeth demanded of the older man. "Those *things* are after *us*. When we take off again, you'd better head to wherever the rest of the villagers hid."

Peter shook his head. "Can't do it. Dug out my old clothes, the ones I died in."

Andy focused on the fact that Peter was wearing worn jeans, a cowboy shirt, and dirty white sneakers without any socks. "If my fellow Mediocrities see me like this," Peter explained, "I'll be no better off than if those *things* catch me. I'm thinking of making some changes, so I'll stick with you."

"You're out of your mind," Andy said.

"Maybe. But at least I'm not mediocre." Suddenly, though, a stab of doubt struck him and he self-consciously added, "Well, uh, at least I *hope* I'm not."

"They're coming our way," Elizabeth said worriedly, her voice as taut as an *E* string on a violin.

"This is hopeless," Andy complained. "We'll never lose them as long as Sir Aleck can point us out."

"That why we no longer run away," Makasha announced.

"What? You mean we're going to fight them?" Andy asked, the fear painfully apparent in his voice. He was instantly embarrassed. Trying to recoup, he quickly went on, saying, "I mean, if you—uh—think that's the best thing to—"

"You crazier than him," Makasha said, gesturing contemptuously at Peter. "Fight them be like sledgehammer on robin's egg. We be egg. Get the yolk?"

Elizabeth punched the caveman in the arm. "This is no time for comedy," she said shrilly. "They're crossing the street! They're coming straight toward us! What are we going to do?"

# CHAPTER 7

"EACH ALONE, WE CIRCLE BACK TO PETER'S house," Makasha commanded. "We scatter—make it hard for giant to see all of us. But not yet. Wait till evil ones are closer."

"They're across the street already," Elizabeth whispered, staring through the hedges. "Isn't that close enough?"

"Not yet."

"But they're looking around, edging this way."

"Not yet."

"They've seen something on the grass. Maybe it's our footprints. They're coming this way fast!"

"Not yet."

"Makasha?" Elizabeth pleaded.

"Not yet. Want them close so when we run they no have chance to cut us off."

Andy glanced at Peter and saw that the sad-faced man was quivering with fear. Andy couldn't blame him—he was shaking, too. So was Elizabeth, though Andy saw that she had balled her hands into fists so no one would see her trembling fingers. Only Makasha seemed impassive and unafraid. Andy wondered how much man had really evolved in a hundred thousand years.

The five gargoyles had gotten so close that Elizabeth was too scared to speak or even gesture. That's when Makasha shouted, "Now!"

Peter jumped to his feet, turned, and ran with his back to the five mutants as fast as his legs would carry him.

Makasha ran to the right.

Elizabeth to the left.

Andy didn't move. Not at first. He watched as Sir Aleck's men, who had been bunched close together, reacted to the sight of their prey on the run. Their group broke apart also, two of them coming forward toward the hedges, while two others began running after Elizabeth, and one started after Makasha. As the gap between the mutated ghosts widened, Andy, like a football player seeing a hole in the line, made his choice to try to run right through it. After all, he reasoned, the fastest way to get behind them was to run past them.

If he could make it.

Andy broke through the hedges as if he had been shot from a cannon. The man whose body glinted like diamonds was closest to him, but Andy surged past him so fast that the blinding effect was minimal. Right behind the diamond man, though, was the beastly being with spikes. It was he who had the better chance of grabbing Andy.

Except that the diamond man spun around as Andy flew by him. The bright, glittering reflection from his body shone like white fire in the eyes of the spike creature, who flinched and had to cover his eyes with one hand. With his other hand he swiped wildly at Andy, who easily dodged him and headed across the street.

''I want the boy!'' bellowed Sir Aleck from above. ''Forget the others! Go after the boy!''

The three remaining mutants were spread out on either side of Andy. They stopped chasing Elizabeth and Makasha and ran back to head Andy off before he disappeared behind a row of indistinguishable houses set back from the street.

The sallow disease carrier had the clearest shot at him. All it would take to bring Andy down was a fingertip on his living skin or the breathing in of the same air that the man breathed out. Coming at him from Andy's left, the disease carrier was fast closing the distance between the two of them. The mutant had gauged their respective speeds perfectly; he raced at an angle that was bringing him directly in Andy's path.

Watching his pursuer out of the corner of his eye, Andy tried not to panic. Keep thinking football, he told himself. Make believe it's a game.

If it was a game, than it was supposed to be fun. And part of the fun of open field running in a football game is trying to fake out the opponents. Andy was going to try. If he failed, he'd be faking himself out of his life.

Timing was everything. Andy waited until they were just a few yards apart and the mutant had started to reach out to touch him. . . .

Pretending to cut to his right, Andy feinted with his head and right shoulder.

The mutant went for it, changing his own angle to compensate for the direction in which he thought Andy was heading. Once committed, the disease carrier lurched sharply to his right.

That was when Andy suddenly spun halfway around and cut sharply and cleanly to his left. The mutant zoomed past his intended victim. And Andy streaked away far from him, a wide grin on his face.

Legs churning, Andy kept on running. He had crossed the street and was just about to run underneath some trees between two houses when someone yelled, "I'll get him!"

It was the lightning creature, who didn't mean he'd tackle Andy. Pointing his finger at the fleeing teenager, he was about to let loose a spark when Sir Aleck thundered so that the ground itself shook with his words. "No! Don't kill him! We want him alive!"

In a heartbeat Andy reached the cover of the trees. Sir Aleck couldn't see him anymore. And once he circled behind the row of houses he had reached, the rest of the giant's henchmen had lost sight of him, too. He had made it to safety.

Moving swiftly, yet staying under cover, Andy worked his way back to Peter's house. He figured he'd be the first one to get there, but he was wrong. Peter, who had fled in the exact opposite direction, and who should have been the last to return, was waiting inside.

"How'd you get here so fast?" Andy questioned.

"You're not thinking like a Mediocrity," Peter answered with a half smile. "Mediocre people worry a lot. They're really more careful than people like you and your friends— they don't take chances. They think, 'What if this bad thing happens? What if that bad thing happens? What will we do?' "

"So?"

"So they worry that someday the lake next

to the village might overflow and wash away their homes. So they dig drainage tunnels under the town, so the water will have a place to go. I took a tunnel here.''

''Where do the drainage tunnels lead?'' Andy asked.

''Back to the lake, of course.''

Andy snapped his fingers. ''Perfect!''

The plan was simple. They sneaked out of the house to the nearest entrance of a drainage tunnel. Once inside the dark, dry passageway, they made their way toward the lake. The ground above them reverberated with every movement made by the giant.

Dirt began cascading down from the roof of the tunnel.

''Do you think it'll collapse?'' Elizabeth asked Andy in a hushed voice, afraid that if she made a loud noise, she might, herself, cause a cave-in.

''I wouldn't be surprised,'' he answered nervously. ''After all, it was built by the Mediocre.''

''Say no more,'' Elizabeth said with a shudder. ''Let's get out of here as soon as we can.''

More dirt fell from the tunnel roof, but the structure held.

Makasha kept his silence through all of this,

stoically squeezing his bulk through the narrow chamber.

"Shouldn't we have reached the escape opening to the surface yet?" Andy wondered aloud.

"Soon," Peter replied.

But not soon enough. The earth shook again as Sir Aleck angrily stomped the ground above them. The force of his footfall caused the tunnel to cave in—right in front of them!

# CHAPTER

THE TUNNEL FELL IN FROM THE ROOF. TONS of earth and rock poured down in front of their startled and terrified eyes. But the tunnel only collapsed in front of them, not on top of them. Nonetheless, the avalanche barred their way—until they saw something move in the debris.

What they saw was Sir Aleck's leather-booted foot as it lifted out of the tunnel. He left a crater, a crater out of which they quickly climbed. Their luck was holding. They were exactly where they wanted to be: directly under Sir Aleck, not where he or any of his sidekicks would ever think to look for them. They had only to remain unseen long enough to slip behind Sir Aleck and circle around the side of the lake. At that point they'd have reached the butte at the far end of the valley. Once they put the butte between themselves and Sir Aleck, everything would be all right.

There was just one thing they hadn't counted on: the Mediocrities fighting back. Elizabeth saw them first, a long line of gray people who, despite their lack of imagination, were not totally lacking in courage when their homes were at risk. Sure, it took them a while to organize, but even mediocre leaders are better than none in a crisis. Finally, and ferociously, they counterattacked the monstrous mutations that had invaded their village.

The battle that followed should have provided the perfect diversion for the four people who stood near Sir Aleck's right foot. At first they saw it that way, too. The problem was that the battle was horribly one-sided. The Mediocrities had no weapons to equal the arsenal of destructive power wielded by Sir Aleck and his bunch.

A strange look crossed Andy's face. He turned to look at the others and said, "I know this is ridiculous. I know that these people— these Mediocrities—are just ghosts, that they can't be killed, that they're just going to reappear somewhere else in this world, but I can't stand what's happening to them. It's wrong. I guess what I'm trying to say is, I can't turn my back on them and run away. I've got to help."

Elizabeth's first reaction was fear. She didn't want to lose Andy in a hopeless cause. She also felt enormous pride—she was proud to know him, proud to call him her friend. In that moment she wondered if she actually loved him. Even if he didn't love her back, she decided then and there to stand shoulder to shoulder with him and do the right thing.

Meanwhile, Makasha took Andy's right hand in his own and pumped it up and down. "You have makings of good Neanderthal man," he offered. "You no run away from fight."

Peter, however, felt different. "You can't do anything to help them," he said, gesturing at the slaughter that continued at the edge of the village. "None of us can. We should get away while the getting is good."

"Now you're thinking like a Mediocrity again," Andy gently chastized Peter. "Maybe with a little imagination we can think of a way to help them."

"Like what?" challenged Peter.

Put on the spot, Andy pursed his lips and studied the battle. The Mediocrities, by sheer force of their stolid will, had pushed forward despite terrible losses. They had driven Sir Aleck's five henchmen to a point on the shoreline of the lake that jutted out close to the village. So far, Sir Aleck himself had not bothered to take part in the massacre. He was too busy scanning the village for any sign of Andy.

"I'm not saying we can defeat these freaks," Andy finally said. "But we could make a difference by at least turning off the juice of that lightning-bolt guy. All we've got to do is knock him into the lake. Last I heard, water and electricity don't mix, and he's pretty close to the water's edge. What do you say?"

"I say count me out," Peter answered firmly. "You got me thinking about the hopes I once had for myself. Well, I decided to leave here so I could do something about those lost hopes. I can't let anything stand in my way now. I'm going."

He got no argument from the other three. They thanked him for his help and said goodbye, all this right under the nose of Sir Aleck. That, however, was soon going to change.

As soon as Peter was gone, Andy, Elizabeth, and Makasha crawled among the stunted trees and high reeds that grew along the shore of the lake. Hidden there, they worked their way closer to the five mutants who had chosen to retreat toward the water's edge. In that way, none of the Mediocrities could sneak up behind them. Convinced that there was no danger from that direction, the mutants ignored the slight bit of movement they should have noticed in the reeds.

Andy found a long tree branch floating just an arm's length beyond the shore. He reached out and grabbed it, causing only a small ripple in the water.

He crawled closer to the lightning-bolt mutant. When he lifted his head above the reeds to get his bearings, Andy saw that he was just ten feet from him. Quickly he ducked back down, fearing he might be spotted.

He was. But not by any of the mutants—not even by Sir Aleck. Several Mediocrities saw him and excitedly began pointing and shouting. Trying to distract an enemy by pretending someone was behind him was the oldest trick in the book, a cliché so obvious that only a Mediocrity would think to try it. At least that's what the lightning-bolt mutant must have thought. Not bothering to glance back over his shoulder, he laughed at the Mediocrities' pitiful attempt to fool him. He sent a quarter of a million volts of electricity streaking at them in five bolts of lightning. In a flash the Mediocrities were vaporized.

As the echoing thunder of the lightning strikes died down, Andy crawled as fast as he could on his hands and knees toward his target. He wasn't sure whether Elizabeth and Makasha were behind him, but he knew this was going to be his only chance, so he took it. When he thought he was close enough, Andy took a deep breath, jumped to his feet

—and realized with gut-wrenching terror that he had overshot his mark. He wasn't behind the mutant, he had jumped up in front of him!

Even the mutant was startled for an instant. But not for long. As Andy thrust the point of his branch at the chest of his enemy, the mutant raised his right hand to send a bolt of lightning at Andy's head. Sir Aleck's warning to take the boy alive meant nothing to him now. He reacted out of a warrior's instinct to kill.

Another warrior, however, took action even faster. An ancient stone ax thrown by Makasha, who had had a thousand centuries to practice his aim, struck the mutant square in the back before the blue bolt of death could be unleashed. Though the stone blade dug deep into the mutant's back, it did no more than surprise him. He was not seriously hurt. But he did make the mistake of temporarily turning his attention from Andy to check who had thrown the weapon. Andy kept his concentration and finished what he had started. He jammed the end of the branch hard against the mutant's chest and knocked the deadly menace off his feet, sending him sprawling backward.

As the mutant fell into the lake, he howled his rage at Andy. Out of his mouth came not curses but lightning. Andy would have been crackling embers if Elizabeth hadn't immediately tackled him. The lightning bolts sizzled through the air over their heads as they hit the ground.

There was a splash, immediately followed by the loudest ZZZZZING imaginable. The water, from one end of the lake to the other, / roiled with streaks of blue, red, orange, and yellow, turning the surface into a prism of liquid light. Then the water began to boil madly, until an awesome explosion from somewhere deep below sent a geyser of water shooting more than a mile into the sky. The top of the geyser soared high above even Sir Aleck's head.

The Mediocrities cheered the defeat of one of their enemies and pressed on.

The four remaining mutants were unnerved by the suprise loss of their comrade and the surging army of villagers who continued to charge them. They began to retreat along the edge of the waterfront, heading in the direction of Andy, Elizabeth, and Makasha.

Intending to hide from them, the threesome dove back into the reeds again and began crawling toward Sir Aleck's feet. What they didn't know was that the giant had seen their battle with the lightning mutant and had spotted Andy. Hiding from Sir Aleck was now no longer possible.

Oblivious to the full degree of their danger,

Makasha good-naturedly whispered to Andy, "You sure 'shock' bad man back there."

Andy smiled.

Elizabeth crawled up beside Andy and added, "Yeah, like a 'bolt out of the blue,' that guy's plans got totally 'short-circuited.' "

Andy joined in, saying, "Well, I've got to admit, this whole thing has been an 'electrifying' experience."

They stopped crawling and muffled their laughter until Makasha suddenly raised his head from the ground. "Shhhh." He put a finger to his lips. "I think I hear something in reeds."

The caveman couldn't quite identify the sound. It wasn't anything like footsteps or even crawling. It was something else, something different—something they hadn't foreseen. . . .

# CHAPTER

## 9

A DARK SHADOW, LIKE A SHROUD, BLOTTED out the light that had filtered through the reeds. Then the threesome heard it again, the sound of something moving through the undergrowth, ripping right through it and getting closer. They had no idea what was happening. Whatever it was, though, they knew it was trouble. And they were right.

Then they saw the gargantuan fingers sweep through the reeds next to them like a comb through thick hair. The outside edge of Sir Aleck's pinkie grazed Makasha's side. The force of it lifted him up out of the cover of the reeds, sending him spinning over Elizabeth's and Andy's heads. He landed at the very edge of the still-boiling lake. He missed falling in the scalding water by only a couple of feet.

Sir Aleck felt something touch his little finger and then saw the caveman fall. He could have easily reached down and crushed the stunned Neanderthal, but he didn't care about Makasha. It was Andy who he wanted, and he knew that the living one had to be close by. He knelt again and feverishly ran his fingers through the same area of reeds again.

He came up empty.

Andy and Elizabeth had moved away by then, crawling toward the fallen Makasha. It took all their combined strength to pull the caveman off the shoreline and into the reeds. Luckily, he wasn't hurt—he'd only had the wind knocked out of him. "Can you run?" Andy asked him.

Disoriented and breathing with difficulty, Makasha managed to nod. After a pause he wheezed, "Which way?"

It was a good question.

The four retreating mutants had seen Makasha's short flight, and they were closing in from one side. Sir Aleck blocked the other direction. The giant's searching fingers could appear from anywhere, the only warning given as the palm of his hand blotted out the light.

"We'll run toward Sir Aleck," Andy said boldly. "It makes the most sense. If we run the other way, we've got to get past four mutants and the Mediocrities. If we run toward Sir Aleck, we might be able to slip past him. We've got a chance to get clean away."

"Let's do it," Elizabeth said.

They helped Makasha to his feet. Then the three of them took off, racing in a low crouch through the undergrowth as fast as they could. Though their heads were not above the reeds, their movement was plainly obvious to Sir Aleck. What he could not see, however, was which one of the three figures scurrying wildly through the undergrowth was the living one he so desperately sought.

He swooped his gigantic hand down through the reeds to pick up one of the small figures. . . .

Elizabeth saw the hand descend. She glanced over her shoulder and saw fingers raking through the reeds behind her. When they were almost on top of her, she dove to the ground, head first, skidding through the mud. The fingers swept over her, coming up empty.

Angry at missing his victim, Sir Aleck closed his huge fist and banged it angrily on the ground. The earth shook with the pounding.

Another figure scurried past his foot and was almost behind Sir Aleck when the giant cupped his hand and swung it down, hoping to capture his prey. . . .

The swinging hand came down so hard and fast that Makasha could hear the wind whistle through the openings between the giant's fingers. Forewarned, he jumped out of the way, crashing into Elizabeth, who had decided it was safer to crawl on her hands and knees.

Elizabeth asked, "Have you seen Andy?"

"No."

The ground shook violently as the giant stepped away from them and closer to the village.

"Why is he doing that?" she said anxiously. "Do you think he spotted Andy?"

"Don't know."

"But you don't think so, do you?" she asked worriedly, taking a chance to lift her head above the top of the reeds to look for Andy.

Makasha pulled her down. "You no help him by making trouble with giant."

"Who's making trouble with the giant?" Andy asked as he silently pushed his way through the reeds.

"Nobody I know," Elizabeth answered with a broad smile. The relief on her face was as plain as the embarrassment on the caveman's.

Andy grinned. "Surprised that I could get so close without you hearing me, aren't you, Makasha?"

Red-faced, the great Neanderthal hunter admitted it was true.

"Hey, don't feel bad," Andy said, stifling a laugh. "I was there the whole time. You guys just missed me when you crashed into each other."

"Then why didn't you let us know you were there?" Elizabeth asked sharply.

"Just curious."

"About what?"

"About what you might say," he said sheepishly. "I wanted to know if you were thinking about me."

"Gee, did we say anything about Andy?" she asked Makasha, pretending she couldn't remember.

"Who's Andy?" the caveman replied.

"Very funny. And now, if you two jokers are finished, maybe we could get out of here, huh?"

"Why not?" Elizabeth exclaimed. "We're behind Sir Aleck now. We're free and clear."

With that, they set off for the base of the nearby butte, being careful to stay hidden in the reeds. But the reeds thinned out as they moved away from the lake and closer to the towering butte. They planned to cut right along the base of the butte and get behind it as soon as they could. Though it seemed as if they'd never get there, after trudging for more than an hour they were finally about to turn the corner and put the whole valley, the Mediocrities, and especially Sir Aleck and his crew behind them.

That was when the earth shook once, twice,

three times, each of Sir Aleck's booming foot-falls louder than the one before. He must have moved off on purpose, hoping that Andy would grow careless and show himself.

The gamble paid off.

Beyond the lake, near the base of the butte, there was little cover for hiding. In a few short seconds Sir Aleck's humongous strides spanned the same distance it had taken the threesome a full hour to walk.

Except now they weren't walking anymore—they were running, out in the open, fully exposed to Sir Aleck's gaze.

"This way!" shouted a familiar voice up ahead.

"Look!" Elizabeth cried out. "Over there, at the side of the butte. It's Peter!"

"Hurry!" screamed the sad-faced man. "Follow me!"

They reached Peter at the base of the butte and, running right behind him, turned at a sharp angle to put the rock face between themselves and Sir Aleck.

It was only a temporary salvation.

The giant leaned down low and peered over a pile of boulders at the edge of the butte. One huge, monstrous eye watched as they ran headlong through a rock-strewn maze of broken stones.

Finally, taking one more small step, Sir Aleck eased around the base of the butte and reached down, hoping to scoop Andy off the ground.

"We're almost there!" Peter shouted, urging the others on behind him. "You'll soon be safe! I promise!"

"Where?" Andy called out breathlessly, his side aching and his legs heavy and cramping.

"Just behind these rocks. You'll see!"

They swerved past the rocks and into a cloud of black mist that offered them shelter in its impenetrable darkness.

Peter was the first to disappear inside the black cloud, Makasha only a half step behind. Elizabeth, with Andy not far behind her, hit the cloud with her arms open wide like a runner breaking the tape at the finish line. She kept right on running through the inky darkness until she heard Makasha call out, "No more run. Come to your right. I guide you by sound of your steps."

She did as she was told, making her way through the mist like a blind person until she eventually touched Makasha's face. Peter was there, too, and Elizabeth wasted no time in thanking him.

"Forget it," he said. "I saw you guys take on that lightning mutant and beat him. I didn't think you could do it. When you did, I said to myself, 'Peter Washburn, you should have been there. You could've written a play about it and then starred in the production.' And, you know, maybe someday I will.''

"I hope so," Elizabeth said toward the direction of Peter's voice. Then she finally asked what was on her mind. "What is this cloud we're in? Is it dangerous?"

"No. I think it's ghost night. It's very rare."

"But there's no night here."

"That's why it's so rare."

"You're kidding me."

"He tells truth," the caveman uttered in the darkness. "Me, Makasha, saw ghost night before two times."

"Then this is really it?" Peter said.

Makasha grunted.

"What are you talking about?" Elizabeth demanded. "I never saw a ghost night or even heard of one before."

"You not ghost very long," Makasha said. "Much to see and learn here."

"I only heard about it once," Peter explained. "The way it was described to me was that, in the living world, every once in a while, something truly spectacular happens on earth during the night. It's a time when the night itself seems to come alive. When that night ends, when it dies in the morning, the dark comes here. It turns into a fine black mist, the ghost of a night that does not want to end. But it does slowly fade away—even here."

Elizabeth swept her gaze all around, seeing nothing but the blackness. Yet it was not a fearful, spooky darkness. Not at all. The cloud gave her comfort. There was a coziness and special warmth there; a sense of belonging.

"Andy," she whispered. "Do you feel it?"

No answer.

"Andy?"

"Andy no here yet," Makasha said.

"But he was right behind me when I ran into the ghost night. He has to be here."

"No here."

"Okay, I get it, Andy," she called out into the darkness. "You're playing games again, right? Well, if you think I'm going to say a single nice thing about you, you've got another thing coming."

Silence.

"Andy!"

Silence.

"Andy?"

# CHAPTER
## 10

HIS MOUTH BONE-DRY, HIS HEART POUNDING like a jackhammer, Andy watched as the others vanished into the black mist. He was right behind Elizabeth, struggling to keep up with her.

Andy's legs ached almost as much as the stitch in his side. No question about it, he thought, it'd be good to be a ghost if you were a marathon runner. You'd never get tired. And I'll be a ghost soon enough, he told himself with lungs burning, because I'm just about ready to drop dead from exhaustion.

Death *was* close, but not from exhaustion. Just as Elizabeth disappeared into the dark cloud, something that seemed like a wall fell out of the sky between him and the black mist, blocking his way. Andy tried to stop, jamming his heels into the ground. When he did, a muscle in his left leg spasmed and he went down like a tree that had just been felled. He grabbed at his leg to ease the pain.

As he rubbed the knot out of his calf, he saw that the "wall" that had come down in front of him was moving toward him, encircling him. It was Sir Aleck's hand!

Lying there helpless, alone, unable to run, Andy was plucked up off the ground. Sir Aleck gave an exultant cry—he had his prize.

"We've got to find Andy," Elizabeth said firmly.

Peter couldn't believe his ears. "With those creatures out there? Are you crazy?"

"He's my friend," she said simply. But the way she said it implied much more than friendship. Makasha heard it and his heart went out to her.

"That's your decision," Peter said coolly. "I wish you luck. Me? I have unfinished business. I was on my way somewhere when I lost my courage and ended up staying with the Mediocrities. Thanks to you, I got my courage back. I did what I could for you, but now, I think I'll pick up the trail again and finish what I started. Or at least I'll try. If I stop now, I might never do it. You know what I mean?"

"I know," Elizabeth said. "You helped us

a lot. Good luck—and I hope you find what you're looking for."

"Thanks."

Turning in the darkness, she spoke to the caveman, saying, "Will you come with me, Makasha?"

"Foolish question," was all he said.

They didn't wait for the ghost night to fade. Instead, Peter took off in one direction and Elizabeth and Makasha set out in another, all of them leaving the memory of one wonderful dark night on earth that slowly drifted off into oblivion.

It didn't take long for Makasha to find Andy's tracks in the dirt. He saw where Andy had fallen. And it took even less time to see that Andy had never walked away from that place. The only logical explanation was that Sir Aleck had picked him up off the ground.

If it was relatively easy finding Andy's footprints, it was ridiculously simple to find Sir Aleck's. They were twelve feet long and nearly four feet wide and left deep craters in the soft earth. In other words, one almost had to be unconscious not to be able to follow him. Being dead, of course, was no excuse.

Following was one thing, catching up was another. Sir Aleck had a head start and each of his steps almost covered an acre. One thing was clear: the trail was taking them toward the great river that flowed throughout the ghost world.

Elizabeth and Makasha might never have caught up to the giant if he hadn't traveled slowly enough for his fellow mutants to keep up with him. Even so, it took a long time before they spotted Sir Aleck bobbing in and out of the white mist that rose off the river. After several hours of keeping the mutant in sight, Elizabeth noticed that he was suddenly half his size.

"Look! He shrunk!" Elizabeth exclaimed.

"You make 'giant' mistake," Makasha replied slyly.

"What are you saying?"

"Giant get smaller because he sit down. Now we catch up quick, like Heinz."

"Heinz—*catch-up?*"

Makasha laughed. "You get joke! Good."

"Since when does a Neanderthal man know about ketchup?" she said, shaking her head in disbelief.

"Know much about ketchup," he answered proudly. "Know it come in twenty-eight flavors. Melts in your mouth, not in your hands. Good stuff. Put hair on chest."

Elizabeth doubled over with laughter, finally supporting herself by leaning on Makasha. When she got herself under control, the caveman innocently asked, "What so funny?"

She didn't think she'd ever stop laughing.

Finally, though, she managed to gasp, "I can't wait to tell Andy this. He's going to go wild."

Makasha smiled at her. "Good plan. We go save Andy. Then you tell him Makasha funny man. Okay?"

Her eyes shining, she met his gaze and firmly said, "Okay."


Sir Aleck's massive face hovered close to Andy's. It was like a face in a close-up shot in a movie viewed from the first row. His breath was like a hot, putrid wind. The wildness in his eyes was that of a madman. And whenever he spoke the sound reverberated like thunder.

"You saved the ghost world with your living magic," Sir Aleck bellowed. "You did it because your heart beats, because you're alive, because you can do things here that no ghost can do—not even mutants like us. You did it for the Guardian. The whole ghost world knows about it. These things cannot be kept quiet. The Guardian is sending you back to the living world to resume your life. And do you know what you're going to do?"

Andy shook his head.

"Then I'll tell you," Sir Aleck announced. "You're going to take me and my mates with you."

"I can't," Andy blurted out. "I can't even get myself back."

"Liar!" boomed the giant, nearly deafening his prisoner. Andy flinched but couldn't really move. He looked and saw how he was staked out lying on his back. Each of the four normal-size mutants had a rope tied around his waist; the other end of each rope was tied around one of Andy's limbs. A fifth rope linked Sir Aleck's little finger to Andy's waist. Andy wasn't going anywhere without the five mutants.

"The Guardian has powers," thundered Sir Aleck. "You have powers. I saw how you brought the mountain down out of the sky to seal the hole between the two worlds. No, you're going back to your life and you're taking us with you!"

"I can't do it!" Andy repeated. "Don't you think I'd have left already if I could?"

The giant paused. The other mutants glanced up at their leader with questioning expressions. Slowly Sir Aleck's puzzled look changed to a knowing smirk. "You almost fooled me," he admitted. "But I have figured out why you haven't left—it's because of the girl. You won't leave without her. That must be it." The smirk on his face twisted until it became evil. "Maybe I made a mistake in capturing just you," he said. "Yes, maybe you would be far more cooperative if she were my captive, too."

80

"You keep Elizabeth out of this!" Andy shot back.

"You doth protest too much," Sir Aleck mocked.

Andy closed his eyes, realizing he had foolishly sent the wrong message to the giant. "Look," he finally said with a sigh, "it's true I like Elizabeth. And it's true I'm trying to get home and the Guardian is trying to help me. But even if I find out how to return home, that doesn't mean I can bring you back with me."

"Enough! I am not debating this. I am telling you! Return us to the living world. We will live again with the powers and strengths we now possess. We will be brought back to life. Do it now!"

Andy didn't think of himself as brave. He just did what he had to do. Though he was terrified, he managed to sound brave because he had no alternative. "I'm not taking you back," Andy declared. "Even if I could, I wouldn't. Do you think I'd want it on my conscience that I brought creeps like you back to the living world? Do you think—"

"Save your speeches! Make them when you're a ghost. Which, if you don't change your mind, will be very soon indeed. But not before you first suffer the most exquisite agony. Feel free," Sir Aleck added sarcastically, "to change your mind at any time while you are being tortured."

Sir Aleck motioned to one of his followers. "Show the boy what a 'burning' need we have to change his stubborn mind," he said to the man whose fingers dripped acid.

As the mutant moved closer, the clear liquid that fell from his fingertips sizzled and bubbled when it splashed on the ground. Andy's eyes went wide.

# CHAPTER 11

PSSSHHHH. A DROP OF ACID SPLASHED ON the dry grass just six inches from Andy's right ear. The brown grass instantly turned black. But it didn't stop there. The sizzling continued, burning right down through dirt and rock until there was a hole one inch in diameter and six inches deep.

"That acid will bore a hole through your skull and into your brain," Sir Aleck said. "You had best transport us back to your world now, while you still can."

Andy shut his eyes as tight as he could and clenched his teeth. The pain would begin soon, and he wanted to be ready for it.

The mutant's right hand was nearly directly over Andy's head now, a droplet of acid beading on his fingertip, ready to fall.

83

"Open your eyes," the mutant said in a hushed voice that carried more than a hint of menace. Compared to Sir Aleck's voice, though, his was reassuring or at least different. Andy opened his eyes and saw the droplet poised to fall on his forehead.

The mutant flicked his finger. Gravity took over. The drop of acid broke loose from his fingertip—and total terror gripped Andy. He screamed.

The acid struck an inch above his head, burning through the edges of his splayed-out hair and then eating its way down into the ground.

The mutants laughed, enjoying the power they held over Andy.

"I must have moved my finger too much," the acid mutant said in mock apology. "I'll try again."

"What do you say, my fine, young, living gentleman?" Sir Aleck offered Andy. "Should he 'try again,' or will you give us what we want?"

Andy screwed up all the courage he had left—which wasn't much—and spit back, "You guys were losers when you were alive, and you're still losers. Stuff it!"

"Burn him!" thundered Sir Aleck.

The mutant began raising his hand over Andy's head again but stopped in midmotion to cry out, "Fire!"

Flames swept across the dry grass like an oncoming tidal wave. The fire was more than two hundred yards away, yet it was bearing down on them relentlessly, the wind already raining black cinders down on them in warning.

The mutant with the spikes sticking out of his body took the warning and cut the rope binding him to Andy—and he fled.

Sir Aleck roared at him to come back, but the fire roared louder, the wind pushing it toward the mutant encampment. It was only one hundred yards away.

The three remaining mutants figured their leader would soon have to run, but he, with his huge legs, could get away from the fire much faster than they could. They needed a head start and took it. They cut their ropes and ran.

The fire was only seventy-five yards away and showed no sign of slowing.

Elizabeth waited, fear gnawing at her. She lay in her hiding place, a shallow pit covered with a thick layer of sod that she had built right under the noses of Sir Aleck and his mutant crew. She was downriver from their camp, but very close to it. Close enough to hear Andy's earlier bloodcurdling scream.

She and Makasha had come up with a good

plan, but she was afraid they wouldn't have enough time to pull it off.

Peeking out of her hiding place, she saw that Makasha, on the far side of Sir Aleck's camp, had finally started the grass fire. When the mutants ran right over her sod-covered dugout, Elizabeth got so excited that their plan was working that she almost thought her heart started to beat. The only problem was that Sir Aleck had not fled the fire.

When the giant saw his men fleeing, he cursed them all. But it *did* change his mind about escaping himself. The difference was, he did not cut the rope between him and Andy. The giant intended to take Andy with him. He reached down to pick up his prize.

Sir Aleck did not finish the movement. Makasha had hauled himself out of his pit similar to the one Elizabeth was hiding in. The fire was almost upon him, but that didn't stop him from throwing a new-made ax straight and true. It slammed into the back of the giant's hand. Reacting only as if he had been stung by a bee, Sir Aleck shook the hand, wresting the primitive stone weapon free, and brought the stinging wound to his lips. Then he spun around to see who had thrown the ax. He saw no one. Makasha had ducked back into his pit, and a moment later the oncoming fire roared safely over his hiding place.

All that Sir Aleck saw was the blazing grass fire cutting across the dry grass right toward him. It was now less than fifty yards away and consuming everything in its path.

The giant, perplexed at not locating the source of the attack, took a couple of small steps in the direction of the fire. The flames leapt up at him, singeing his black coat. Whoever threw that ax, he reasoned, had to have been consumed by the fire. He didn't want to be the flames next victim. Sir Aleck turned and pulled on his rope to drag Andy toward him. . . .

The instant Sir Aleck had turned to look for Makasha, Elizabeth took her one and only chance. With the giant's back to her, she leapt out of her hiding place and sprinted the short distance to the mutant camp. Elizabeth reached Andy and, with a knife Makasha had given her, slashed the rope that was tied around his waist.

"I can't believe it," Andy said, staring into Elizabeth's eyes.

"Hey, you look like you've just seen a ghost," she quipped, helping him up.

"You're getting as bad as Makasha," he replied happily, racing with her to her hiding place. They dove into it and pulled the sod cover over the top, leaving an opening for

Andy to breathe. Just then Sir Aleck tugged on his rope and found that it had been cut.

The giant appeared to be in shock, frantically searching everywhere for Andy. The fire licked at his legs. Sir Aleck had no choice. He retreated—and kept on retreating to find his men.

Sir Aleck had been defeated—for the moment.


Grass fires cover a great deal of land and they burn hot. They do not, however, last long. Once the grass is consumed there is nothing left to feed the flames and they die out. Makasha emerged from his pit after the fire exhausted itself, retrieved his ax, and rejoined Andy and Elizabeth.

Andy had asked what had happened to Peter.

Elizabeth finished telling him, and summed it up by saying, "Peter Washburn was no Mediocrity."

Something clicked inside Andy's head. "Washburn? Was that his last name?"

"Yeah. Why?"

"Oh, no! My mother's maiden name was Washburn. She had an older brother who died when I was a little kid. She used to tell me all about my Uncle Pete. That had to be him! That's the person from my past that the Guardian said I had to find. How stupid can I be?

He was right in our hands and now he's gone!"

"Left him many miles ago," Makasha noted solemnly. "Trail be old and hard to find."

We've got to track him down," Andy said desperately. "We've just got to. If we don't, I'll be stuck in the ghost world forever!"

# CHAPTER 12

"HE WAS OLDER THAN MY MOM," ANDY explained as they tracked Peter through stark, hilly country. "My mother rarely talks about him. When she does, she always says, 'It wasn't the sickness that killed him, it was the sadness.' When I asked her what she meant, she said, 'Your Uncle Pete always wanted to be an actor but he finally gave up.' The way I remember it, Uncle Pete tried acting for a while, but never got anywhere. According to my mom, he was miserable for the rest of his life."

"Do you think our Peter is really him?" Elizabeth asked. "Does he look anything like your mom?"

Andy shrugged. "I wasn't looking at him

with that in mind, so I really don't know. But maybe a little. Or maybe I'm just trying to convince myself. With my luck, we probably won't find him again, anyway."

"Hey, don't think like that. We'll find him, won't we Makasha?" Elizabeth said, wanting the caveman to reassure Andy.

"Uh—don't know," Makasha tentatively replied, sounding more worried than Elizabeth could remember.

"What's the matter?'

"Peter go where we cannot follow."

They had come to the crest of a hill that swept down and away from the great river. The lush landscape was far different from the sparse, rocky ground they had just traveled. Nonetheless, Makasha stared, looking strangely unnerved to both Andy and Elizabeth.

"What are you talking about?" Andy said. "Why can't we follow him? I mean, I'm just a junior in high school and the only tracking I've ever done is on my parents' VCR, but even I can read Peter's tracks in that thick green grass."

"Can track. Just can't go."

"Why?"

"Down there," he said, gesturing, "is Valley of Fears."

Elizabeth, who had taken a couple of steps down the slope, instantly jumped back up to the top of the hill to rejoin the others. "Makasha's right," she said nervously. "It's too dangerous to go in there."

"But Peter went that way," he pointed out. "And I'm supposed to help Peter. The Guardian said so. Besides, I don't see anything down there that we ought to be afraid of. I mean, what's the big deal?"

Elizabeth licked her lips and took a deep breath. "Down there, everything you fear can—and very well might—come to 'life.' There isn't a more dangerous place in all of the ghost world. It would be a terrible mistake to go down there. We'll have to circle around it."

"But Peter went straight in."

"He may not have realized where he was going."

"All the more reason to go after him and help him."

"Forget it, Andy," Elizabeth practically shouted. "We're just not going down into the Valley of Fears."

"I understand," Andy replied calmly. "That's why I won't ask you to come with me."

He started down the hill.

"But you can't go without us," Elizabeth insisted. "You wouldn't stand a chance alone."

"You may be right," Andy conceded. "Or," he added with the hint of a smile, "you may be wrong. I'm hoping that because I'm not a ghost the 'fears' won't attack me. You wait here. When I find my uncle Pete, I'll bring him back.''

"Don't risk it," Elizabeth pleaded.

"I have to," he called out over his shoulder, heading farther down the hill. "If I don't do what the Guardian said, and find my uncle, I'll die an old man in this place."

"There are worse things," said Elizabeth, a cry in her voice.

Andy didn't hear her. He was hurrying toward his destiny.

Except for being lonely, Andy was doing just fine. He was following Peter's trail quite easily and making good time, as well.

Elizabeth and Makasha really scared me about this valley, he thought to himself. But they were wrong. It's beautiful. I just wish it wasn't so hazy; I'd like to see more of it.

With nothing horrible or evil in sight, Andy started to think he was probably one heckuva courageous guy; obviously there was nothing in the Valley of Fears that scared him. His confidence soared.

Up ahead, a movement caught his eye. He stopped—suddenly not quite so confident, after all. Having Elizabeth and Makasha on either side of him would have gone a long way toward calming his nerves. Just the same, he kept up his courage and eased forward to get a better look at the trail ahead.

After gently pushing his way through low-growing blooming bushes, he gazed up a tree-lined path. Though he had trouble seeing through the haze, he thought he could pick out Peter at the top of the path, just before it dipped down a hill.

Andy took a deep breath to shout, but the sharp intake of air gave him a coughing fit that made him double over in pain.

When the coughing subsided, Peter was out of sight, obviously on the downside of the hill now.

Andy hurried up the path, surprised that every single one of his joints was aching. Knees and elbows creaking, he had gone only halfway when he had to stop to catch his breath. Glancing down at his hands, he was shocked to find the skin leathery and covered with large brown freckles.

Andy felt panic starting to take hold of him. Something was happening to him and he didn't know what it was. For a moment he even forgot what he was doing in the Valley of Fears. Then he remembered Peter, and forced himself to climb the rest of the hill. Uncle Pete was nowhere in sight, but there was a pond off to the right. At least he could get a drink of water. He couldn't believe how parched he had become.

Limping to the water's edge, Andy was just cupping some water to bring up to his lips when he stopped. Horrified, he stared, with failing vision, at his reflection in the pool of water. . . .

He was an old man.

His hair was white, and his skin was slack and deeply wrinkled. He was withering away, dying of old age in the ghost world, just as he had feared.

# CHAPTER 13

"DO YOU THINK WE MADE A MISTAKE?"
Elizabeth fretted.

Makasha folded his long arms around his
chest, frowning. He did not answer.

Ignoring her fear, Elizabeth went on, "I've
been thinking about how much Andy and I
have been through together. A lot of it was
scary. Somehow, though, we faced all of it.
How could I face all those horrible, frightening things before, and not have the courage to
face my own fears now? You know what I
mean?"

"Makasha know exactly what you mean.
You want go after Andy."

"Is that stupid? Is that wrong?"

"To enter Valley of Fears? Is stupid. Is

wrong." He unfolded his arms, fighting an overwhelming fear that seemed so alien to him. Slowly, defiantly, he said. "But we go after him, anyway."

"You just said—"

A smile crept across his lips. He said, "Educated girl from nineteen-sixties take advice from caveman?"

Elizabeth gave him a playful punch in the shoulder.

He pretended to draw his ax to defend himself.

They laughed.

The more they talked and kidded, the more their fear begin to fade. It was almost physical, like taking off jeans that are too tight— the relief was unmistakable. Elizabeth was the one who put it into words, saying, "It was the valley—its power—that stopped us from going with Andy."

"It stop us no more!" Makasha declared. "We go find him."

Elizabeth and Makasha moved surely and swiftly, following after Andy. Though he had an hour head start on them, they steadily closed the gap. They knew they'd catch him eventually because Andy had to rest and they didn't. It was only a matter of time before they were all reunited.

Elizabeth silently worried that something terrible might happen to Andy before they caught up to him. But the beauty and peace of the valley started to soothe her.

After pushing through brightly colored, blooming bushes, they climbed up a tree-lined path. At the crest they saw an old man sitting forlornly beside a pond.

"It's about time we ran into someone," Elizabeth said, relieved. "Maybe he saw Andy and can tell us how long ago he passed by here."

Aware that his presence sometimes put strangers off, Makasha gestured for her to go ahead and question the old man without him.

Elizabeth circled up next to him, offering him her right hand. The old man raised his eyes to her, trying to squint away the haze that clouded his vision. She seemed so very familiar. Was she someone he knew from a long time ago? But who? He wished he could see better.

They touched hands.

Through his gnarled, arthritic fingers, he felt a sensation that he had known in his youth. More than that, the familiar warmth he felt told him that she was someone he once cared for. His mind wandered, searching for memories, for any clue that would explain who she was.

"Excuse me, mister," came a lilting voice that played softly on his ears. "I'm looking for someone. Did you see anybody come by here recently?''

The old man changed the angle of his head to try to get a better look at the girl, to make out the features of her face. He wanted to see her so much.

When the old man didn't answer, Elizabeth assumed he was hard of hearing. She spoke louder, nearly shouting, "I'm looking for a boy. He's sixteen, kind of tall and thin." She gave a crooked smile and added, "He's kind of cute, too. Have you seen him?''

The voice, the touch, the warmth—it all came together in his mind. Though he couldn't see her through his cataract-covered eyes, he knew it was her. It was Elizabeth. He desperately tried to speak, to tell her who he was, but all he could manage was an incoherent mumble.

Elizabeth heard the old man make a few indistinct sounds. He wouldn't be of any help at all. Feeling defeated, she began to withdraw her hand.

It wasn't that easy. The old man would not let go.

"I've got to leave now," she explained, trying to wriggle her hand free from his grip without hurting the frail old man.

Overcome with emotion, he shook his head no.

"Makasha!" Elizabeth called out. "This old

man won't let me go. Can you give me a little help, please?''

The caveman stepped closer, expecting his mere presence to frighten the old one into submission. The effect was just the opposite.

Though Andy couldn't see well, he could make out the sheer bulk of the Neanderthal man, and that told him that Makasha was there also. Andy reached for the caveman's hand, grasping it tightly despite the pain he was suffering from the exertion.

"You please let go?" Makasha asked plaintively, unwilling to use his considerable power against a feeble old man.

Andy shook his head, trying to speak, to form words. Nothing came out.

"I don't know what to do," Elizabeth said to Makasha. "I don't want to hurt the old man's feelings, but we've got to go. Andy might need us."

Upon hearing those words, a tear formed in Andy's right eye. It welled there and then rolled down his cheek.

She noticed the tear and watched it make its way down the old man's face. She knew that ghosts couldn't cry—they have no tears. Instead of trying to free her hand from the old man's grasp, she held his hand with a firmer grip. He nodded his head.

Could it be? Elizabeth checked out the old man's clothing. He was wearing jeans, a white

T-shirt, and white sneakers—the same as Andy. It was strange how the clothes looked so different on an emaciated and aged body.

"It's really you," she whispered.

Another tear rolled down Andy's face.

Elizabeth put her free hand to her mouth. If her greatest fear was losing Andy, she was on the verge of having that fear come true. Even as she watched, Andy grew older. His white hair began to fall out, his nose grew larger as his face became smaller. The wrinkles deepened and he became even more stooped.

He was dying of old age, and there wasn't much time left to save him.

# CHAPTER 14

"IT'S ONLY FEAR!" ELIZABETH CRIED OUT TO him. "You can change back, Andy. You can beat it!"

Her words fell, literally, on deaf ears. Because of his advanced age, Andy had now lost his hearing.

Elizabeth turned to Makasha for help, but the caveman didn't know what to say or do. He was having a hard time recognizing Andy amid all the wrinkles and sagging skin. The old man who sat in front of Makasha seemed to him to be one hundred years old. All Makasha could think of to say was, "Fear is very strong. Must be only thing he feels now."

"Wait! I think you're on to something."

"I am?" Makasha looked at her, perplexed.

"Yes. It makes perfect sense," Elizabeth said excitedly. "If the fear is the only thing he's feeling, we have to drive it out of his mind. We have to replace it with something stronger."

"But what?"

Andy began to wheeze—his lungs had started to fail.

Elizabeth racked her brain trying to come up with something she could do that would drive the fear out of him, but she couldn't think of a thing.

Sensing the end was near, Andy gave Makasha's hand a slight shake to say good-bye. Then he lowered his head to the other hand he held—Elizabeth's—and let his lips touch the fingers. It was his good-bye kiss.

"No!" she cried. It didn't matter that he was old and wrinkled. It didn't matter that he was crippled, blind, and deaf. It didn't matter that he was barely recognizable as the boy she once knew. All that mattered was that he meant so much to her.

She fell to her knees in front of Andy, wrapping her free arm around his head. She didn't see him as old and decrepit—she saw him the way she loved him. That was when she passionately kissed him full on the mouth.

The emotion was so raw, so deeply felt, that it flew from Elizabeth to Andy. Andy felt the winds of it blowing inside his mind, swirling there, uncovering remembered feelings from his youth. All he wanted to feel right then was the passion of her kiss, and all he wanted to do was kiss her back. The emotions that welled up inside of Andy could not be denied. The hurricane of feelings buffeted his fear, sending it flying back to the dark recesses of his mind.

As they kissed, Andy's breathing got stronger, his wrinkles faded, his sight and hearing returned, and his crippled joints no longer ached. And once more he had a full head of brown hair. He was himself again—even down to being shy. Realizing that Makasha was standing right next to them, he pulled away from Elizabeth and blushed.

"Uh—uh—she—we like each other," he finally uttered.

"Makasha notice," the caveman said and might have winked, but Andy wasn't sure.

Andy blushed an even deeper shade of red. "What I—I mean is—"

"What he means," Elizabeth interrupted, trying to help him out, "is that Andy and I are going to his high-school prom together— if we ever get him back home."

"That's exactly right," Andy said with a happy grin on his face. "We're going to the prom together. One ghost and one real guy." Then he added, "And I'll be the proudest guy there even though no one but me will be able to see the prettiest girl at the dance.''

It was Elizabeth's turn to blush.

Andy soon told them about the man he had seen right about the time he started aging. He thought it was his uncle Pete, but he wasn't sure.

Makasha found the tracks and they followed them at a fast pace. For his part, Andy was bouncing along as if he had all the energy in the world. It was great to be young again.

A couple of hours later they saw a man in the distance, a man sitting beside a rushing stream with his feet in the water. He was staring off at something far in the distance, his mind seemingly a million miles away. According to the tracks he ought to have been Peter. Anything, however, was possible in the Valley of Fears, so they approached the man warily, sneaking up on him from behind.

When they got close, Andy accidentally kicked a small stone. The man up ahead was startled by the sound, and Andy watched as the stone skittered past him and then plopped down into the stream near his dangling feet.

The man raised his head and faced them. They were relieved by what—and who—they saw.

"It's you!" Andy exclaimed joyfully. "Uncle Pete!"

"It's me all right, but why are you calling me Uncle?"

Andy told him everything, including the stories his mother used to tell about her older brother. Peter seemed genuinely pleased to have been reunited with his sister's boy. Naturally, Peter wanted to know every single detail about everyone in the family. Andy did his best to give him all the facts, including how his aunt Rose (Peter's other sister) had become a model.

"Rose always had a weight problem when she was a kid. You know, she loved to swim but hated having to wear a bathing suit because she looked so fat in one. So she actually modeled them. Good for her!" Then he glanced up at something far away and muttered, "I guess anything is possible as long as you don't give up."

"According to my mom," Andy offered, "you really tried hard to be an actor."

"Not hard enough," he said, shaking his head sadly. "I got discouraged too easily. I listened to everyone who said it's too hard, it's too competitive, you'll never make a living at it. I became convinced they were right and gave up. I was sorry for the rest of my life. I shouldn't have let my hopes die before I did. That was what really killed me, but I'm going to change that now. I may be stuck here, but my hopes don't have to be. Freeing them may

106

not bring me my final peace, but it will sure give me some peace of mind."

"Uh, you lost me," Andy said, trying not to upset his uncle. "What are you talking about?"

"I'm talking about going there," he said gesturing in the direction he had been looking when they first approached him.

Andy saw nothing but swirling clouds of mist rising from the distant river.

"It's there—don't worry," Uncle Pete said. "Sometimes the mist parts and you can see it."

"See what?" Andy asked.

"The Prison of Hopes. It's the place where our hopes go when they die. And I'm going there to liberate mine!"

Andy recalled the Guardian's instructions: "Remember, you must help the person from your past if you ever want to return to the living world." With those words reverberating in his mind, but having no idea how helping his uncle might get him home, Andy said, "I'll go with you."

"Me, too," said Elizabeth.

"Me, three," added Makasha.

"Does he say things like that all the time?" Uncle Pete asked.

"All the time," Andy said. "Might as well get used to it."

\* \* \*

After they had been marching for what seemed like the better part of eight hours, Elizabeth asked, "Where exactly is this Prison of Hopes?"

"At the very center of the Valley of Fears," Peter replied. "We should be pretty close soon."

Upon hearing that, she said, "Now I know why this is the Valley of Fears: fear always surrounds hope."

"You speak much wisdom," Makasha said.

Andy was also impressed by her insight. He was just about to say so, too, when Peter shouted, "There! The mist is parting. Look!"

They strained to peer through the mist as its veil of white lifted. Not far away, on a bluff overlooking the river, they caught a glimpse of a castle, a beautiful fairy-tale castle, encircled by a glowing purple ring of light. Except for the strange purple light, the castle could have been used by King Arthur and his knights of the round table.

"If they had prisons like that in the living world," Andy said, "people would be fighting to get in."

"Hopes are often larger than life," Uncle Pete explained. "So why shouldn't the prison that holds them be as magnificent as what's contained within its walls?"

Andy had no answer. A moment later the

mist drifted back in, shrouding the prison once again in a mysterious white blanket.

Hurrying on with the others, anxious to reach the prison now, Andy figured out the riddle the Guardian had told him. He had said that Andy would have to "travel to a place that is always close but far away, that is always in mind but not always in sight, that is at the center of everything yet is as ephemeral as the mist." The Guardian was referring to hope.

After marching through the cloud of white mist, they could see that the Prison of Hopes stood on a bluff, bright now under the clear yellow sky.

Except for some large clumps of bushes, there was nothing between them and the prison except the band of purple light. And they knew that the light had to be there for a reason. None of them, however, knew what that reason was.

"No touch," Makasha warned as they cautiously eased up next to some bushes right next to the purple light.

Because they were so focused on the band of purple, they were caught totally off guard when someone leapt out of the bushes at them!

# CHAPTER
## 15

THE PERSON LANDED RIGHT IN FRONT OF Elizabeth. Makasha balled his right fist, ready to defend his friend. Peter immediately swooped down with his right hand to pick up a rock for a weapon. But it was Andy who acted first and dove at the man's legs to bring him down.

"I don't mean you any harm," the stranger shouted as Andy pinned his shoulders to the ground. "I just need to talk to you."

He was a skinny man wearing threadbare clothes. With dark eyes flashing, he insisted, "I didn't mean to startle you. I just wanted to stop you before you went any farther. I have things to tell you."

The others checked the bushes to see if anyone else was lurking nearby. Finally satisfied that the stranger was alone, Makasha said, "Let man up."

After Andy took his knees off the man's arms, Makasha lifted the skinny fellow to his feet by grabbing a handful of shirt, which also made sure that the stranger couldn't run away. In the meantime, Andy turned to Elizabeth and asked, "Are you all right?"

"I'm fine—thanks to you." She smiled at him warmly. He smiled back. Andy could hardly remember ever feeling so pleased with himself. He wanted to bask in the glow of her approval, but he knew there wasn't time.

"Who you be?" Makasha questioned the skinny man.

"I am Randall Neames, and I will tell you all about me. I promise. I wouldn't dream of not telling you, because I really need for you to listen. I really do."

"So far, you're talking, but you're not saying much," Peter challenged, still clutching his rock.

"I know exactly what you mean. I am here, you see, because I must talk to you about me. I am fated to start every sentence I speak with the word *I*. I know it drives people crazy, yet I can't help it. I really blew it when I was alive, and now I'm paying for it.'"

"What did you do wrong?" Elizabeth asked.

"I was one of those people—you know the

type—who was totally self-centered. I had to be the focus of everyone's attention. I had to dominate every conversation. I had to have everything my way all the time. I was, in a word, a bore. I know that now. I just can't do anything about it, though."

"But why are you here, just outside the Prison of Hopes?" Andy asked suspiciously. "Are you some kind of guard?"

"I am just the opposite," he said, chuckling. "I want you to enter the prison. I want you to come out, too, because I know that that's when I'll get to talk to you about myself for who knows how long?"

"I don't get it," Andy complained. "What are you saying?"

"I draw your attention to the purple light that surrounds the prison," said Randall Neames. "I can assure you that it's not meant to keep you out. I can tell you, though, that it is meant to keep you from leaving. I have seen it work. I have seen people walk right through it to get to the prison, and I have seen those same people get entangled in it when they try to leave. I, naturally, speak to those who get trapped in the purple light, because they cannot run away from me. I must admit, most of those I've talked to under those circumstances have been driven mad."

"Why are you telling us this?" Andy wondered out loud. "Why warn us about the purple light when it's in your best interest not to?"

"I can't help myself," he admitted. "I have to tell everyone everything I know. I don't stop there, either. I'll tell you things I don't know, and I'll tell you things I wish I knew, and then, when I can't think of anything new to say, I'll just repeat everything I've said all over again."

"Well, thanks just the same for the warning about the purple light, Mr. Neames," Elizabeth said. "I hope we won't be talking to you later."

He grinned. "I know what you mean."

They left the skinny man behind and stepped through the purple light. As Neames had said, it offered no resistance—at least in that direction. They continued on toward the prison.

There appeared to be no sentries or guards. Spectacular iron gates stood closed to them, but they had never expected to enter the prison through the front door, anyway.

After scouting along the walls, Makasha found a metal grating that covered the opening to a room built below the ground. He was strong enough to bend the grating so that they could all enter the building that way.

Andy was the first to go in, sliding through the opening feet first and holding on to the grating to lower himself into the room. It was dark and he couldn't see how far it was to the floor. There was only one way to find out. He had to let go and hope. He was relieved when his feet touched the floor just a short yard below.

Even if his eyes had adjusted to the darkness—which they hadn't—Andy was too busy helping the others down to check out the room. Though they tried to be quiet, four people climbing down onto a stone floor makes a fair amount of noise. When they were all safely inside the Prison of Hopes, however, they stood and silently tried to analyze their surroundings.

The sound of breathing seemed to fill the room. At first Andy thought he was hearing the others. Soon, though, he realized that the breathing was much too loud to be coming from just four people.

Unnerved, he didn't move and put out his hands to hold back the others. They were not alone and they knew it. The question was, did whoever else was in the room know that the four of them were there?

Slowly, they each began to make out something in the dark shadows, something too terrifying to contemplate—hundreds of glowing eyes were staring at them from every direction!

# CHAPTER 16

HOLDING HIS BREATH, ANDY SLOWLY TURNED his head and was confronted by a pair of eyes blinking at him no more than three feet away! The shock of it made Andy jump back—right into what felt like a hand.

Whipping around, Andy lurched to his right and his shoulder smacked up against a door, knocking it ajar. Light streamed into the room from a hallway.

The first thing they all saw was that the room—and it was incredibly huge—was filled with cages. In each cage was a human. The light had another effect beyond letting them see—it also acted like a switch for the prisoners. They all began talking at once—not to one another or Andy, Elizabeth, Makasha, or

Peter. Each person launched into what sounded like a prepared speech. They were speeches in every conceivable language, spoken by people from every part of the world and every historical period.

"Who are they?" Elizabeth shouted above the ear-splitting din.

Peter leaned in close to Elizabeth and said, "They must be the dead hopes of everyone who ever wanted to be a politician."

"We go," Makasha bellowed, pointing to the door. "Very warm here. Politician talk mean much hot air."

The corridor they entered was long, with hundreds of doors leading off it. And that corridor was hardly the only one in the prison. They opened the next few doors in the hallway and found each to be filled with people in cages.

It soon became clear that each room in the prison housed a different category of dead hope. There were so many, though, that they soon realized they'd find Peter's hope faster if they split up, each of them searching for it independently. They agreed to rendezvous at the door to the politicians' room when they finished checking. They also agreed that there was one thing they could count on—the room containing the hopes of everyone who had wanted to be an actor would have to be an incredibly large room.

\*     \*     \*

Elizabeth had seen rooms filled with aviators, cowboys, judges, and ballerinas. So far, though, no actors. She continued racing down her hallway, throwing open one door after another.

After she threw open the sixteenth door, she stopped dead. In that room were all of those who had once wanted to be doctors but had given up hope. They wore white coats and had stethescopes draped around their necks. She should have continued her search, but she had to know. Would she be there in that room of thousands?

Running past row after row of cells, she noted that most of the people were in their teens and twenties. How sad, she thought, to give up on something so young.

She turned a corner and gasped. There she was. Just as she had been at fourteen. Except for the two-year age difference, the girl in the cage was her mirror image. Elizabeth looked at her younger self, dressed as she had always imagined herself if she had become a physician. But it was not to be. That girl and her dreams had died two years before Elizabeth lost her life. She hated seeing that part of herself caged in a cell.

She reached for the cell door, only to be accosted by voices inside her head, saying, "You can't be a doctor." "Only boys can be doctors." "You're not smart enough." "You'll be happier if you're a nurse.'' The closer her hand got to the cell door, the louder and more insistent the voices became. She couldn't take it and backed away.

The girl in the cell stared at her with imploring eyes. Elizabeth felt ashamed. This time, she threw herself at the door, shouting at the top of her lungs to drown out the voices telling her to quit, to stop, that she was no good, that she should settle for less. Her hands grasped the cell door. She pulled on it, and it swung open. There was no key. It hadn't been locked. Yet no one could have opened it—no one but Elizabeth.

She put out her hand to the fourteen-year-old girl, who stared back at Elizabeth with a wonderfully confident gaze. Their fingers touched. . . .

*Whooooop!* The two Elizabeths became one—the hope was alive inside her again, reabsorbed.

Just like Elizabeth and the others, Andy was busy opening doors, searching for his uncle Pete's lost hope. He had seen violinists, clowns, race-car drivers, and all sorts of other exotic career choices. By the time he was almost finished with his assigned doors, he had begun thinking how neat it would be to free all of those hopes. Wouldn't it be incredible, he thought, if everybody's hopes suddenly were reborn? He even tried to free one particular clown. The cell had no lock, but it would not open. No wonder they hadn't bothered with guards here, Andy thought. Who needs guards if the doors can't be opened? And if the doors couldn't be opened, then their journey to the prison was for nothing. He felt bad for his uncle because now it seemed that he wouldn't be able to free his dead hope.

A few doors down from the clown room, Andy found the room filled with writers. There were more cells in this room than in any other he had entered so far. In fact, the cells seemed to disappear into the distance. He didn't mean to stay, but, as far as he knew, finding his uncle Pete's hope now wouldn't do him any good, anyway. So he poked around in the writer's room.

That was when he came face to face with himself. Even though he was still alive, there was a part of him that had actually died and come here.

Andy had once hoped to write great books with swashbuckling heroes. He had filled notebook after notebook with ideas for stories, chattering endlessly about how someday millions of people would read his books and see the movies on which they were based. And then the hope of being a writer died when his English teacher massacred a short story he had written; when a fantasy story he submitted to a magazine was sent back with a rejection form letter; when his best friend, Steve, laughed at a story he had written about his grandmother. Discouraged, he had given up any hope of being a writer. The hope had died. But there it was—or, rather, there he was, sitting in a cell, writing busily in a fat writing tablet.

With butterflies of excitement fluttering in his stomach, he moved toward the writer he had hoped to be to get a better look. It was an image just a few years younger than his present sixteen.

As he got closer to the cell, he suddenly began hearing voices. Yet no one appeared to be talking. "You can't do it," one of the voices taunted. Another said, "It's impossible. You don't have the talent!" Still others advised him, "It's a pipe dream." "You don't have a chance." "Do something more reasonable, safer, smarter."

At first the voices weren't all that loud, but there were many of them and each one was telling him why he couldn't, shouldn't, and wouldn't be a writer. And the closer he moved to the cell, the stronger the voices became.

Disoriented and confused by what was happening inside his own head, Andy stumbled back from the cell. The voices stopped. He shook his head. What was that all about? he wondered.

Not really believing what he had just experienced, Andy decided to try again. He moved briskly toward the image of himself in the cell—and was met, once again, by a barrage of voices, this time more insistent, bullying, and intimidating. He tried to fight through them, to ignore them, but the closer he got to the cell, the louder and uglier they became.

It was like having headphones on at the top decibel level and not being able to adjust the volume. All he wanted was to stand up close to what he had once hoped to be. Ultimately, though, the price he was paying for his simple desire was too great. The cacophony of voices inside his head was driving him mad. Unable to stand it anymore, he cried out in anguish and stumbled backward, beaten.

Andy crumpled on the floor and sat there, holding his head in his hands. He was still in the same position when Elizabeth came running down the corridor to find him.

"Are you hurt?" she demanded. "Are you all right?"

"I'll be okay," he said in a monotone.

"I was out in the hallway when I heard you scream. I came running as fast as I could."

When he didn't say anything, she knelt beside him and gently asked, "What happened?"

He told her.

"And you're giving up?" she asked. "You're not going to try to free your hope?"

"Free it? What are you talking about? The doors can't be opened. I know, because I tried to set somebody else's hope free in another room before I got here."

"You're wrong," Elizabeth said, cupping his face in her hands and making him look right at her. "Maybe you can't open somebody else's cell and free his or her hope, but you can free your own. *I* know," she said, "because I did it myself just a little while ago. I fought the voices in my head and got through. I know having my hope of being a doctor freed won't do me much good here, but freeing *your* hope could change your life, Andy. It might even save it."

He gave her a sharp, questioning look.

"Don't you remember? The Guardian said you had to be 'complete' to return to the living world. Maybe he meant you needed to be whole, that nothing could be left behind, including your hopes."

"And I thought we came here to help Uncle Pete," Andy said, suddenly in awe of the Guardian's clever manipulation. "It was really the other way around, all the time. Uncle Pete, whether he knows it or not—brought us here to help me."

"So, you'll try again?"

Andy swallowed hard. The memory of the voices was still strong and painful. Yet the idea that he really could free his hope buoyed his spirits. He had been beaten back twice and vowed he would not be beaten back again. "I'll try," he said.

"You're going to make it. I just know it." Beyond encouraging him, she also prepped him. "Shout at the top of your lungs. The sound you make drowns out some of the voices in your head."

"I'll give it a shot. Thanks."

Breathing heavily, sweat dripping freely down his face, Andy got up off the floor. Elizabeth rubbed his shoulders to try to relax him. What it did do was to let him know how much she was rooting for him.

Andy gazed across the space between where he now stood and where his image was happily scribbling away in a writing tablet behind iron bars. What story am I writing in that cell? he asked himself. Is it this one? Am I writing about myself, Elizabeth, Makasha, and Uncle Pete? Am I putting down everything that has happened to me here in the ghost world? He wanted desperately to know.

Steeling himself for one more try, Andy told himself that if Elizabeth thought he could do it, he could. He tried to rid himself of the memory of how the inside of his head had felt as if it were going to explode. He didn't want to feel fear. Only resolve. No butterflies. Only eagles.

He took a huge gulp of air, then dashed toward his cell, screaming so loudly that his throat burned from the effort. Even with that, he still did hear the voices. "You can't be a writer." "You don't know grammar." "You haven't lived; what can you write about?" "You'll fail miserably." "You'll make a fool of yourself." He heard all of that and more. It didn't stop him. He bulled his way forward despite the ever-louder voices thundering inside his head.

He reached for the cell door.

The pressure and pain behind his eyes was tremendous.

He wrapped the fingers of his right hand on the door handle.

His head was pounding almost as hard as his heart.

He yanked on the cell door.

He thought he was going to pass out.

The door flew open!

The voices ceased.

Wobbling on shaky legs, he studied himself in the cell. The writer that he had once hoped to become put down his pen, stood up, and walked toward him. Andy stuck out his right hand. So did the writer. When their hands met there was a loud *whooooooop!* The writer had vanished back to where he had always belonged: inside Andy's heart and soul.

Andy turned to face Elizabeth, who would have been crying tears of joy if it had been possible. She ran to Andy and they hugged.

When he let her go, Andy climbed inside the cell to look at the writing tablet on the table. It was blank. Not a single scribble on any page. After the initial shock, he realized that that made sense. His stories were still to be written. They were inside him, waiting to be told. All he needed was the skill—and the will—to put them down on paper.

Glancing at Elizabeth, he promised himself that, yes, he would write it all down. Even if no one believed a word of it, he would tell the story of what had happened to him here. And, he promised himself, he would write most lovingly about Elizabeth.

He climbed down out of the cell and took Elizabeth's hand. "Thanks," he said simply.

"For what? You did it."

"Just the same. Thanks."

She shyly nodded her head.

The look that passed between them was deeply charged. He wanted to kiss her, but couldn't get up the nerve to do it. Instead, he said, "I guess we better head back and see how Makasha and Uncle Pete made out."

She had wanted to kiss him, too, but all she could say was "I guess you're right."

Yet neither of them moved. Something was happening between them. Something that was interrupted by a huge fist that smashed through the ceiling of the prison above their heads!

# CHAPTER 17

WHEN THE FIST BROKE THROUGH, A SLAB OF stone weighing more than two tons crashed down in front of the doorway, blocking Andy and Elizabeth's exit. That, however, was the least of their problems. Chunks of stone fell in a shower of debris, pelting them with pieces of rubble as large as grapefruits. Andy was struck on the back and knocked to the floor, nearly unconscious. While lying there, stunned, smaller pieces of stone rained down on him, bruising him. Elizabeth was only slightly luckier. A chunk of wall caved in next to her, but she dodged most of the damage. When jumping out of the way, though, she smashed her shoulder against a cell and her arm went temporarily numb.

With her one good arm, Elizabeth pulled Andy to the relatively protected place beside the slab of stone near the door. There, he recovered slightly and looked back into the crumbling room. Giant fingers coiled and uncoiled, searching for something to grab hold of. Cells were knocked over and crushed, hopes destroyed, with every wild movement of that one humongous hand.

The hand was suddenly withdrawn, escaping through the ceiling. More debris fell. When the dust cleared, though, Andy and Elizabeth peered up through the massive hole in the ceiling and saw exactly who they feared would be there: Sir Aleck.

"He followed us," Andy said in a panic. "He hasn't given up."

As if to punctuate their fears, they heard the giant bellow, "He's in there someplace. Find him!"

"It sounds as if he has his 'troops' with him, too," Elizabeth said sourly. "We've got to round up Makasha and Peter and get out of here," she added. "Let's go."

With the doorway blocked, they left the room through the space in the broken wall. Once in the corridor, they raced to their rendezvous point. Makasha, alone, was waiting for them there. "Hear big boom," the caveman said worriedly. When he saw Andy's bloody and stained T-shirt, he asked, "You hurt bad?"

"Not serious," Andy said quickly, dismissing his wounds. "Sir Aleck is here. He's looking for me. We've got to find Uncle Pete and scram."

"Scram?"

"Get out. Vamoose. Beat it."

"Mean 'leave'?"

"That's exactly what it means."

And that's exactly what they did. The three of them went in search of Peter, calling out his name like parents looking for a lost child. He didn't answer. They did eventually find him, in a state of semiconsciousness, face-down on the floor. He had found the actors' room. But so had Sir Aleck. There was a massive hole in the ceiling, and dust and debris were still falling from all the floors above them.

At least Peter hadn't been buried under the stones. A cell had fallen on top of him, pinning him down. It wasn't any cell. Inside this cell was a younger version of Uncle Pete. The sad-eyed man had found the actor who had once lived inside himself.

"Hurry!" shouted Andy. "We've got to get the cell off him before he's driven insane by the voices."

Makasha didn't know what Andy was talking about, but he trusted his young friend and went into action. He lifted one side of the cell while Andy and Elizabeth took the other. At the count of three, they picked it up off Peter's leg and set it right side up. When they dragged Peter away, he was groggy—but grateful.

He was not, however, prepared to leave. "I'm not going," he insisted, "until I free my hope. I had almost opened the door when the floors above came down."

Elizabeth explained about Sir Aleck, but it didn't dissuade Peter. "I'm not going until I've done what I came to do. Period."

Noting his single-minded determination, Andy couldn't help saying, "You know, you've changed an awful lot since you were a Mediocrity, Uncle Pete."

"I guess that comes from hanging around you," he replied with a grin.

The sound of footsteps in the hallway caused the grinning and talking to come to a sudden halt.

Makasha grabbed his ax handle. Whoever was coming would not be a friend.

Two mutants appeared at the door. One of them was the disease carrier and the other was the one whose body was covered with sharp-tipped spikes. "I told you I heard something," the spiked mutant said, locking eyes with Andy. "You go tell Sir Aleck," he ordered the disease carrier. "I'll keep the living one here until the master comes for him."

It was four against one. The odds were clearly not in the remaining mutant's favor, although he didn't seem to either notice or mind. He controlled the doorway to the room. No one could leave without passing him.

He didn't have to move. It was up to the four of them to either fight to get past him, or wait for Sir Aleck. The choice was clear to them all—except Uncle Peter. "I told you," he said, "I'm not leaving until I free my hope."

With that, he charged the cell holding his younger self. No one but Peter could hear the belittling, taunting voices that besieged him. As he got closer to the cell, they screamed like banshees inside his head. He countered by screaming back at them with a blood-curdling howl that sounded barely human.

Neither the mutant nor Makasha had ever witnessed anything like this. Their attention was riveted on Peter's bizarre behavior.

Andy and Elizabeth, however, not only knew what Peter was doing, they also knew what to expect when he started his charge. Instead of watching him, they kept their eyes on the mutant. As soon as he was distracted, they nodded and leapt into action.

In one fluid motion Elizabeth bolted toward him, swinging her hands down to the floor to scoop up two handfuls of the gritty dust that had come down with the roof.

At the same time, Andy took off at a dead run for their spiked guard.

Elizabeth was slightly ahead of Andy when their paths crisscrossed in front of the mutant. Elizabeth swerved to the left just as the mutant reached out for her. Eluding his grasp, she threw her handfuls of dust in his face, temporarily blinding him. Meanwhile, his arms were extended toward her, and Andy cut across to his other side, leaping at the mutant like a battering ram, feet first. He avoided the spikes and smashed full force into the mutant's body.

He struck the mutant high on the chest, sending him sprawling backward into the corridor. Unfortunately, Andy hit the deck hard, too, and bounced the back of his head off the stone floor. He lay there close—too close—to the spiked creature, who started to rise with the intention of revenging himself upon Andy.

Except that wasn't going to happen—not if Makasha could react in time. The caveman was quick to follow up on Andy and Elizabeth's bold actions. He ran for a slab of stone that must have weighed at least four hundred pounds. Straining and heaving, he hoisted it up and ran with it toward the doorway. Makasha was strong, but he was no Hercules. He could only hold it so long before he had to drop it. Screaming and racing as fast as he could, he heaved the slab at the mutant.

The spikes got flattened. And so did the mutant.

At that moment, from behind them, they heard: *Whoooooop!* Makasha turned to see what had happened. Elizabeth already knew. Even with his head spinning, Andy knew as well. Uncle Pete's hope of being an actor was alive again inside his ghostly body.

'Now I can leave," Peter said with a flourish.

They rushed down the corridor, intending to sneak out of the prison the same way they had sneaked in. Before they reached the end of the hallway, though, a gigantic hand broke through the side of the building. It gripped the wall and yanked with a tremendous force, ripping the hallway wide open and giving them a view of not only the mist-shrouded river at the bottom of the bluff, but also the face of Sir Aleck.

The giant mutant, on hands and knees, was peering into the crumbling building. When he saw Andy he gave a wolfish smile. "You did well to guide me here," Sir Aleck announced, his booming voice loosening more sections of the corridor walls. "It bodes well for the future—my future. You see, I once had very grand plans. Oh, my hopes were small at first. I merely wanted to rule the land that my ancestors had ruled. But my dreams grew larger. Soon I wanted to dominate England, and then use that as my base to conquer Europe, Russia, the Americas. There were others who had hopes like my own. Like them, I finally had to give it up as impossible. But now it's not! As soon as I retrieve my hope, I will come back for you. And then you will take me to the living world, not as a ghost, but as a human being brought back from the dead.''

''You don't get it,'' Andy said. ''I don't know how to get back, and even if I did, I wouldn't take you. End of story.''

''No,'' Sir Aleck replied coolly. ''End of life. Yours. But not right away. Either you help me or, one by one, each of your friends will be destroyed. If you haven't helped me by then, you'll be the last one to go. On this, my boy, you have my solemn promise. Oh, and by the way,'' he added, ''don't even think about trying to leave. My associates would not like that.''

When Sir Aleck left, his associates appeared where the wall of the corridor had once stood. They were all too familiar: three mutants, one as bright as diamonds, one a carrier of ghostly diseases, and one whose fingers dripped acid. The three knew that Andy was the only important one, so they were at pains not to hurt him. That was not the case with the others though. In fact they were hoping for an "example," someone they could use to scare those that remained.

Just then Peter stepped forward. Andy and Elizabeth tried to stop him, but he wouldn't listen. They were afraid they'd be the ones who would have to listen—to his screams.

# CHAPTER
## 18

ANDY COULDN'T BELIEVE WHAT HE SAW. HE watched, astonished, as his uncle Peter strutted toward the mutants, speaking in a forceful, rich voice that seemed so unlike him. He announced, "I know what you're thinking! You're thinking that that overgrown leader of yours is the greatest thing since buttered popcorn. You're thinking that he's going to take you back to the living world with him. Well, think again, because your thinking is all screwed up!"

Makasha and Elizabeth both gave Andy the same questioning glance, each of them silently asking, What is he doing? Andy only knew that his uncle had certainly grabbed the mutants' full attention.

Peter grinned at his guards with a thousand-watt smile, sounding as if he knew everything and they knew nothing. His presence was no longer wishy-washy—it was dynamic, intense, and blazing with confidence now.

Pointing in the direction in which Sir Aleck had just gone, Peter scornfully said, "If you think bigger is better, just remember the dinosaurs. If you think he's taking you back to the living world"—he laughed derisively—"then get your mutant heads examined. He knows full well that only *one* can go, and he intends to be that one. And if you think you're better off crossing him rather than me, just consider that I have powers you cannot conceive of, powers so strong that I am forbidden by the Guardian to use them—except in dire emergencies. If you force my hand, however, the pain you'll suffer for the rest of eternity will be the price you pay for your foolishness. You have been warned."

By this point Andy understood two things: his uncle was a terrific actor and he was either very stupid or very brave for attempting the most outlandish bluff ever made on this side of the grave!

The disease-carrying mutant seemed worried. "What kind of powers do you have?" he asked.

Andy smiled. Uncle Pete had that one hooked.

Gesturing for Andy and the others to follow him, Peter continued to ease closer to their captors. All the while he kept on talking, saying, "My powers, my strengths come from the most powerful source there is: the mind. But you have nothing to fear from me as long as you do as you're told."

"I don't know—" the acid-dripping mutant began.

Peter threw his arm out at him like a whip, pointing his finger at the mutant, cutting him off and shouting, "You don't know anything!"

The acid dripper flinched and shut his mouth, listening.

He was convinced, Andy thought. Now, if we can just get close enough—

"Your only problem," Peter went on, "is that you should be with us." He gestured to his right. "Andy," he said softly, making the mutants lean forward and concentrate on his every word, "has a power even greater than mine. And it isn't the power to bring just one person back to the living world. That's nothing. That's the very large Sir Aleck thinking very small. No. Andy has the 'living touch.' He has the power to bring you back to life right here! He did it for me. He did it for her," he announced, gesturing grandly at Elizabeth, who walked beside Andy. "He even did it for this caveman," he proclaimed, sweeping his hand to his left, "a human who had been dead for tens of thousands of years. That is Andy's gift—life. All he needs to do is touch you. Then you'll know that everything I've said is true. Once you're convinced, you'll be spared the grief and agony that come from crossing me!"

Andy was no actor, but he played his part well. He simply nodded his head and said, "One touch of my hand is all it will take."

"You mean, even if I don't go to my final peace," the diamond-covered mutant asked, "I can sleep again and lose myself in it for a little while?"

That's three, Andy said to himself. They're all buying it! To the mutant he said, "That's exactly right."

They had gotten to within just a few yards of the three mutants. Suddenly the diamond-covered being squinted his brilliant eyes at Peter and cocked his head to one side. "Wait a minute," he said cautiously. "I think I saw you before." He furrowed his gleaming brow, nearly blinding Peter, whose fingers had begun to tremble. "You—you—ah, yes, I remember now. You were a frightened little Mediocrity who ran from us in that village."

The acid dripper shook his head angrily. "Then he has been lying to us?" He stepped toward Peter with violence in his eyes.

"It's true I was a Mediocrity," Peter said,

trying to keep his performance going, "but that was just an act."

"They've played us for fools!" The acid dripper said, turning his head toward his fellow mutants for just one instant.

Before the acid dripper saw him, Andy lunged at him, ramming both his hands into the mutant's side. The mutant, of course, did not come to "life"—instead, he came to grief. Andy shoved the acid dripper into the disease carrier. Instinctively, trying to avoid a collision, both mutants reached out with their deadly hands. Too late, they realized their mistake. Acid seared through the disease carrier, eating away at his body, and ghostly diseases spread like wildfire in the acid carrier. They had grasped each other in an embrace of mutual destruction.

There was only one mutant left. He remained standing, barring their escape. Makasha dove at the diamond-covered being, knocking him off his feet. It was almost enough, but not quite. Before the mutant banged his head on a piece of rubble and became unconscious, he turned up the level of his brightness and caused a yellowish red flare of light to explode like a sunburst.

Peter, Andy, and especially Makasha were temporarily blinded. Just in time, however, Elizabeth had covered her face with her hands. She wished she could have also covered her ears, because Andy's terror-stricken cries pierced her like a knife.

"I can't see!" he wailed over and over again, fear seizing him.

Elizabeth took Andy's right hand and soothingly said, "You'll be all right soon." Then, more urgently, she added, "But we can't stay here. We've got to go. Now!"

He ignored her. "We're finished!" he insisted, lost in his own personal darkness.

"Don't give up," she pleaded. "I can see, so do as I tell you. Okay?"

Surprised to learn that at least one of them was not blind, Andy tried to steady his breathing, desperately fighting to get a grip on himself. "Okay," he said, but he was still on the edge of total panic.

Elizabeth guided him to Peter and placed Andy's free left hand into Peter's right. Next, she brought her growing human chain to Makasha, placing Peter's left hand in Makasha's right.

"Don't let go of one another," she ordered. "I'll lead. We're getting out of here!"

Elizabeth wasn't the only one left who could still see. . . .

Sir Aleck had found his evil hope and had just freed it. Soaring with the confidence that his dream of conquest would soon come true, he was about to return for Andy when he saw the flash of light. Sir Aleck knew that some sort of battle had likely taken place between his men and the captives. His only concern was that the living one might have gotten harmed.

The giant had to take several monstrous strides to get around the massive building before he saw that his prisoners had escaped. Sir Aleck didn't care about the mutants who had been transported. Their bodies had vanished to someplace else in the ghost world and would be returned to their previous, unmutated forms. Nor did he care about the diamond being who lay moaning on the ground. He cared only for himself. On that score, Uncle Pete had been totally right.

Scanning in every direction, Sir Aleck searched for Andy and the others. It took only a moment to find them. They were heading for the outlying band of purple light that surrounded the prison. They would be easy to catch. This time, however, he would waste no time before destroying the others.

He took a long stride in their direction. . . .

# CHAPTER

## 19

"WE'RE ALMOST TO THE PURPLE LIGHT," Elizabeth called out as she led her blind friends away from the Prison of Hopes.

"How get past purple light?" Makasha asked, giving words to the thought that was on all of their minds.

"I don't know," she admitted. "But let's get there first before we worry about it."

"Me worry now, okay?" Makasha said.

Before she could answer, the ground shook under their feet. They all knew what that meant: Sir Aleck was on the move. Elizabeth couldn't help herself; she looked back to where they had escaped the three mutants. The giant was there, and his huge booted foot was already in the air, coming their way!

Because she wasn't watching where she was going, she accidentally led them across a patch of rough, uneven ground. Before she could warn them about where to walk, Peter, who was third in line, tripped on a rock and fell flat on his face. He pulled all of them down with him. They might have survived that, but when he hit, Peter let go of both Andy's and Makasha's hands. The chain had been broken.

Frantically, Elizabeth pulled Andy to his feet and then half dragged him to the other two. "Don't move!" she ordered Peter and Makasha. "I'm coming."

But Sir Aleck arrived first, his boot thundering down next to the four of them. The ground quaked so hard that Elizabeth and Andy both lost their balance, falling yet again—and this time *their* hands unclasped.

Andy rolled onto his back. Lying there, looking up, he could just begin to make out the vague outline of Sir Aleck's gargantuan body against the yellow sky. His sight was finally beginning to return. He didn't figure it would do him much good.

"You are a resourceful group," Sir Aleck conceded, leaning down over them. His breath blew over the foursome like a hot wind off a garbage dump. "I give you credit," he added. "I also give you no chance for survival." So saying, he swept his right hand across the ground and scooped up Elizabeth, Makasha, and Uncle Pete.

Andy saw the dark shadow of the hand go by and heard the screaming of the others as they were lifted high into the sky.

"What are you going to do?" Andy shouted up at the giant, madly blinking his eyes.

"I'm going to do what I should have done before," Sir Aleck announced. "I'm going to crush them."

"Wait! No!" Andy cried. "I—I'll make you a deal," he promised, having no idea what he'd say next. He was just stalling for time.

"I'm listening. I'm also squeezing."

The screams that fell on Andy's ears made him wild with terror. "Don't hurt them! Please!" He bit down on his lower lip, trying to see, to think, to come up with something to offer. Then it came to him. He'd offer Sir Aleck exactly what he wanted—and a little bit more.

"You win," Andy shouted up at the giant. "Here's the deal. You put them safely down on the ground, and I'll take you back to the living world."

"When?" the giant challenged, suspiciously.

"Right away."

"Tell me why should I trust you."

"What do I have to gain by lying?" Andy replied. "If I don't do as I've promised, all

144

you have to do is pick them back up again, right?''

"True. Except there will be one difference. I'll pick you up, too. And I'll squeeze you the hardest.''

"Fair enough," said Andy, barely keeping the quaver out of his voice. ''Now put them down.''

Sir Aleck began lowering his hand, intending to drop the three of them next to Andy.

"Not here!" Andy said, his vision getting better. "When I take you back to the living world a—a cyclone will be created where we are now standing," he improvised. "They'll get hurt, and I don't want that. Put them down out of danger, on the other side of the purple light, say.''

Sir Aleck shrugged his massive shoulders. It made no difference to him where he put them down. He leaned over the top of the purple light and casually dumped them where Andy had suggested.

Elizabeth, Makasha, and Peter scrambled to their feet. They didn't bother running; they knew there was no escape. All they could do was stand up and watch.

"I've done my part," Sir Aleck said meaningfully. "Now do yours.''

"I came to this place for two reasons," Andy began. "To retrieve my lost, dead hope, and to go home. Both had to be done from here. The secret,'' he announced, ''is the purple light.''

"What do you mean?"

"Didn't you notice that the purple light appears to be like a barrier to the prison, yet you could walk right through it without getting so much as an itch? You probably walked over it when you came here, but your friends had to pass through it. So you know what I'm saying is true.''

"Go on."

"So, if it isn't a barrier, then what is it? Well, the Guardian told me—and I'm telling you. He said it's a power source.''

Sir Aleck looked dubious.

"A very great power source," Andy insisted. "Notice that it's circular," he added, trying to sound credible. "That represents the connection between life and death. It's all a great circle, where those who know how can go back and forth between the two worlds. Of course, first you have to be complete within yourself, absorbing all your dead hopes from the prison. Did you do that yet? I can't take you back unless you have.''

"Yes, yes. I'm complete," Sir Aleck said hastily. "Let's get on with it."

"Right. Good—fine." Andy swallowed. This was what he was building to. "We have to tap into the power of the purple light. And here's how it works. While I perform a chant that the Guardian taught me, you put your hand in the purple light and let it flow against your skin. When I give you a signal, you pick me up in your other hand. The next thing you know," he added with the hint of a smile, "you'll be someplace you never thought you'd ever be."

Sir Aleck stared down at Andy. In a harsh voice that was as loud as it was chilling, he said, "If this doesn't work, you and your friends will be very sorry. *Very* sorry."

"I'm not worried," he replied. He wasn't— he was petrified.

"I'm starting," Andy said. "Get ready to touch the purple light." In a soft voice he began mumbling the words to "Bustin' a Gut," the song he had been singing when Elizabeth first showed up in his room. It seemed so long ago. As he chanted the words, he stared through the purple light and saw that she was watching him with such hopeful, caring eyes. In that moment, he felt the bond between them grow even stronger; he wished he could tell her how he felt. And, now, knowing that if he failed he would die, Andy made a silent vow that if this was to be his end, he would never stop searching the ghost world until he found Elizabeth again. Even if it took eternity.

The moment had come. Andy finished mumbling the last verse of the song, then pointed to Sir Aleck, giving him the signal.

Andy suddenly saw the giant begin reaching down for him. No! he thought with wild horror growing in his brain. That's the wrong order! The purple light has to be touched first! Now, he feared, he'd never be with Elizabeth in life *or* death; he'd be trapped with Sir Aleck in the purple light for all time! It was the end of everything. He took a deep breath to shout out Elizabeth's name before it was all over, but then, without warning, just before the giant's hand enveloped him, there was a monumental *snap,* followed by an equally loud, but longer *whiiiiiip!*

Blocked by Sir Aleck's huge body, Andy hadn't seen that the giant had, in fact, put his hand in the purple light. The band of light had not been intended to protect against giants. It wasn't supposed to break. But it did, and then the entire length of it whistled through the air to wrap itself around the one who broke it.

Sir Aleck wasn't going to the living world. He wasn't going anywhere. He was going to stay right there to listen to Randall Neames talk about himself for a *very* long time.

148

# CHAPTER
## 20

"I'M THINKING OF STARTING A TRAVELING troupe of actors to tour the ghost world," Peter announced as they sat on the bank of the river, well away from the Valley of Fears. "What do you say? You folks want to join up with me?"

"Thanks for the invitation, Uncle Pete, but I'm going home," Andy said. "At least that's what the Guardian promised. I just wish he'd show up."

"How about you, Elizabeth?"

"Please," she said and laughed. "I'm no actress."

Peter looked at the caveman and said, "I don't suppose you—"

Makasha shook his head.

149

"Well, I missed a lot of years I could have been acting," Peter said, "so I'm just going to have to make up for it here. I'm sure there are plenty of former actors around who'd be glad to join me."

"I'm sure there are, Uncle Pete," Andy said. "And I wish you all the luck in the world—mine and yours."

Peter walked purposefully over to his nephew and put out his right hand. Andy shook it. "When you get back home, Andrew—and I know you will—do me a small favor, huh?"

"Anything."

"Tell your mother that I'm okay—and that I love her."

"I will," he said simply, wondering if his mother would believe any of this.

"And there's one other thing."

"Yeah?"

"I just want you to know that I'm very proud to be your uncle."

"And I couldn't be more proud to be your nephew."

They hugged.

The Guardian did not come, even after Uncle Pete had left.

"He promised," Andy said.

"Must be trouble someplace," Makasha said. "But Guardian come. You see." The caveman patted Andy on the shoulder.

"I scram now. You make nice talk with Elizabeth."

Reassured, if only for the moment, Andy took Makasha's advice and sidled up to Elizabeth. He gently kidded her, saying, "I've been meaning to ask you what hopes you've got that aren't in prison."

"You mean the ones that are out on parole?"

"Yeah. Those."

"I've got one in particular that comes to mind," she said, smiling. "It has something to do with dressing up, music, and dancing."

"The prom!" he guessed.

"If you're still asking."

"I'm asking."

"Then I'm going."

They stared at each other for a long moment—and then they kissed, which was one less hope they had left to fulfill.

Makasha looked on from a distance, smiling contentedly at their happiness. He had a hope, too. His hope was that the three of them would stay together a little bit longer. And until the Guardian arrived, Makasha's hope would be very much alive.

# About the Authors

Barbara and Scott Siegel are the authors of thirty-nine books, six of which have been national bestsellers. Internationally, their works have been published throughout Europe, as well as in Asia and Australia.

Two of their books for teenagers have been honored by the American Library Association, and a good many of their other titles, both for teens and adults, have been selected by leading book clubs.

The happily married couple's most recent bestseller is the Dragonlance fantasy saga, *Tanis: The Shadow Years*. Among their current non-fiction titles are *Jack Nicholson: The Unauthorized Biography* and *The Encyclopedia of Hollywood*, which Jeff Strickler, movie critic of the *Minneapolis Star-Tribune* called "Remarkable! One of the most impressive film reference books I've seen. It's destined to become one of the most useful and most used Hollywood reference texts." They are also the authors of *The Celebrity Phone Book*, a popular reference volume that lists the names, addresses and phone numbers of 4,250 famous people.

Their expertise in the popular arts has led the authors to do regularly featured film and theater reviews on radio stations throughout the U.S. and Canada. In addition, they are the directors of an annual film festival at a well-known New York City college.

Barbara and Scott are also the owners of the Siegel & Siegel Ltd. literary agency, representing a wide range of celebrity and bestselling clients. As both authors and agents, they are often asked to speak at universities, schools, and writers' conferences.

The Siegels are as pale as ghosts because they're rarely outdoors exploring nature; they're usually indoors, reading books, seeing theater, and watching movies—in other words, exploring *human* nature.